WAL

WALK

By

John Mooney

RB
Rossendale Books

Published by Lulu Enterprises Inc.
3101 Hillsborough Street
Suite 210
Raleigh, NC 27607-5436
United States of America

Published in paperback 2013
Category: Fiction
Copyright John Mooney © 2013

ISBN : 978-1-291-46073-5

This is a work of fiction. Names, characters, corporations,
institutions, organisations, events or locales in this novel are either
the product of the author's imagination or, if real, used fictitiously.
Any resemblance to actual persons (living or dead) is entirely
coincidental.

Dedication

To Wilf, the eldest, Freddie, the youngest, and all of the
Mooney family in-between, past and present. And to
trawlermen everywhere and Fred Cone.

Acknowledgements

Many thanks to my friend, racing journalist and award-winning
playwright Chris Wilson, for pointing me in the right direction. Also
to Ray, Judy and Derek Hilton for some excellent photos and to my
rugby-watching pal Roy Bielby, also for photos. John and Elinor
Edson provided that snapshot of Flinton St Coronation party - John
is the handsome young chap grinning in the centre. Vincent Walsh of
Rossendale Books made the publication of this book possible with
his patience and skill for which I will be eternally grateful.
Finally to my family - this is for them.

The Last Year — No More Scandals

Most of you upright citizens will find what I did unethical to say the least, and probably downright crooked, but wouldn't you have done the same given the opportunity? Financial meltdown was staring me in the face when I was presented with a last minute 'get out of jail' card, so there was surely only the one option, unless of course, unlike me, you are blessed with a few scruples.

Believe me I've been involved in more than my fair share of scams and dodgy dealings and haven't always come up smelling of roses, but I've mostly managed to keep my head just above the water-line so was hardly likely to let a little setback undo all of my hard-earned and mostly ill-gotten gains.

Being an 'illegal' street bookie doesn't put me or my like in the Al Capone bracket and none of us, as far as I know, are on the 'Most Wanted' list at MI5 or the FBI. But there's still a certain stigma attached to the job despite the fact that the majority of working men in the country avail themselves of our services, even if it is, for most at any rate, only once a year on the Grand National.

Where I came from though once is never enough as there's an event that attracts more heavy gambling than the great Aintree spectacular, the Derby and the FA Cup Final put together, even if it has had more than its share of drama, betting coups and scandals in its recent history – and I should know - I've been involved in most of them.

The Annual St George Club Walking Race is a hugely popular event that has gathered strength in the immediate years following the end of the Second World War and has become the most eagerly-awaited spectacle of the year in the fishing community of Hessle Road in Hull. Not too surprising really as Hessle Roaders love a good scandal – the meatier the better - and there's little evidence of shrinking violets taking part this year.

The Walking Race is said to have originated in the early 1900's and was confined to members of the Fish Trades Association. It lapsed for many years until reappearing in the early 1930's as the Walking Match where it took on a different format to the one having its final fling today, becoming a major gambling event in the process.

The event was originally a handicap, though how on earth the handicapping committee decided on the allotted starts for those taking part is a mystery. Some of them must have been deranged, drunk or crooked, possibly all three but most definitely the latter as there were numerous incidents of massive gambles taking place. It was staged over a very long and gruelling 13-mile round trip from Hessle Road through Hessle and right up to the upmarket village of Swanland. Although it attracted plenty of entries there were very few serious competitors as it needed a thoroughly fit and dedicated athlete just to complete the marathon course.

One of those athletic types who became synonymous with the event and won it a couple of times was the popular Johnny Williams, who has become a very well known figure in the rugby league world as the physiotherapist and trainer of Hull Kingston Rovers. Johnny's son Mike has been keeping goal for Hull City schoolboys and has just signed for the Tigers so athleticism certainly runs in that family.

Although these days it's a serious business for many of the participants, especially those who have had a wager on themselves, the event still manages to take on a carnival atmosphere with thousands of onlookers lining the route and dozens of youngsters riding along on bikes behind the walkers. Few of the ragamuffin kids can afford a bike of their own so many of them hire one at an hourly rate, some of them clubbing together and running alongside their pals until it's their turn to ride. It's an event that has been gathering momentum for the past few years, building up to today's final countdown.

Another major and enjoyable part of the day is the parade of horses. Traders from all over the city dress up their horses with bunting, multi-coloured rugs and flags making a colourful spectacle - no doubt treated as an annual holiday by the nags themselves - who are more used to pulling coal-carts, beer wagons and fruit and veg carts around the streets, dodging the numerous pot holes and mad dogs in the process.

It's been a fantastic sight over the last decade or so but this year will be very poignant as it will almost certainly be the last time the event will ever be staged. Hessle Road is now changing in a major way and traffic has become a big problem for both organisers and competitors. There's also the spectre of a new and much-needed flyover at Dairycoates level crossing which is certain to bring major disruption to the area for a considerable time. The days of forming an orderly queue for half-an-hour while three trains steam past – at least one of them taking the driver home for his tea - should be long gone in a couple of years. Thank God for that!

This year's race has once again attracted hundreds of entries, even though the Club's Rules and Regulations have had to be tightened up dramatically after a few unsavoury incidents, and almost everyone taking part wants to have a wager on themselves, however large or small, to be crowned the champion on the day and receive a very welcome winner's cheque as a bonus.

And that's where I come in! Although just a small cog in what has been a huge illegal betting operation in the city for more years than anyone cares to remember, my pitch in Liverpool Street is amongst the best on a road that's teeming with people and industry, the vast majority of it based around and depending completely on fishing. I have also through various ways and means become the 'main man' to have a bet with in the race and this year has been truly exceptional with the amount wagered reaching fever pitch.

Come On You Bounder

One of my regular punters is Gordon 'Bounder' Bradley, who was a surprise entry in the Walk to say the least. Gordon had at the starting point arrived supported by an untidy looking woman and half-a-dozen offspring, chanting 'Come on you bounder' at every opportunity.

The object of their support was Gordon 'Bounder' Bailey, a typical hard-bitten deep sea fisherman with over 20 years experience, man and boy, in the Arctic wastes trawling for fish. Like most of his kind he returned from a fishing trip just long enough to get drunk, measured for a new suit at Waistells, pay off a few debts, lose his money in the betting shop and sire a new offspring, not necessarily in that order.

Gordon, who had been a punter all of his working days, would leave Raynors pub at kicking-out time around 3.15 then proceed to the recently opened betting shop at the corner of Subway Street. He would place his bet than attempt to shout it home with the immortal words 'Come on you bastard' which in truth hardly ever helped.

One day, a new lady betting office manager with slightly more refined view on life than is the norm around these parts, asked Gordon politely if he would mind refraining from shouting out obscenities. Gordon, rather flummoxed by such a request, was in the process of listening to his latest nag struggling home in last place in the 3.45 at Beverley. He was just about to shout out his usual encouragement when, remembering the manager's request, changed it at the very last minute to 'Come on you bbbbbb ounder', which had the regulars in uproar.

Incredibly, the oath appeared to have the desired effect on the said nag, which took hold of the bit and stormed up Beverley's stiff uphill climb to snatch the spoils right on the line. From that day on Gordon's war cry never altered and he was christened The Bounder by all who knew him, which was just about everyone in the drinking and betting fraternity on Hessle Road.

Apparently his wife had encouraged him to enter the great Race in the hope of picking up some prize money but he was a 100/1 chance and even with half the waiting crowd shouting 'Come on you bounder' it was unlikely to have any effect.

My pitch is in a disused stable that had previously housed the nag which pulled the coal cart around the streets, but who had expired a couple of years back and not been replaced - the coalman having gone all modern and got himself a lorry. It may not be the most salubrious of surroundings, and certainly not the sweetest smelling, but I have hundreds of clients each day, the vast majority having a few bob on the gee-gees in the hope of winning enough to buy ten Woodbine; pay the rent; have a few pints in the Club; or if very lucky, hire a caravan for a week at the seaside resort of Withernsea.

Thankfully for my sake, few are successful and I have able to build up a nice little pot with which to keep me and my family, and a couple of others, in the manner to which we have become accustomed though it's fair to say the last few years haven't been without their traumas.

Friday is Bath Night – Get in Line!

My parents are typical of those of the era in that, apart from the annual pilgrimage to Withernsea, they hardly ever venture out of their own little domain. In that respect they are undoubtedly typical of most citizens of this country, especially in the north, as travel has been very restricted since the end of the war for one reason or another. My dad, Harry, supposedly works on the railway, at least it's they who pay his wages, though God knows what he does - sweeps the floors and cleans the toilets in the sheds probably. Whatever he does it was enough though to keep him out of the war in a 'reserved occupation' capacity so he must have been doing something worthwhile at the time.

In all honesty he was always a bit of a bore – no, let's be honest here, a crushing bore. One of his main hobbies is doing jigsaw puzzles; another is collecting matchboxes from around the world. He would come home from a trip to the docks with a new matchbox and you would have thought he'd won the football pools. He'd start telling us a story about where the matchbox came from, what it's Swedish/Danish/Finnish name was etc etc and after a few minutes we were all hoping for the kettle to boil or someone to knock on the front door and release us from our misery. It would have been more entertaining reading the Hull and East Yorkshire telephone directory.

I hatched my own escape plan whenever dad started out on one of his interminable lectures. I would bang on the back of my chair and pretend it was someone at the door.

"What's that", dad would shout mid-sentence.

"It's OK dad, it's just the door, I'll go", I would say and shoot up the passage and out into the street.

That worked a couple of times until one night, I banged loudly on the chair and my sister beat me to the door.

Me and my two sisters were brought up in a terraced house in Westbourne Street. As we were relative latecomers to West Hull we weren't surrounded by uncles, aunts, cousins and grannies like everyone else though they had begun to trickle into the area once mother and father moved here and we weren't short of cousins to play with.

The house was at the end of the terrace and was probably slightly bigger than the others in the row. My parents had one of the bedrooms; my sisters another; and I slept on a make-shift bed in what was euphemistically called the veranda but was really just a wooden lean-to. Not surprisingly it was freezing in a winter and stifling in a summer. I regularly asked to move into the front room but no chance – that was only for 'special' occasions.

Just take a look around at the houses, not just where I had lived but all along the streets of Hessle Road and beyond. In fact the whole of the City of Hull has been a mess for years. The majority of the houses are just about functional where the bombs haven't struck and are mostly kept immaculately clean by mothers and grandmas everywhere. Scouring the front step with a pumice stone is a weekly chore and anyone who doesn't do it is regarded as 'that mucky woman from number six'.

It's most definitely a tight-knit community – everyone knowing, or thinking they know – everyone else's business, whether they like it or not.

Many of the terraces are characterised by fishing nets criss-crossing them as hundreds of women earn a few extra pennies by a process called 'braiding'. Walk down the likes of Havelock Street and Flinton Street on a Monday and it's a sight for sore eyes – washing lines strung across terraces and fishing nets scattered all over the street.

Our house, rented of course, was always heated via a coal fire, or if things are really tough, cinders or coalite, neither of which give out much real heat and are almost worthless in the depths of winter. We spent many a morning scraping ice off the kitchen window before getting washed and changed in double quick time in the sink.

Bath night was usually a Friday when the tin bath gets taken out of the coal shed and filled by boiling pots of hot water on the gas stove. We bathed in front of the fire - everyone in the family taking their turn - usually in age order so in our house I always ended up last. Those not bathing had to crowd round the kitchen table – it was always a long wait!

As youngsters we played football, cricket and rugby in the streets as there was hardly any traffic and the biggest hazards came from stepping in droppings from the dozens of horses who ploughed up and down pulling the carts. In the early 1950's there were just 10,000 registered cars in Hull but by the end of the decade that figure had swollen to 40,000. My grandma loved those horses – she collected the manure in a bucket to use on her allotment and had the best rhubarb in the area.

Stray dogs were a major hazard as there were always hundreds of the scruffy mongrels roaming the streets, some of them viscous and many likely to run off with the cricket ball just as the game is getting interesting. I spent many an hour chasing some demented animal up the street in the vain hope of retrieving the ball.

Oh No – not Hedley!

My parents had me christened Hedley Doyle, about as embarrassing a name as is possible when all my mates are Tom's, Dave's, Fred's and Les's. Dad was a great cricket fan and his favourite was the Yorkshire bowler Hedley Verity, hence the name.

Dad had been completely in awe of Verity, who was one of the great spin bowlers of his generation but like so many international sportsmen his career was interrupted by the war. Unfortunately he was badly injured during the allied invasion of Sicily and died of his wounds while in captivity.

Hedley Doyle doesn't exactly trip off the tongue but thankfully just about everyone called me Ed, even dad, though mother, whose name is Vera, insisted on calling me by my given name, or 'edley as she pronounced it, that was when she was around, which wasn't too often in my early days.

Mother had just two interests in life – bingo in the afternoon and bingo in the evening. Some days the two sessions would combine into one and she didn't come home until the last bus left the town centre at 11.00pm.

One night she walked in nonchalantly to be greeted by dad: "Were the 'ell have you been, the kids haven't had any tea."

"You should have gone to the fish shop," was the reply, said in the contemptuous manner that was by now the norm in our household.

"I didn't 'ave any money, said dad.

"You took it all to play bloody bingo all day and night."

"If you didn't booze it all away on a weekend we wouldn't have to worry about money," was mother's barbed retort, though what she didn't know was that dad didn't spend his money on drink, it was gambling that was his downfall.

The arguments went on and on so life wasn't exactly a bed of roses in Westbourne Street. I suppose, looking back, mother must have decided that a life of drudgery wasn't for her. Like most women she was expected to do all the household chores and with three kids and a husband to see to it won't have been easy.

Wash day must have been an absolute nightmare. We had a dolly tub in the back yard and a mangle in the kitchen until a few years ago, that's when the enterprising Syd Roscoe started hiring out the new-fangled washing machines at half-a-crown an hour. Syd had four machines and every Monday he would roll up to the top of our terrace with his van, load one of the machines onto a sack barrow, and drop it off at our house. Once he'd gone half the neighbourhood descended on our back kitchen and shared the washing duties. That's about all I know about washing, apart from our clothes appearing clean and ironed every Tuesday after mother slaved away the day before.

As for cooking – we had lots of fish like everyone else, and plenty of mince and on one occasion a plateful of tripe and onions appeared, but all three of us kids refused to touch it and it went into the dustbin. We seemed to make do with bits and pieces of things but

I don't ever remember going hungry - egg on toast and bread and jam were always on standby.

Mother despised housework so why she didn't go out and get a job I don't know though it just didn't appear to be on the agenda at any stage and she eventually gave up most of the chores for her beloved bingo. Thankfully I spent almost all of my days and nights playing outside in the streets and on the bombed sites from a very early age. There was only one tree in the near vicinity. Me and my pals must have climbed it a thousand times; how it survived I'll never know.

Dad's betting habit led to the usual ups and downs – mainly downs - in the world of gambling. He backed the winner of the Walking Race last year and bought a bottle of sherry in the hope of earning some brownie points, and a possible rare interlude of passion, with mother – fat chance! She resented every minute of her life with us - and let us know about it in no uncertain terms most of the time.

My sisters came off much worse as they more or less had to run the household once mother downed tools and they were very pleased to get out when an opportunity arose.

Dad had plenty of affection for all three of us but he was a weak character who daren't show it too much in case it offended mother. She walked all over him and though I knew I would be relieved when it was my turn to get out of that nightmare I also felt sorry for dad being left on his own with someone who quite obviously couldn't care less about him. Mother had turned into one of those women who wouldn't give the ball back when it landed in the back yard.

However, I didn't have too long to dwell on such problems as the whole scenario took a completely unexpected and disastrous turn of events, just a few weeks before I was due to leave school.

Mother – The Mad Poker Woman!

Dad had experienced what all punters go through at some stage and, after the euphoria of that nice win in the Walking Race had evaporated, couldn't back a winner to save his life. He started having bets on credit and was in hock to a local bookie, Gerry Malloy, to the tune of £20, about a month's wages. Malloy had been pressing dad for payment for weeks, threatening him with violence and, even worse, much worse, telling mother. One night just after I had finished my tea, a knock came on the door as mother was about to leave for another bingo session.

"Who on earth's that at this time of night? said mother.

"It's probably that scrounger Mrs Dosdale wanting to borrow a cuppa sugar again.

"Tell 'er we 'aven't any," she said looking at me.

"I'm not telling 'er, I said.

"It's nowt to do wi' me."

"I'll go," said dad, attempting to keep the peace as ever, though he got the shock of his life when he opened the door as it wasn't Mrs Dosdale stood there with her begging cup; it was Malloy and his henchman 'Gormless Gordon' Spradbury, a total half wit with hands the size of shovels and a brain the size of a pea.

"Twenty quid you owe me Doyle, the bookie said to a shocked dad.

"You either pay me or I'll let Spradbury loose and he'll tear this place apart."

Mother was absolutely astonished at this development. She had no idea whatsoever that dad was a betting man never mind owing a small fortune to a bookie. It didn't take long for her to gather her thoughts, however.

"Tear this place apart will yer? she said.

"I'll show you about tearing apart."

She picked up the poker from the fireplace and set off in a frenzy for the front door where Malloy and Spradbury were in the process of defending themselves against an attack by a mad woman.

Mother lifted the poker high above her head and struck with real venom, but it wasn't the bookie or his minder she hit, it was dad!

"That's where all our money's gone is it"? She said, and struck dad again, this time even more forcefully, battering him to the floor in the process.

Malloy and Spradbury had scarpered by this time and the neighbours, including 'that scrounger' Mrs Dosdale, were gathering in clusters around the front door, as they always did when there was any sign of a commotion. I had an armchair, or ringside view of what had happened but it was all a blur and the only thing I could see was dad lying on the floor with blood spurting from his nose, ear, and several other orifices that mother had lain into with the poker. Thankfully – and be thankful for small mercies here – the offending object hadn't been used for the purpose it was designed for within the last hour so wasn't red hot.

Mother was still hurling abuse at him and was in the process of clouting him again when Mr Glossop from number 8, who had been watching the spectacle from outside with the rest of the nosey parkers, shot through the front door and disarmed her, though she continued kicking and scratching despite Mr Glossop being a ship's welder with forearms like Popeye The Sailorman.

I yelled at Mrs Dosdale to call the cops and she hurriedly sent her teenage son Gary to the police box at the top of St George's Road where a bobby was always in attendance, usually having a cup of tea and reading the paper, hoping that nothing would disturb his peace and quiet, which it rarely did.

It was a helluva shock to him when young Dosdale came bursting through the door yelling of attempted murder but sure enough PC Wilkins was quickly on the scene and had the presence of mind to call for an ambulance, which was very much required with dad still lying there semi-conscious and bleeding all over the lino.

To say the scene was chaotic is an understatement. Another of the neighbours also went round to Brighton Street where my sisters were renting a house and they both arrived, adding to the confusion in the process and yelling and screeching at mother, who was now being restrained by both PC Wilkins and Mr Glossop.

The ambulance came quickly and carted dad off to the infirmary in King Edward Street while a Black Maria took mother away in handcuffs, jeered on by a crowd that had gathered from nowhere at the end of the terrace. No doubt the 'cuffs were for the protection of the bobbies who had arrested her on suspicion of GBH.

One of my sisters, Molly, decided she needed to stay with me for the night 'for my protection' though from who or what I have no idea while the eldest, Kathleen, went to the hospital. Dad spent a week in the infirmary and had to have 20 stitches in various parts of his head. Naturally the police interviewed me about the incident but I told them I couldn't remember anything, that's because dad had said he wasn't going to press charges and that I had to keep my mouth well and truly shut.

It Could Have Been Laurel & Hardy

The bobbies had spoken to the neighbours before interviewing me and wanted to know who it was at the door when mother attacked dad; what were they there for and were they the cause of the trouble. I certainly wasn't telling as I had come up with a bit of a brainwave, one that hopefully would turn the situation round in our favour. I found out where Malloy spent most of his afternoon's - in one of the local clubs - and went to see him with my plan.

He recognised me straight away.

"The police are very interested to know who it was at our house that night and who was the big ugly-looking thug, I said.

"Some of the neighbours know but of course they won't be telling though Mr Glossop thought it might have been Bing Crosby and Bob Hope and Mrs Dosdale swore blind it was Laurel and Hardy. I could have temporary amnesia and not recall who it was but that's dependant on dad's debt being wiped out."

Malloy was flabbergasted by the suggestion - he wasn't at all happy about losing twenty quid - but quickly realised he had little option but to agree as he didn't want any problems with the police. So the end result was that mother got off scot-free and dad got off owing the bookie a score.

Mother did eventually return home after a night in the cells without charges being made – she wouldn't have had anywhere else to go anyway – and once dad got back things did seem to turn slightly less frosty – just as long as he kept away from betting, which he managed to do though not surprisingly he turned to drink as a substitute.

The whole episode was a massive turning point for me. Until then I had no idea whatsoever about the way my life would unravel, but now I had a clear sight of how I wanted to spend my days. Gerry Malloy had inadvertently become my hero.

Billy Really Was That Daft

I had been no lover of school, and no-one, including the teachers, would have known what the national curriculum was, but I had a real penchant for mental arithmetic and often surprised the teachers with my speedy and accurate calculations. Most of them in fact were astounded as I had no inclination to try an inch at any other subject, apart from sport, and they all thought I was a dunce.

Life was more or less set out for us – we were expected to leave school at fifteen without any qualifications and head straight for the fish docks to find work. The cleverer ones had passed an 11-plus examination and went on to Kingston High, Riley High or the catholic Marist College, but I can't recall a single person in my area who graduated to university – it just wasn't considered an option.

Most streets on Hessle Road had a school and ours certainly did. Westbourne Street School was situated at the Dairycoates end, about a minute's walk from our house. We started at the age of five; went into juniors at eight; and seniors at eleven, that is unless you were one of the clever clogs who went to high school, which was probably about one in five of us.

I recall learning to read and write at a much earlier age than most thanks to my grandma's love of books and I could do my times table before anyone else in my age group. Apart from that the only things I learnt were how to play soccer and cricket – oh yes - and the words of the hymn 'For those in peril on the sea' which we sang in the school assembly every morning.

It was also useful to know how to look after ourselves and while I was no Joe Louis or Freddie Mills I had a couple of quite major fights in my schooldays and drew 1-1. The knack was to know the pecking-order and stay out of the way of those who were obviously likely to give you a beating, and there were always a few of them.

In junior school all of our teachers were men, as were most in the seniors section. The majority were quite happy to participate in extra-curricular activities so the school thrived at sports - soccer and cricket for the boys and netball and rounders for the girls. For such a small school it had an outstanding record in soccer and one boy, Alec Dawson, went on to play for Manchester United in the post-Munich Cup Final.

Alec was actually a Scot who had come to live in Hull with his family. He was a really nice, unassuming lad despite the fact that he was playing, and scoring goals regularly, for England Schoolboys from the unprecedented age of thirteen and was always destined for great things.

My best pal in those days, Billy, wasn't at all bright though he bragged to one and all that he didn't finish last in lessons – 40th out of 42 – though that was due to Freddie Green being absent throughout the term with scarlet fever and 14-year-old Beryl Briggs, who was always a bit more forward than the rest of us, getting pregnant by a Swedish sailor.

Billy spent half his schooldays in the dunce's chair and I'm certain he was putting it on most of the time – then again I'm not so sure – he really could have been that daft.

For most of us lads, girls were as mysterious as aliens, even to those of us who had sisters. They didn't play soccer or cricket so what use were they to anyone? We did though occasionally get into closer contact when the teachers made us play rounders against them on sport's day.

And boy don't they cheat! Everything in the school was about competition – we all hated losing at whatever was set before us so when the chance came to thrash the girls at rounders we were obviously convinced it was hardly any use them turning up. Big mistake!

Most of the girl's rounders team were also in the netball side and they were invariably in the top two or three teams in the city. They were incredibly competitive but also much more athletic than we could have envisaged so, coupled with their ability to cheat at every opportunity, they beat us more often than not, much to the amusement of the lads who weren't picked to play.

Girls hadn't really come onto our radar at that time though there were rumours and sniggers emanating from the slightly older boys about Nancy Pickles allowing them to feel her 'bits and pieces' for half-a-crown.

I heard the rumours but thought that if I had half-a-crown to spare I would be buying a new cricket ball not fumbling around in Nancy Pickles underwear down some back alley.

School sports day was the most eagerly awaited day of the week. Like the majority of schools in West Hull, we didn't have the luxury of a playing field so had to traipse all the way to Pickering Park in order to play soccer and cricket. I seem to remember it was always raining!

Not everyone was sporty of course, girls or boys, but all had to join in at some level. One particular girl, Jennie McDonagh, was known as 'Fattie McDonagh' for obvious reasons, and we all laughed ourselves silly when she attempted the vaulting horse in the assembly hall. She would bound up to the ramp – slam her feet down hard – and attempt to take off. Invariably though she ended up in an undignified heap and while her friends had endless sympathy for her plight the lads all thought it was a huge joke.

She lived in the next street and her mother was a regular bingo partner of my mother. They were always attempting to bring us together, mother suggesting one day: "Jennie's mam said she would love to go and see the latest Doris Day film at Eureka," insinuating of course that I could take her.

"Not likely, I replied.

"I'll be the laughing stock of the school if seen out with her.

"She's like a great big elephant."

The last remark earned me a clip around the ear, causing me even more reason to dislike 'Fattie'.

English literature, history, geography, science – none of them had the remotest appeal to me and as for woodwork and metalwork, I generally managed to dodge them one way or another. I also managed to stay out of any major bother though there was one incident where I had a very close call.

Don't Play With Colin's Gang

Being quite a good soccer player, and a regular member of the school team above my age group, I usually played with the older boys on an old bombed laundry site off Patrick's Lane close to Carlton Street. One of them, Colin Boynton, was a real tough nut who was rarely out of trouble though as a close neighbour whose dad was a workmate of my dad, he would always keep an eye on me and ensure I didn't get a kicking.

One autumn evening, after a mammoth game of football on the bomb site, Colin and two of his pals went off on their own, much to my disgust as I was rather hoping to join their gang as they were regarded with fear and dread by most of the kids in the area. Obviously I was far too young to be mingling with the likes of them but that didn't prevent me being annoyed at them leaving me to play alongside boys of my own age.

"Can I come with you Col, I shouted.

"I don't have to be in until late."

"Nah, not tonight, Colin replied.

"We've got summat to do and we don't want to involve you."

Of course I was crestfallen, though as things turned out, I was well out of what happened that night. Colin and his two mates, Les Goodman and Artie Stanworth, made their way to the house of one of the teachers at the school, Graham Benn.

Benn was regarded as a strict disciplinarian; in fact he was more of a sadist. He regularly handed out the stick to his pupils, more often than not for extremely minimal offences, and Stone had been one of the recipients a couple of days earlier for a minor transgression that to any other teacher would have meant nothing more than a telling off.

Benn lived in Sunningdale Road, close to the Regis cinema. He had never married and lived alone. His main hobby was his small garden and potting shed where he grew all varieties of plants and vegetables and was a founder member of the local fuchsia society.

As darkness fell, Colin and his henchmen crept along the passage at the back of Benn's house and stayed there for a few minutes until everything was quiet. They then did something extraordinary. Each had three lemonade bottles filled to the brim with paraffin which they lit with Stone's cigarette lighter and hurled at Benn's shed. Where on earth they had got that idea from no-one knows though it's quite likely they had been watching American gangster films starring the likes of James Cagney and George Raft and that may have prompted them to re-enact a scene from the movies.

Wherever the idea came from it caused mayhem.

Before too long the shed, and all of its contents, were lighting up the sky around North Road and Gypsyville and the recalcitrant trio were heading quickly back along the passage leading from the house, laughing to themselves at having given Benn the shock of his life.

Unfortunately for them, heading in the opposite direction, undoubtedly to Benn's house as she was only a few yards away, was none other than Westbourne Street's naughty schoolgirl Nancy

31

Pickles. As the trio swept past, she raced to Benn's house and, along with several neighbours who had heard the commotion; set about putting out the fire.

Benn had several water containers in the garden which were put to good use and the fire was eventually put out. The fire brigade weren't called and after about half-an-hour there was just a pile of cinders where once stood a shed full of prized blooms, not to mention a lawn mower, a couple of deckchairs and several garden tools.

Nancy urged Benn to call the police as she could easily identify the three boys who she had spotted running away from the scene but much to her surprise Benn was most reluctant to take that option though he wasn't about to let the matter rest.

Of course none of us were aware of what had happened, not until the next morning anyway. Benn and the headmaster, Mr Strickland, confronted the errant trio before assembly the next morning. All three were paraded in front of the whole school and administered a severe thrashing by the headmaster, a man who rarely lost his temper but judging by his demeanour was enraged at what had happened to a member of his staff the previous evening.

As for Nancy Pickles, she disappeared from school for a few months until emerging one day in the school playground – pushing a pram! Believe me there was more than one Westbourne Street schoolboy heading for an early exit that day – and quite possibly an errant teacher as well.

To be fair to my friend Colin and his partners in crime, they took their punishment without a whimper and as far as I know nothing more was said about the incident, well, nothing apart from everyone, teachers and pupils alike, asking why on earth Nancy Pickles had been going to Benn's house that evening — it certainly wouldn't have been for homework!

Blood & Guts In The Fish House

Thankfully my prowess at maths was a real godsend which was why, after the incident with mother attacking dad, I decided I had to use my ability with figures to the best possible advantage otherwise I would never get out of that environment.

I did have a part-time job working on the petrol pumps at my uncle's club in Stoneferry. My uncle paid me eight-bob a day, which wasn't bad money, unless you realise that I biked from Hessle Road to work, started at 8.00am and finished when uncle came to open up the club for the evening at around 6.30pm. No breaks, of course, just a bottle of Murdens lemonade and a bag of crisps.

I was able to augment that meagre salary by a little 'creative accounting'. I was the only worker on the pumps so got to serve every customer. Petrol was four shillings and ten pence a gallon and most customers would give me a quid then wait for their eight pence change. I always took my time, fiddling around before telling them I had to go into the cabin for some change. Usually by the time I got back they had got fed up and driven off leaving me with a nice little earner. I often made more in a good day through those 'perks' than my actual wages.

It wasn't to last for too long though. One afternoon while the club was closed I heard a noise coming from inside. Uncle had given me a key and when I opened the door I saw a local guy, Mick Crenshaw, attempting to prise open the till with a crowbar. I shouted at him and he beat a hasty retreat through the back door which he had badly damaged when forcing his way in.

In my naivety I called the police. Uncle was absolutely livid when I called him later as he said he would have sorted it himself, which I have no doubt he would have. Anyway, the police knew all about Crenshaw and quickly arrested him though he denied all knowledge with his parents and brother swearing blind he's never left the house all day.

That meant it was my word against his, of course, and I had to go to the magistrates court a few weeks later. As I arrived Crenshaw's family were waiting for me.

"You stinking liar, Doyle, Mick was nowhere near that club and you know it, screamed his father.

"You'd better not say otherwise or you'll live to regret it."

I was between a rock and a hard place but didn't have much option but to tell the court exactly what I saw despite the Crenshaw's glaring at me. The defending barrister made me look a right Charlie but in the end Crenshaw was found guilty. His punishment? A suspended sentence or a 'second chance' as the magistrate put it.

The prosecuting lawyer told me that this was Crenshaw's fourteenth 'second chance' as far as he was aware and there could have been more. Needless to say he was back in court a month later for burgling a house in Saltshouse Road. Maybe he'll get another 'second chance'.

Not surprisingly that was the end of my days in Stoneferry as the Crenshaw family were obviously out to get me and I spent quite a few weeks looking over my shoulder. Still, it wasn't such a wrench as petrol had gone up a penny a gallon by now so may little 'scam' would only have brought in fourpence instead of twice that amount.

Anyway, my visit to see Malloy at the club had a lasting effect on me. Malloy was not only a street bookie with a major financial interest in the club, but also had one of the best pitches at the local dog track. He had arrived at our house that night in a big shiny black Wolsley car with footplates and leather interior and was dressed in a very smart suit, silk shirt and tie and black brogue shoes.

There weren't too many people dressed like that in Hull but Malloy always liked to make a big impression and he certainly made one on me as I was just about to leave school and make my way in the big wide world.

It was rumoured that Malloy made a huge amount of money every year taking bets on the Walking Race and he was certainly the main bookie of the event. I was determined to become part of his world as soon as possible and make my own fortune.

I went back to see Malloy and asked if I could be a sort of 'apprentice' to him, fetching and carrying and generally learning all the tricks of what looked to me to be an incredibly interesting and glamorous business, though of course there was a side to it that was rather less than uplifting which, as a wet behind the ears callow youth, I couldn't see at the time.

Malloy must have taken a bit of a shine to me the day I did the deal with him and he offered to tutor me in the ways of the gambling world, though he wouldn't be going so far as to pay me for my troubles but would give me the occasional 'backhander' when things were good.

I would have to get a regular job of course but as long as I finished reasonably early and didn't have to work Saturday's, it was feasible enough. But where would I find a job like that? Dad tried his best to persuade me from going onto the docks but that appeared to be the only option open to someone like me, a product of Westbourne Street School with no qualifications and very little prospects.

There were always vacancies on the docks for all types of work and through a friend of Malloy's I went for an interview with Grubb Brothers Fish Merchants at the bottom of Manchester Street.

When I entered the building it nearly frightened me to death. A dozen or so men were filleting fish at about 100 miles an hour and chucking them into boxes, which were then barrowed through a stinking mess of blood and guts to a waiting lorry.

"Who sent yer?" was the greeting I got when reporting to Tommy Grubb, who appeared to be the only Grubb brother involved in the business.

"Gerry Malloy, I said.

"He said you might fix me up."

"Fix you up wi what? said Grubb.

"I 'ope you don't expect to walk straight into a well paid job straight from school with no experience."

"Anything will do, I said.

"Just as long as it's an early finish."

"Christ, he's already dictating his hours and he's not even started yet," yelled Grubb at the top of his voice and the workforce were looking at me with a mixture of contempt and pity.

"We start at six and finish at two, no breaks, just a cuppa tea and a Penguin around ten.

"It's two quid a week cash in hand so it's up to you if you want it."

So that was that, my first job interview. I started work the following Monday and to say I hated every minute would be the understatement of all time.

It was a desperate job for desperate people working in desperate conditions. The workforce were mainly older men who had been in the fishing industry most of their lives, many of them ex-seamen now too old and worn out to do the arduous work of a trawlerman and seeing out their working days in this dump.

They were a rough lot who gave no quarter but to be fair they treated me well despite the fact I took a long time to learn the ropes. My task was as a barrow lad, taking the boxes of fish to the lorries that were waiting to transport the goods to all parts of Yorkshire. You wouldn't think that would be too difficult, would you? But side-stepping empty fish boxes, clogs, dozens of pallets and cod-heads wasn't as easy as it looked, especially when expected to do a dozen or so journeys in an hour – and those barrows were bloody heavy!

The lorry drivers were better paid than the fish workers but were always in a great hurry as they were on piecework and a couple of extra loads a week went a long way in extra wages.

One of them, Baz Shorthouse, was a bully who delighted in giving me a clip round the ear every now and then just to let me know who was in charge. We all knew him, not surprisingly perhaps, as 'Baz Shithouse' though not to his face; never to his face. The other workers hated Shorthouse as much as I did and one of the older guys took his life in his hands one morning and told him to stop knocking me about.

"Who the fuck are you talking too? Shorthouse said.

"You have two options, either you shut up or end up with a cranking handle round your head."

Not surprisingly my defender took option one as no-one else appeared in a hurry to back him up.

Most people in life have at least one redeeming factor – but not Shorthouse – he was simply one of life's bad buggers. He was also known by another nickname – Baz the Bastard. That wasn't just a slagging off name – though of course he really was a bastard – but Baz was also illegitimate and we all knew it. His mother, Millie, was married at one stage to Alan Shorthouse but he'd long since bit the bullet, leaving a trail of devastation in his wake.

Millie was known for 'putting it about a bit', probably even for the short period she was married to Shorthouse and most definitely post-him. Shorthouse senior obviously knew what his wife was up to and was quite simply sick of all the jibes and innuendos he had to take from work colleagues and neighbours. One afternoon, after downing a full bottle of cheap vodka, bought off a Russian seaman on the dock, Shorthouse swallowed a handful of Asprin before slitting his wrists with a rusty razor blade. He then turned on the gas oven and lit a Swan Vesta, blowing up not just himself, the kitchen and front room, but half next door's lounge in the process as well as most windows in the immediate vicinity.

When the inquest was held a couple of weeks later, Millie told the coroner 'it was a cry for help'.

When Baz was born the locals were taking odds on who was the father. A Russian seaman was favourite as he was a regular visitor to the house; a long-distance lorry driver from Aberdeen was also in the frame as were the milkman and the window-cleaner, who was suspect number one in my book.

The postman was definitely not on the list as he was known to be a fan of Noel Coward and had once been to a ballet but there was a quartet of possibilities and I don't believe even Millie knew for certain.

That's probably a good reason why Baz turned out like he did. It can't have been easy going through schooldays being called shithouse and bastard but it certainly turned him into a viscous bully who was roundly detested by everyone.

One time in the fish house when he hit me across the back of the head with a rolled-up magazine, probably Tit Bits, I stared him down and told him I would get my revenge in a couple of years when I was fitter and stronger. He just laughed in my face but I was convinced he'd get his come-uppance at some stage though maybe not from me.

Not All Bookies Are Filthy Rich

Having to begin work at 6.00am was a massive upheaval for someone used to starting school at 9.00am - that's when I could be bothered to go at all - though of course the good part was that I finished at 2.00pm sharp and was home, washed, changed and ready to go out by 2.30.

I wasn't officially allowed in the club but that never seemed to bother anyone there. I had to go in through the back door but the clientele, all bookmakers and punters, welcomed me with open arms as I did all their running around, made the tea, swept the floor of losing betting slips and generally made myself useful.

I was in a completely alien world to that which I had been brought up in. No scornful mother, no weak-willed father, no nasty, smarmy schoolteachers and no Baz Shorthouse to belt me around the chops at his will. It was bliss – I was living the dream.

Not only did I thoroughly enjoy the fetching and carrying, the bookies and punters were always generous when they had a win and I sometimes more than doubled my wages from the fish house in a week. Shillings, two-bobs, half-a-crowns and one glorious Saturday, a ten-bob note, all came my way and I thought I was in easy street.

The only person who wasn't particularly generous was Malloy. He more or less treated me like a skivvy and hardly ever dipped into his deep-seated pockets – so much for the 'backhanders' he was supposed to pay me on the good days. Still, I was there to gain valuable experience and was absolutely delighted when one day he suggested I go to the dog track with him. I was about to travel in his big shiny car for the first time.

I was earning more money in a good week than my dad and he had been at work for a lifetime. Although officially not allowed to work at the track I acted as a go-between for Malloy and some of the other bookies and quickly picked up the art of tic-tac. Malloy also showed me his field book for that year's Walking Race – he'd taken a fortune and had such a well balanced book that he would have won whoever came home first.

I was in my element and when Malloy allowed me to help his clerk one very busy night my passion for maths shone through and I was able to impress him with my speedy calculations in what is a very fraught job that can prove costly if not done correctly.

Working at the track for the next few years not only provided me with much needed extra cash but also with a huge font of memories – good and bad – of the characters who frequent the sport of greyhound racing.

Many of the track's bookies had little money – some would start a night at the dogs with virtually nothing in the hod. One ruse to get money to start off the evening was to bet on the Daily Double, which were always the first and last races of the night.

Punters would have to back two dogs to win and even if the bookie had taken money on the first winner the punter still had to wait until the last race before even having a chance of collecting. Many a night ended with one or more of these characters doing a runner with nothing in the satchel to pay out with but incredibly they still managed to bounce back for the next meeting with some untenable excuse as why they had to leave early the previous night.

It's almost impossible to explain to people that not all bookies are filthy rich. There's an old saying: 'You never see a bookie on a bike', but I have known many bookmakers who wouldn't even have the money for a bike in the first place. Some bookies are just plain unlucky while others enter the business believing it to be paved with gold only to find it can be just the opposite.

An old school friend of my dad's called Charlie Bagshaw was in the fish and chip trade and doing very well thank you very much. He'd been in the family business all of his life and certainly knew exactly what he was doing in what is an extremely cut-throat environment. Charlie decided that he would invest a big chunk of his savings (and his dads) in one of the new betting shops that were springing up all over the city and spent many thousands setting up the business.

He decided he would run the shop himself despite having no experience whatsoever - like many he thought it was just a case of taking the mug punter's money and watching it accumulate in the till. He employed a till girl and a deputy manager, neither who had ever had a bet or knew anything about betting, and everything went OK for a few weeks apart from it being a little quiet.

In the second month of trading, one fairly busy Saturday, Charlie was looking through the betting slips he had taken and noticed an 11/6d flag bet plus a five-bob each-way accumulator in which the first two selections had gone in as big price winners in early races. This is where his inexperience showed. Although he made a mental note to keep an eye on the bet as it could turn out nasty, by the time he came to look at it again the last two selections had also won at huge prices.

Charlie then got out his ready reckoner to work out how much the punter had to come and, after about half-an-hour, came to the conclusion that the bet would come to about three hundred and fifty pounds, very bad for business but not a complete disaster. He called me and asked me to confirm the amount. It took me a few minutes to work out but I then called him back.

"I've checked that bet Charlie and it comes to one thousand, one hundred pounds, fourteen shillings and sixpence."

The line went dead – Charlie had fainted!

Not surprisingly he very quickly got out of the bookmaking business, at a great loss I might add, and went back to doing something he knew about – fish and chips!

No Mug Punter

Obviously most bookmakers make a profit or, like any other business, they couldn't stay solvent but not every punter is a 'mug', far from it. I have known numerous punters in my time who are just genuinely lucky people. The one saving grace for the bookies is that few of them realise just how lucky they are.

They are so used to winning that when a little misfortune comes their way they are always quick to point out just how unlucky they had been.

In my early days as a fully-fledged member of the bookmaking fraternity, one incident stands out like a beacon. A regular Saturday punter, who I knew as someone who invariably had more than his fair share of good fortune and was rumoured to have backed the winner of the Walking Race three years on the trot, had a week off work and started betting with me one Monday. The first day he had his usual stroke of luck when a favourite he had bet against fell at the last fence allowing his selection, who was struggling along in second place, to romp home.

He then decided to tempt his luck and go for a forecast – picking the first and second in a particular race. Sure enough it came up thanks to another enormous stoke of good luck when a horse he had left out of his calculations but was cantering along well in the lead, took fright and ran off the track with the race at his mercy, leaving his pair to fight out the finish.

And guess what? His selection just managed to hold on in a photo-finish.

That set the tone for the whole day and he quickly followed up with more winners, ending the day a long way in front and me kicking next door's cat on the way home.

Naturally I was hoping he would come back the following day so as to allow me a chance to get my money back but once again he went from strength-to-strength and ended the day even further in front.

Wednesday was a day of relief for me as the punter decided to take his wife and kids on a day trip to Bridlington with the winnings – he could quite easily have gone on a Caribbean Cruise!

By Thursday he was back – this time chancing his arm not with forecasts but tri-casts, a bet which requires the punter to find the first, second and third in a particular race. I was mightily pleased when the first two bets went down and hoped he would continue with this strategy which is absolutely loaded against the punter.

His third tri-cast was in a 24-runner handicap in a sprint at Ripon – impossible - or so I thought. His first two selections were fighting out the finish, a long way clear of the remainder with the third selection well out of sight much to my huge relief. The punter could hardly believe his 'misfortune' and shouted out in despair: "Where's Donut?" the name of his third selection.

Sure enough, from out of the clouds and to much cheering and shouting, appeared Donut to snatch third place right on the line.

The starting prices for the three selections were 10/1, 12/1 and 8/1 and the tri-cast paid £253 for a ten-bob stake. I had to pay out through gritted teeth and then make my way to see Gerry Malloy for a loan as I wouldn't have had enough money to open with the next day without substantial input from my backer.

So, the moral is that not all bookies are millionaires and not all punters paupers though thankfully for me the guy did manage to put a few quid my way on the last couple of days betting and I at least finished the week solvent – just.

Wouldn't Win A Best-Dressed Contest

Teddy Jelley, or TJ as everyone called him, was a bookmaking 'character' and without question the tightest, meanest man on God's earth. Everyone at the dog track has a story about TJ's penny-pinching exploits and none would be exaggerated. Unlike most bookies, who enjoy giving off the appearance of being cash-rich, he revelled in the idea of being 'careful' as he put it and often berated a winning punter for taking his money off him.

TJ wasn't the world's flashiest dresser either. No-one ever saw him in anything other than the clothes he had been wearing for twenty years – winter and summer. However, one night he arrived at the dog track in a brand spanking new pair of shoes, astounding everyone with their shininess and style.

I couldn't believe my eyes.

"TJ, I said.

"Those shoes look like brogues, where on earth did you get them?" expecting him to say some relative had passed away and left them to him in their will.

"I was passing a shoe shop in Beverley and saw them in the window for ten-bob, he said.

"The last pair of new shoes I had were my army boots and I thought these looked a bit cheap so went in and asked if there was anything wrong with them or were they second-hand."

"Was there something wrong," I asked innocently.

"Not really, he replied.

"Except one's a size six and the other an eight so I just wear a thicker sock."

I occasionally helped Jelley out at the dog track if his poor down-trodden clerk didn't turn up – for the bare minimum pay I might add. It was always a chastening experience working for him. He'd never stop moaning from start to finish, always about how much he should have won on a particular race though his odds were so tight he hardly ever lost on a race and never in my experience at a meeting.

I almost had to beg for my wages at the end of the night but it was all good experience for me even though I was always pleased to see the back of the evening. Jelley had a pitch at many northern racecourses – always in the cheap ring – and he was just as mean and tight with his odds as he was at the dog track.

Jelley hated paying out to winning punters – it was as though they were robbing him of his last penny. I was working as a clerk for him one night when a punter we had not seen at the track previously had £20 on a dog that was running there for the first time. Its trial times had been nothing special but the dog was the subject of an almighty gamble and the punters had got on at odds of 5/1, meaning he stood to win £100 plus his stake money back if it was successful.

Jelley had been unable to lay off much of the bet as the odds had shrunk quickly in the face of sustained support so he was staring at a loss if the dog won. In fact the dog was in a totally different class to its rivals and was back in its kennel having its supper before the others had finished. It was obviously a 'job' well done and all of the bookies had to face a big payout.

Jelley was distraught – he actually lost on a race – almost unprecedented. The punter, a wiry looking man probably in his early 70's, came to the pitch to draw his winnings.

"You should be locked up pulling stunts like that, Jelley said as he counted out the £120, grimacing with every fiver he pulled out of his pocket.

"It's no more than fraud and I've a good mind to report you to the authorities".

The punter didn't bat an eyelid. He took the money, carefully placed it in his inside pocket, then grabbed Jelley by the throat, pinning him up against the rail where the pitch was located.

"Report me will yer, he said in what sounded like a South Yorkshire accent.

"Report me for what? The cops and everybody else will be delighted that we've taken money from a greedy bastard like you so go ahead, you'll be a bigger laughing stock than you already are."

He then let a trembling Jelley go and walked casually off. Although obviously a pensioner, he didn't look someone to mess with, something I had confirmed a few minutes later. George Danville was a regular punter of ours. He was also in his 70's and had been a well-known pugilist in his time but was now obviously retired though still very active. He called me over just as the lucky punter was walking away.

"Ed, he said, I remember that guy from my fighting days.

"I took a last-minute fight one Saturday in Doncaster, his home town, and knew I was on a hiding to nothing as I would have had to knock him out to get a draw.

"I managed to keep him at bay for a few rounds until he hit me with a right hook that almost knocked me senseless. I went down on one knee and for the first and only time in a career spanning 130 fights I deliberately stayed down.

"I can still feel that punch now so if he'd have hit Jelley, even at his age, he would have ended up on the dog track and might never have woken up."

One Saturday night Jelley asked if I would go with him to Ripon the following Monday – a Bank Holiday – for the Great St Wilfred meeting as it was forecast to be a warm sunny day and there would be a big crowd.

"There won't be any pay, of course, he said.

"But you'll enjoy the ride and can help out if I need you."

I reminded him of an old saying.

"Men who work for nowt and women who shag for nowt are always busy", and declined his offer.

He must have stewed over it for a while or offered someone else the same deal and got turned down as before the night was out he backed down and said he would pay me 'the going rate' whatever that meant.

He lived on Holderness Road and said he would pick me up on the corner of Dairycoates Avenue as there was a Co-op butchers there that would be open despite it being a Bank Holiday. I went into the Co-op with him as the butcher, Billy Bishforth, was a friend of mine and a regular punter.

"Now then Bill, said TJ as he walked briskly through the entrance to the counter.

"Can you weigh me two thin pork sausages – oh, and have you any old mutton that's been hanging around and you don't want? It's for the cat you know".

Bill knew TJ from old, and knew very well he didn't have a cat.

"Christ TJ, are you throwing a party?" he said.

We got into his old banger of a car and called in Ferriby for some petrol. He asked the attendant for one pound, eight shillings and four pence worth of fuel – no more, no less. He'd worked out that was exactly the amount of petrol it would take to get there and back to Ripon. Good job there were no diversions!

Greyhound punter Jack Wallis told me that Jelley once had had an old banger that had given up the ghost and had to be towed away when returning from Beverley races one day. He wasn't too concerned as the insurance was worth more than the car but he was absolutely crestfallen as he'd put almost two pounds worth of petrol in the day before.

He'd gone to the scrap yard the next day with a can and siphon to retrieve the fuel but someone had already beaten him to it. Apparently he never slept for a fortnight which is why he never bought more fuel than absolutely necessary from then on.

There was an enormous crowd at Ripon that day – a post-war record in fact – and we never stopped taking bets from half-an-hour before the first race. The results were good for the bookies with several outsiders winning and Jelley had a very good day. There was no chance of a bonus of course and we never had a thing to eat or drink from setting off in the morning. He did disappear for a few minutes after the third race and I thought he would come back with some refreshments which to be fair to him he did – a lemonade bottle filled with water out of the tap in the toilet.

However, Jelley did say he would pay for fish and chips on the way home and we called in at his regular feeding place in Wetwang. As we entered the chip shop Jelley's face turned almost white. He'd looked up at the notice board and saw that the haddock had gone up from one shilling and three pence to a shilling and sixpence.

"What! – that's extortion, Jelley said.

"You can't do that – I can't afford it".

The chip shop owner told him that was the price and he could take it or leave it so Jelley said he would leave it. I told him he'd promised me fish and chips and he very reluctantly had to buy mine but there was no way in the world he was going to the extreme of purchasing a haddock for himself.

He asked the proprietor for a bag of chips and some scraps. On receiving them he was beside himself with joy. I'd never seen him so happy.

"There's bits of chips in these scraps, he said.

"Brilliant - this is what I'll be having from now on."

That from a man who had just had an excellent day at the races – God knows what he would have done if he'd lost! – no doubt starved to death.

If You Don't Like Someone, Buy Them A Greyhound

There's another old saying – 'If you don't like someone, buy them a greyhound' and that's been a feature throughout my life. Everyone who enters the sport should do so with a health warning as 'Going to the dogs' can seriously damage your wealth, and in some cases, health. However, as long as you have your wits about you and are not shocked when a well plotted plan goes wrong, as it often does, then the sport can offer massive entertainment and enjoyment for very little money.

I never owned a greyhound despite having numerous opportunities to do so. Several of my clients who have owed me money have offered their dogs in payment but I was never tempted and usually told them not to bother and wait for a better day.

The main reason for such reticence was an incident concerning a good friend of mine, Charlie 'Chuck' Harrison, a real rough and tumble character from Liverpool Street. Chuck was a fine amateur rugby player with a reputation as one of the hardest of them all but like so many of his kind he had a soft side, especially when it came to animals.

Chuck won a greyhound puppy from a so-called pal in a game of cards and kept it in a life of luxury in a converted shed in the back yard. At some stage of its pampered life, the dog began to show something of the ability its breed were meant for, especially when chasing moggies around the back alleys of Liverpool and Witty

Streets. Chuck therefore decided that the dog, which had been registered and tagged at birth, should go into training as a 'proper' greyhound and that he was the man for the job.

So began a regime of training that the immortal Mick The Miller would have been privileged to have had. The dog, whose racing name was Mad Lad but was known to one and all as Laddie, was fed the very best of nutritional food from Maltbys with supplements costing Chuck a small fortune. He took Laddie to Pickering Park every afternoon and let him loose, watching in pride as he gradually began to look the part of a racing thoroughbred.

Another friend of his, a veteran of the greyhound world, Cyril Bolter, set up a contraption called a ball hare which Laddie chased to great effect, seemingly enjoying the chance to show his prowess as a racer and both Chuck and Bolter believed he had the speed and ability to go right to the top of the greyhound racing ladder.

After a few months of this regime, Chuck decided that the time was ripe for Mad Lad to make his debut on the racetrack. I had just passed my driving test and had old banger of a car and Chuck asked me if I would take him, Bolter and the dog to Askern racetrack near Doncaster where he had been entered in the 7.45.

The plan was that the three of us, plus canine superstar, would travel to South Yorkshire where a coup had been planned and we were set to make our fortune. We believed no-one would know the dog at the track - an unlicensed venue known as a 'flapping track' - so we were certain to get a good price about him and win a tidy sum.

Unfortunately for us, the word had gone around the streets of Hessle Road, probably from Bolter, that Chuck Harrison had a real

55

'flying machine' who was an absolute certainty in the 7.45 at Askern - it was just a case of putting the money on with the unsuspecting bookies and coming home with a fortune.

On the way to the track, Bolter sat along side of me in the front of the car with Chuck in the back with Laddie, who was wrapped in a blanket to ensure he didn't catch a chill and being fed honey from a spoon. He was being offered plenty of encouragement for the task ahead by a smitten Chuck, convinced he had found a passport to fame and glory as a greyhound trainer as well as a considerable financial reward from the betting coup.

On arrival at Askern we were rather dismayed to see what seemed to be half of Hessle Road's greyhound punters, all there obviously to take advantage of Mad Lad's undoubted prowess and put one over the local bookies. That was bad news for us as it would mean we might not get the top price we were hoping for but nonetheless we were still certain that we would be pulling off one of the biggest betting coups seen in these parts for a long time.

The dog was taken to the paddock before racing where he was weighed and inspected as he still had to be a registered greyhound to run even though it was a flapping track. The first race came and went and all eyes were now on the 7.45 where Bolter paraded Mad Lad, who was due to race from trap four.

I said to Harrison and Bolter: "Just look at him, he's in fantastic shape, much more like a real greyhound star than the five mangy looking specimens also being led around.

"Let's get on and bet like men."

The five owners of the opposing dogs were obviously in the mistaken belief they could take on our superstar and most were by now backing their own dogs.

The bookies, who were definitely not stupid and had noted the influx of strangers with the easily observed Hull accents, were taking no chances and chalked Trap 4 Mad Lad as a 2/1 favourite, a much lower price than any of us had anticipated. That didn't deter the Hessle Roaders however who plunged on him to such an effect that his price quickly contracted to a very short 6/4 favourite.

We had missed the boat in that respect and had to take the lower price which meant staking more than intended – still, what did it matter?, the money was surely in the bag as Mad Lad was an absolute certainty – wasn't he?

Once the dogs were loaded into the traps, myself, Chuck and Bolter made our way to the winning line to cheer our hero home. The hare started up and the anticipation was incredible. The traps opened with a jolt and Mad Lad got the perfect flying start we had hoped for. We were all screaming "Come on Laddie" as he raced to the first bend just in front of a scruffy looking trap 1 with a tiny bitch on his outside also challenging for the lead.

The six dogs shot into the first bend at incredible pace and we held our breath as they turned the corner – but only five came out! Where was Mad Lad? That became obvious when we espied a lone animal in the black jacket of Trap 4 rooted to the spot at the bend. As the remaining five headed swiftly for the finishing line, Mad Lad was watching them disappear into the distance, seemingly oblivious to what was required of him.

The problem was, we later found out, that Bolter's ball-hare only went in a straight line so that when Laddie entered the bend in that strange environment he had no idea what to do.

He then decided to trot back to the kennels where no doubt another nice meal and the usual warm friendly greeting would be waiting for him. Not this time Laddie!

Not surprisingly it was a long drive home. Chuck sat in the front seat alongside me with Bolter and the dog, minus blanket and receiving a torrent of abuse from his owner, in the back. When I say a long drive home, that didn't strictly apply to Bolter. To be fair to him, he'd advised us to give the dog a trial before we attempted a betting coup as he'd seen many a young greyhound fail to make the grade for all sorts of reasons.

Of course Chuck and I would have none of it – we knew better didn't we? Unfortunately Bolter, who was a really nice guy who would help anyone at any time, simply couldn't keep his opinion to himself and all the way home he kept on repeating how he'd told us to have a trial. If he'd said 'I told you so' once he said it a dozen times and Chuck was getting more and more exasperated. By the time we reached the top of Boothferry Road and Bolter had repeated it one more time Chuck had heard enough. He stopped the car abruptly, got out and slowly walked to the rear, opened the door and threw poor Bolter out. It was a long walk down Boothfreery Road back to Edinburgh Street as Bolter had no money left to hail a cab and buses had long since stopped running.

On his return to Liverpool Street, if Mad Lad expected the pampered life he had so far been privileged to have he was very

58

much mistaken. It was stale bread and water for him – at least until Chuck's anger and humiliation subsided and life gradually got back to normal.

Will You Do Me A Favour?

Greyhound owners are drawn from every possible walk of life though the vast majority are working men and women who enjoy the cut and thrust of the sport. Owning a top-class dog is everyone's dream and of course it's impossible for them all to be world-beaters though many of their owners wear rose-tinted glasses when it comes to their greyhounds.

One of the best dogs in Hull was owned by a character called Mally James, who loved to issue personal challenges to other owners who believed they had a dog to match his. The track regularly staged 'matches' where James' dog, Flashy Outlook, would take on rivals for a substantial side bet – 'Flashy' would shoot out of the traps like an arrow and almost always came up with the goods and was virtually unbeatable on his own patch.

James was quite a big gambler though it wasn't betting that led to his eventual demise – it was a vice of a completely different nature. He had left school and joined the army at a very early age – long before being conscripted. He had no particular talents and would never had made an engineer or signals expert but an incident in training sent him down a path that he could never had visualised, and eventually led to his demise, though not without a somewhat licentious rewarding spell on the way.

One of his platoon colleagues was quite badly injured in a fall while scrambling along a rope ladder and it was James who attended him and comforted him until help came. An officer saw his obvious empathy with the injured man and suggested he transferred into the Army Nursing Corps, something that James had never even contemplated.

It all made good sense and was an occupation that James could make a good career for himself, even when he eventually left the Army.

He was duly transferred and began training at an Army establishment in the Midlands where that year's intake of nurses had 150 new recruits – 146 girls and four blokes – two of who were puffs!

James wasn't a particularly handsome individual but had a very strong personality and always did very well thank you very much with the ladies – and now he could hardly believe his good fortune. He and the other guys were billeted with the girls in Army barracks and for three years James was in paradise – both at work and at play.

After another three years as an Army nurse, James left the service and went into the NHS and quickly rose through the ranks, becoming a nursing tutor at a top training hospital. He never married but had numerous girlfriends, many of them nurses, but his demise came when a nurse who had been turned down for promotion accused James of offering her an advancement for certain 'favours'.

She believed she had been knocked back because she didn't go along with what James had wanted and was obviously extremely bitter.

That appeared to set a ball rolling as several other nurses came forward to accuse James of requesting favours for advancement and the NHS managers took drastic action, suspending him from work indefinitely while it carried out an enquiry. A whole can of worms had been opened as it turned out that many of the senior nurses had been 'girlfriends' of James' at one time or another and were under suspicion of having obtained their positions by favours.

It was no great surprise to anyone that James lost his job and his pension but he was undoubtedly very fortunate indeed not to be prosecuted and sent to jail. It never really deterred him and he bounced back large as life after a few months – and 'Flashy' kept on winning enough to cover his living costs for a long time afterwards.

Skint In His Own Country

Jack Wallis, who I mentioned earlier, was a regular punter who had owed Malloy a small sum for a few weeks. Malloy told me one night to go and ask him for the money and I enquired of him, in the most diplomatic terms I could muster, when we were likely to get paid.

Wallis, one of Hull's greatest characters who had a wealth of anecdotes for every occasion, went into his inside pocket and reached for what I hoped was the few pounds in arrears.

Instead, he took out a pocket notebook with a list of people he owed money to and said:

"You were number six on the list for payment – you're now number 42."

Wallis was an inveterate gambler who thought he knew everything there was to know about dog racing yet, like so many, he hadn't a clue about the most useful aspect of the sport to any punter – backing winners.

Every loser he backed had been unlucky or 'tied up' by the cheating trainer – it was never his own judgement that caused his downfall. One particular night, after yet another failure, he recounted to everyone within earshot how the winner couldn't possibly have won but for his selection having the worst possible luck in-running.

Most of the regulars took Wallis's whining with a pinch of salt but one of them, a Polish guy who had arrived in the city with a group of

1000 of his countrymen in 1951, had heard the excuses just once too often.

"The winner was a certainty, he said.

"That's why I backed it and you're skint."

That sort of thing was like a red rag to Wallis, already smarting from losing the last of his wages and having to listen to someone ridiculing his judgement.

"I might be skint, he said.

"But at least I'm skint in my own country."

The Pole shouldn't have been too concerned. Wallis hated just about everyone, especially blacks, Asians, foreigners, Chinese, Jews, bookmakers and most of all, Hull FC supporters as he was a die-hard Hull KR fan. In fact the only people he appeared to get on with were fellow losing gamblers and thankfully for him and us there were always plenty of those around to empathise with him.

He especially despised bookmakers and Malloy was definitely on his hate-list. When I asked him for the money he owed he said: "Your boss is the meanest, hardest man I've ever come across. The softest thing about him is his teeth."

Wallis was born and bred on Hessle Road but like many his home had been flattened and had moved to the newly-built Bilton Grange Estate with his long suffering wife Edna. He hated it.

"In Wassand Street we had an outside lavvy and a dirty coal-house, he said.

"But at least you couldn't hear the next door neighbours putting salt and vinegar on their chips!

"The walls are that thin you can hear the old fella putting his teeth into a glass."

Wallis was one of the very few men I ever met who joked about his wartime experiences. He'd definitely served his country in some capacity but said that when the first shot was fired he was in Calais – when the second went off he was in Gypsyville Tavern!

Apparently he'd been slightly wounded in the leg. He'd be having an argument with someone, telling them how he'd fought through blood and bullets to save the likes of them, then he'd shake his leg and asked them to listen to the shrapnel rattling.

That Polish guy, we called him Ludo as we could neither spell, say, nor understand his real name, hadn't had much luck in his time though I suppose he was better off in Hull than many of his countrymen.

He'd been captured by the Russians during the war and when it was over transferred to the British. He ended up in an internment camp in Kenya and didn't get out until 1951. What on earth he must have though when landing at King George Dock is anyone's guess but like so many of his fellow travellers he wasn't averse to hard work and earned enough to become a regular and sometimes sizeable punter at the dog track. He and Wallis did have one unlikely thing in common – both had wagered a lot of money on the St George Club walking race and had backed the same guy – Denis Batte – who had been telling everyone for months that he was a certainty.

Money Making Machine

Most of the track's bookmakers had a sort of relationship with a trainer. The bookie would get to know when one of the trainer's dogs 'wasn't wanted' for whatever reason and laid it to plenty of money. When it lost, as it invariably did, the bookie would hand the trainer a sweetener though there were often occasions when the dog inadvertently won, usually by a fluke, and that caused no end of friction,

One such trainer was Ginger Lomax, a huge bull of a man for whom the word 'bent' was surely invented. Lomax couldn't have lain straight in bed and though thought by many as a bit of a character was far from that and mixed with all the wrong kind of people.

He should have been warned off the track on numerous occasions but the stadium owners realised he always had plenty of people willing to purchase and race greyhounds so put up with his ways when the correct thing to do would have been to throw him off.

Malloy and I had a few run-ins with Lomax at the track but he also gave me information on a couple of occasions that I naturally took advantage of. He believed I owed him a favour or two so I occasionally transported a dog from one venue to another in my van and even had one of his dogs in my shed for a few weeks though I never asked why as I realised it would almost certainly be the forerunner to some sort of scam.

Lomax called me one day and asked if I would do him a big favour.

"Can you bring your van and pick up this money-making machine," he asked.

A money-making machine is usually a term for a dog that would prove unbeatable if handled the right way.

"You can keep it in your shed for a few weeks until the heat has died down."

Believing I was going to pick up the dog, I drove to his kennels, which were situated out in the sticks near Brough, knocked on the door and was greeted by a friend of his who I knew vaguely called Nick Chivers.

Chivers was what you might call a 'Jack The Lad' and had his fingers in many pies, most of them either bordering on, or just over the line of, the illegal , though he was well liked by all and known as someone who always paid his debts, an honourable trait in an often dishonourable business.

"Where's Ginger? I asked.

"I've come for the dog."

"What dog's that then? a voice shouted from the back of the building.

"Who asked you to come for a dog?"

That was Lomax of course and I brushed past Chivers and went inside.

"You told me to come and pick up a money-making machine I said.

"So I've brought the van and I'll take him home and keep him in the shed for a while."

"Who said anything about a dog? Chivers piped up, and I was beginning to get more than a little nervous when realising he was involved.

"There's no dog, it IS a money-making machine."

Lomax then pulled a huge tarpaulin cover off a strange looking object that was standing in the corner of the room.

"This is it, he said.

"We've been making ten-bob notes with it but the market's been flooded and things are getting a bit uncomfortable so we need it hiding until they cool down."

Needless to say I left skid-marks.

Would You Watch Muffin The Mule?

The first few years after the Second World War ended had brought much austerity to the country, especially in the cities that had suffered major bombing damages; London, Coventry, Belfast and especially Hull, as we had to endure more casualties per population than any other.

Our city's strategic position as the country's third largest port, and of course its convenience for the enemy aircraft, had incredibly led to bombings by Zeppelin's in the First World War and in 1915 54 people were killed. It suffered terribly the second time around and over 1200 lost their lives including 400 in two disastrous successive evenings when thousands were also injured.

Not surprisingly the whole area needed a vast rebuilding programme but money to put schemes into operation was virtually non-existent, especially in this part of the world. My dad was very pally with one of the city councillors, a fellow railwayman, who told him they had applied to the Government for grants to begin rebuilding. The original claim was for £1m but the amount granted was £50,000, half that given to Plymouth and Portsmouth.

No wonder we all had the feeling that we were stuck out in a forgotten city somewhere in the bleakest part of the frozen north and we were being left to fend for ourselves.

The first 10 years after the war hadn't been so very different from the pre-war era. Television was very much in its infancy and Gerry

Malloy was the only person I knew who had a TV set in 1951 when the new Holmes Moss transmitter began broadcasting to this area, though why anyone would want to watch Muffin The Mule, Mr Pastry and Wilfred Pickles is beyond me. Pickles, who was also an actor, had a 'great face for radio' and should have stuck to that medium where he and his wife Mabel were extremely popular.

Hardly anyone had a car and people had to make their own entertainment and enjoyment, which they were certainly intent on doing.

Thankfully for most of us by the middle of the decade things were changing on the political scene and many more working class institutions and organisations were beginning to make their mark. Even those of us who had no feel whatsoever for politics – and that was most of us if the truth be known - had that unmistakeable feeling that the days of being ruled by upper class 'toffs' and imbeciles, more often than not the same person, were drawing to a close though it's taken a very long time in coming – approximately 1700 years since the Romans left – and it can't come soon enough!

There was an undeniable feeling of change in the air. Much of the drabness was disappearing from our daily lives, probably thanks to the fact that many more homes had acquired televisions and we could actually see what was happening in other parts of the world for the first time. We'd been able to watch clips on Pathe News when we went to the pictures but TV brought a new dimension to our lives. The change was palpable and rapid and life went from grey to full colour in a very short space of time, even in a backwater like Hull.

Despite that, travelling from the top to the bottom of Hessle Road it was still very easy to see the devastation that the bombs had caused. Almost every street had some damage and many were virtually obliterated. But the strange thing is that it didn't appear to bother anyone too much.

Despite the squalor we just didn't seem to notice – probably a case of everyone trying to forget the horrors and getting on with living our lives as best we could. Mother would go to the old church hall in Carlton Street with her ration book every Monday morning, joining the throng that was already there. While the meagre ration allowance was always very welcome it was fish that was the staple diet of just about every family. Most mothers had seven different ways of cooking fish – a variation for every day of the week.

Pubs, clubs, cinemas, snooker halls and dance-halls thrived and sport has been the major attraction for men since the end of the war. Great sporting icons such as Denis Compton, Freddie Trueman and Sir Len Hutton were ruling the cricket fields while Sugar Ray Robinson, along with Joe Louis, Tommy Farr, Freddie Mills and Rocky Marciano, were treated like Gods in the boxing rings.

Soccer had Stanley Matthews, Tom Finney, Billy Wright and Manchester United's Busby Babes, all idolised and providing entertainment for the masses - local fans paying through the turnstiles.

It's a very rare sight to see a woman at a soccer or rugby ground but go to the Continental dance hall on a Saturday night and they appear to outnumber the men by about three to one. Also, there were many more heartthrobs for the ladies in the cinema, so while I was idolising Raich Carter my sisters were madly in love with Cary Grant and Stewart Granger.

The Glory Days With Carter

As a youngster, my greatest delight was watching Raich Carter lord it over Boothferry Park. Me and my pals would walk down Hawthorn Avenue, into Haltemprice Street, then across Beaky's field towards the back of the huge stadium.

We then climbed a small wire fence surrounding the ground and into the outer regions where we had a secret loose railing which we shot through in turn, escaping the stewards in the process.

Amazingly the gap in the fence wasn't closed for a very long time and though the crowds were always massive they were undoubtedly a lot more there than the official attendance figures thanks to that illegal entrance.

I was at Boothferry Park one Saturday in 1951 and watched in absolute wonder when the first train pulled into the stadium's own platform, called Boothferry Halt. That was the first-ever soccer special to disgorge supporters at any stadium's gates in the country and, as the fare from Paragon Station was only 6d return, the trains were always packed to the hilt with 5000 estimated to have made the journey on that first day.

Unfortunately our secret entrance was found by a particularly nasty steward who, on catching me squeezing through one Saturday, clipped me around the ear before demanding a shilling or he would call the cops.

I reluctantly paid him the bob but he grabbed hold of me by the scruff of the neck and threw me out anyway.

As it happens, my love affair with Hull City was on the wane anyway as the great Raich Carter left the Club in 1952. The Tigers had beaten Manchester United 2-0 at Old Trafford in the third round of the FA Cup but were struggling in the league and Carter played his last league match when they beat Doncaster 1-0 and just avoided relegation.

Myself and 29,000 other went along to Boothferry Park to pay homage one last time to the great man when City drew 2-2 with his former club Sunderland in a friendly. The guy who took over from Carter, Bob Jackson, wore a bow-tie, which completely alienated me and my like. We thought bow-ties only belonged to professors or classical musicians, certainly not to soccer managers.

Carter had also persuaded the likes of Don Revie and Neil Franklin to follow him to Hull and it was no great shock when Revie soon asked for a transfer and went to Manchester City so I decided it was time to switch my allegiance to rugby.

Hessle Road belonged to Johnny Whiteley's Hull FC, who always played to huge crowds at The Boulevard. Rugby League is massive all over the north and what a fantastic treat it is to go along to the ground and watch the likes of Tom Van Vollenhoven, Billy Boston, Eric Ashton, Rocky Turner, Neil Fox, Dick Huddart and Vince Karalius. We wait in great anticipation all week for the arrival of Wigan, St Helens, Wakefield and others and often have to stand in long queues to gain entry.

Hull had a fantastic pack of forwards led by the brilliant Johnny Whiteley and included the fearsome Drake twins and Welshman Tommy Harris, regarded as one of the greatest ever players in his position. Jim Drake, who I got to know well, was a ferocious prop-forward whose sole aim in any game was to cause havoc, and he was very good at it, in fact one of the best.

Jim was a bit unfortunate in his career as it coincided with that of the great Wigan prop Brian McTigue, who was regarded as probably the best forward in the world, even by the Australians.

Jim's brother Bill was a completely different character, laid-back but a very strong-running second-row forward whose speed and strength allowed him to score numerous tries.

The forwards must have been amongst the best ever as the backs were ordinary in the extreme, none ever getting a look in for international selection.

The team were supported by perhaps the most feared fans in the game. The Threepenny Stand was renowned as the place the visiting team hated. Packed in like sardines, the fans would start abusing and insulting the away side before they had even kicked off and many a so-called hardman of the game wilted under the sustained pressure.

However, they also have a reputation for being knowledgeable and I remember a particular game when the great Warrington wingman Brian Bevan scored another of his trademark wonder tries and he was afforded a reception fit for one of the local heroes.

The saying at the time was that the day's attendance was gauged by how deep the piss was in the latrines at the back of the

Threepenny Stand, though there was probably more, much more, running down the terraces.

Hull Kingston Rovers didn't have much going for them for a long time, being made up mainly of young local players. There's a saying in the RL world that if Featherstone or Castleford needed a prop forward for the weekend they need only go to one of the numerous pit-heads in the area, shout down and another prop-forward would emerge.

The same could apply to Rovers, only for pit-heads substitute Alexandra Dock. Thankfully for them by the end of the decade some fine young talent, especially Peter Flanagan, John Taylor, Brian Tyson and Alan Burwell, was emerging and the future is looking much brighter for the Robins.

Other great names from the sporting world include Stirling Moss, Emile Zatopek, Reg Harris, Vladimir Kuts, Gordon Richards, the Yorkshire athlete Derek Ibbotson, my own hero, despite being an Aussie, Keith Miller, and the brilliant young jockey Lester Piggott, who has became both a hero and villain to me. It has certainly been a fabulous era for all those of us interested in sport, and not just for betting purposes.

Almost every home has a musical instrument of some sort. Many have pianos while accordions, mouth organs, penny whistles and even the occasional violin are also in abundance. People are encouraged to 'do a turn' whether it's in the home or on stage on concert night at a local Club.

The Hull v Hull KR derby was often played on Christmas Day with a noon kick-off and many a time as a youngster mother had to tell me to go round to Jim

Sullivan's house in Eastbourne Street to drag dad away from the front parlour where, after watching the game then going on to Miller's pub, a dozen or so men would be singing White Christmas, Danny Boy and I'll Take You Home Kathleen around the piano.

A City Divided

Few people venture far from their own communities; they live there, work there and play there. Each city has separate areas which often differed greatly from another across the divide – and there are few divides like the River Hull, which separates East and West Hull.

The East of the city has its vast docks complex and most of the industry, including Fenners, Priestmans, Imperial Typewriters, Needlers, Blundell's Paints, Rank Flour Mill and Reckitt and Colman, is based there. The opening of the Bilton Grange estate has meant an exodus of sorts for some Hessle Roaders and another new estate at Bricknell Avenue has already taken hundreds of people away from the area.

Although these factories are big employers, I never knew anyone who worked in them, quite simply because they were deemed to be too far away, especially the first three on the list which were all on Hedon Road, about five miles away. My mate Billy was offered a job at Fenners when he left school but wouldn't take it. He said he gets a nose-bleed when crossing North Bridge and anyway, he doesn't go as far as that on his holidays.

In the West of the city it's very much fishing that holds sway and Hessle Road is the heart of a huge industry which the teachers at our school always told us with great pride was the world's biggest.

Virtually the whole of Hessle Road relies on fishing for a living, not just those involved in the industry itself but ancillary businesses such as taxi's, clog makers, the tailors who make the unique fishermen's suits, chandlers and numerous others who have a foothold in this vast industry.

While much of the country has struggled to get to grips with life after the war, Hessle Road's fishermen are providing tens of thousands of people with jobs, some of them with lifestyles unheard of elsewhere in the north.

Trawler owners, skippers, fish merchants and many more are getting rich on the proceeds of fishing trips to far away places such as Bear Island, Iceland and Norway, but of course it's a boom that didn't apply to everyone in the city and there's always a price to pay, unfortunately with the lives of so many trawlermen who have died on fishing trips to inhospitable places.

Hull's unemployment levels have been a major source of concern to all who aren't involved with fishing. The national average in the early 1950's was less than 2% but Hull's was more than double and some 5000 men were out of work at that time.

All were desperately seeking employment and I can remember reading in the Hull Daily Mail that a small deputation of men had hitch-hiked to London in the hope of persuading the powers that be to help the city's regeneration schemes. Thankfully they didn't have to hitch a lift back as the city's MP's put their hands in their pockets and paid their fares.

Dad had never liked the idea of me going to work on the fish dock after school and hated the idea of me running around after

Malloy and his cronies in the club. As I also despised the fish-house work with venom and, because I was earning a few quid at the dog track two nights a week, I gave up my job and allowed him to find me a position on the railways where I was supposed to be training to be a signalman.

I hated that job even more and was delighted when the foreman caught me skiving in the sheds, and not for the first time, so ending a brief and wholly unrewarding stint in the great nationalised industry.

It took me about five minutes to get another job – this time in Rosen's shoe factory on Hessle Road – but once again I had had an aversion to clocking on and clocking off at the same time every day and this time another foreman took umbrage when I 'borrowed' a pair of top-notch shoes for the weekend dance at the Palace and fired me on the spot when I took them back on the following Monday morning.

'Fattie's' Revenge

One Saturday night dance at the Palace, featuring The Billy Cotton Band Show with Alan Breeze, brought about a chastening experience for me, by now more than two years out of school and taking just a little more interest in the opposite sex though my main interest was still sport.

I was there with Billy and Harry, my best mates from schooldays, and a couple of lads I had met playing rugby for Fish Trades Youth Club. We all stood around the outside of the dance floor waiting to pick a 'lucky' partner to dance with as the girls were at this point dancing together.

Billy and I spotted a couple of likely looking recipients of our charms and nonchalantly walked out to split them. Billy grabbed his by the waist and spun her towards him while I took the hand of the rather attractive girl who supposedly was 'mine'.

"Are you dancing?" I enquired in my best James Dean-type tone.

"Not with you I'm not," came the shattering reply as she spun away with a big smirk on her face.

I was left there in the centre of the dance floor on my own waiting for the ground to swallow me up. With the best imitation of a nonchalant walk I could muster under the embarrassing circumstances, I slunk back to the side of the dance floor where my mates were doubled up laughing.

"She's a bit of a dog anyway, I lied.

"I only went so Billy could dance with the other one."

Of course no-one believed me but what happened next was scarcely believable anyway. The girl who had spurned me came over to where we had now all gathered, Billy included, and said:

"Hello Billy, how are you, you don't remember me do you?"

Billy looked at her with his usual quizzical gaze, and then it dawned on him.

"It's Jennie McDonagh isn't it?

"Jesus Christ, you look different."

"That's right, she said.

"Fattie McDonagh,

"I'm pleased you recognised me after all this time"

She then quickly turned on her heels and, looking even more attractive than she had a few minutes before, disappeared into the crowd.

Apparently Jennie had left school and gone to stay with her elder sister, a trainee teacher in London. She was always good at art in Frankie Sugden's and went to London to attend a college of art.

I later found out that she held a part-time position with a fashion designer called Mary Quant in a shop in somewhere called King's Road in Chelsea and that's where she had transformed herself from 'Fattie McDonagh' into a lovely young woman, far too good for the likes of me or my cronies anyway. Whether there's a future in the fashion business I'm not sure as I always thought it was the French who led the world in that industry. I wouldn't be at al surprised to see Jennie heading back to Hull with her tail between her legs in the not too distant future.

There weren't too many opportunities for mingling with girls but Billy and I managed to wangle a couple of tickets for one of Hull University's Saturday night dances. They were held once a month and usually featured at least one very good headline artist, obviously subsidised by the University.

Billy had a cousin, Ray, who worked behind the bar on busy nights and we blagged tickets off him at a reduced price. Ray informed us when we got there that it would be absolutely no use attempting to chat up any of the students who he said "were out of your league," and he was right.

After about an hour mooching around, Billy took the bull by the horns and approached a couple of lasses who were stood near the bar.

"Can we get you a drink, girls? He said.

"What'll it be, Babycham?"

"Thanks very much, I'll have a double brandy and my friend will have a whisky," one of them said in a strange accent.

Ray looked at us like we were a couple of mugs who'd just been had, telling us we would have more chance with Zsa Zsa Gabor, then thankfully only charged us about half of the true cost, though it was still plenty.

"What are you girls doing here," I asked.

"I'm reading history and my friend is in the geology department," the one with the strange accent said.

"Do you mean reading about history," I enquired innocently.

She looked at me with disdain.

"No, reading history," she emphasised.

"You're studying history then," I said, and she gave another contemptuous glance my way.

The conversation had started badly and went steadily downhill. Neither girl could believe it when we said we'd never heard of some guy called Philip Larkin.

"Never heard of Larkin, the other one said contemptuously.

"He's our absolute hero."

"Have you heard of Johnny Whiteley? Billy piped up.

"He's ours."

Not surprisingly once the girls had supped up they got up and left and were last seen smooching with a couple of student types who will undoubtedly have heard of Larkin - one of them even had a pony-tail!

Six-Month Stretch

I was just over a year away from doing my national service but out of work and looking for something to 'fill in' before joining up. I'd had quite an eventful life for someone so young, working in the club and at the dog-track was regarded as quite glamorous by most of my mates who were either on the fish dock or doing mundane work on the railways or for the council.

Things appeared to be going OK but that's usually when something comes along and kicks you firmly in the goolies. Little did I know what was coming next – if I had I would have run the proverbial mile. My lifestyle prospects were to about to take a huge reversal.

Gerry Malloy mixed with some shady characters, amongst them a Liverpudlian called Harold Gallagher. Gallagher had one of those 'criminal faces', you know, like a Scouser with cauliflower ears; a dash of Cockney and a hint of Glaswegian. He'd been a former boxer who had regularly fought out of Hull and decided to make his base here. Gallagher was into all sorts of bent scams, mainly minor stuff like smuggling tobacco and cigarettes from Holland but he was also known as someone who would 'fence' stolen goods in a small-time sort of way.

The rumour was that he'd had to scarper from Liverpool in a hurry after some gang-related fracas in which he'd been heavily involved. All in all not a nice man to do any kind of business with.

Gallagher had treated me quite well when I was running errands at the club and I probably got more back-handers from him than anyone else, including that ten-bob note I mentioned earlier. What I didn't know at the time was that he was grooming me for something else.

Malloy handed me a package one day and asked me to take it to Gallagher's house in Bean Street. I didn't think anything of it at the time, believing it to be money owed from a bet. Gallagher than gave me another smaller package and asked me to take it to Paragon Square and hand it to a friend of his from Liverpool who was getting a train back.

Again I though nothing of it and did as I was told, handing the parcel to a shifty looking pock-faced character who Gallagher had identified to me beforehand.

A week later Malloy told me to go round to Gallagher's house as he wanted me to do an errand. When I got there he asked me to repeat the process of the previous week and there would be a few bob in it for me.

I can't say I was particularly suspicious at this stage though something didn't feel quite right. Anyway, I got off the bus at Paragon Square and looked for 'pock-face' but couldn't see him anywhere.

I stood there for about two minutes when to my absolute horror I was grabbed from each side by a policeman and a detective, who placed handcuffs on me and frog-marched me into Paragon Station. There, alongside two other detectives and a couple of coppers was Gallagher's pal.

"Is this the courier," one of the 'tecs asked him.

"Who's he? said the Liverpudlian.

"Never seen him before."

"What am I supposed to have done?" I asked.

By this time the police had taken the package from me and it didn't take the mind of a genius to know that this was the offending article.

"Is this your property," one of the detectives said.

"No, I'm just passing it on to someone," I said.

"Who might that be, said a copper.

"Is this who you're supposed to be handing it to?" looking directly at the shifty Liverpudlian, who glared at me with venom in his eyes, daring me to agree with the copper.

"I don't recognise him, I lied.

"In fact I've never seen him before."

A smirk came across the Scouser's face, noticed of course by the coppers.

"Who gave you the package?" one of the detectives asked.

That's where I had to think on my feet. I couldn't possibly implicate Gallagher or Malloy.

"A guy I met in a pub, I lied.

"He gave me two quid and asked me to bring it to the station and hand it to someone who would recognise me."

A likely story which the coppers of course knew was a complete fallacy. Naturally I couldn't remember which pub nor describe the so-called handler and was then bundled into the back of a Black Maria and taken to Central police station where I was shoved into a holding cell to await my fate.

A couple of hours later I was taken out and charged with being in possession of stolen goods. I still didn't know what was in the package but it turned out to be some jewellery heisted from Barnaby And Rust just off Whitefrairgate..

While the stolen goods weren't all that valuable they were a little too hot for Gallagher to handle which is why he was sending them on to Liverpool. He had decided to do it in stages and the first one got through but the police had received a tip-off and yours truly copped for the second lot.

I was then taken back to the cell and was provided by the police with the duty solicitor. If I thought my luck was out before I met this guy it took a dramatic turn for the worse once he entered the equation.

His name was Simon Green, who ran a local law firm that had been started by his father many years before. The old man was much liked in the community and greatly respected but his clown of a son had no idea what he was doing, as I was to quickly find out.

He asked me to tell him the exact truth or he couldn't represent me so I spilled the beans to him. He said he would be returning in the morning with his advice but in fact he didn't turn up, which was to become a recurring theme throughout the traumatic events, always with some lame excuse.

Obviously he knew I was guilty and couldn't care less about extenuating circumstances and when at last he did arrive he told me to plead guilty and that as it was a first offence I would get probation and a fine.

At least Malloy stood bail for me and I was allowed out but having to explain the situation to my parents wasn't easy – no-one in our family had ever been in trouble with the law previously, well except Uncle Edgar, but nobody in the family ever spoke about him, and I was suddenly an outcast.

By this time Gallagher had fled to pastures new – some say he was now working for a couple of guys in London called Kray – but left a thinly-disguised message with Gordon Spradbury that any attempt to implicate him in the scam would be dealt with violently, not specifically to me but to my sisters.

That sort of warning is unambiguous but I was still living in hopes that my solicitor could fine a way out – no chance!

I pleaded guilty to receiving stolen goods when my case came up at the Magistrates Court and awaited my sentence. After an interminable wait the magistrate sentenced me to six months in a juvenile correction institution – borstal.

Slit Wrists & Worse - A Rovers Fan

So began the worst period of my life so far. Taken away in a prison van, I ended up in the borstal on Hedon Road – what a nightmare.

The hardships endured as a child in the war and growing up amongst the debris of Hessle Road were nothing compared to life in a juvenile prison. After a thoroughly degrading debriefing which included sticking things into places where I didn't even know I had places I was taken to a cell in C Wing reserved, I suppose, for those of us regarded as 'non-violent'. If that was the passive wing God knows what the violent part was like.

The first thing I noticed when walking to the cell was the smell, a mixture of stale cabbage, piss, sweat and disinfectant. It didn't bother me, after all I was used to the fish manure factory, but it was an odour that lingered throughout my time in this so-called 'corrective facility'.

I was put into a cell containing a skinny guy of about seventeen with a sallow complexion who never spoke as I entered, he just gave me an evil look to suggest I was on the top bunk and don't bother attempting conversation. He didn't look like the type to argue with.

The first couple of hours passed without a word, just the banging and shouting from outside the cell. The screws eventually came banging on all the doors telling us it was supper time – at 5.00

o'clock, not even tea-time at home, and we were all marched down to the dining hall.

There were what seemed like hundreds of young kids hanging about, all of them looking to my eyes like murderers, violent robbers and rapists. I had a quick look around but didn't recognise anyone and my heart sank – it would have been a bit more comforting to have had someone to speak to whatever they'd done but not tonight at least.

After a truly gruesome meal which appeared to consist of cabbage, cabbage and a bit more cabbage, we were led back to our cells and at 8.00 o'clock the doors were locked for the night and the lights turned out. I was in a state of complete shock by this time but had no option but to climb onto my bunk and attempt to settle down.

Everything appeared to go quiet after a couple of hours with just the occasional shouting and I must have dozed off. Some time later I was awakened by a sort of whimpering sound, obviously coming from the bunk below. My cell mate had made it plainly obvious that he didn't want any sort of communication so I was very reluctant to get involved though I thought it strange that he should be crying; he had looked so tough.

After about half-an-hour I plucked up the courage to have a peek down below. What greeted me was the most horrific sight imaginable. He had slit his wrists! There was blood everywhere, a great pool of it lying on the cell floor – no wonder he was whimpering.

I shot out of my bunk, almost slipping in the pool of blood in the process, and began banging and shouting for help on the cell door.

No-one came. It was at least five minutes, almost an eternity, before a screw arrived enquiring what all the fuss was about.

"What the fuck's going on, he shouted.

"Do you want a good hiding on your first night?"

"He's slashed his wrists, I screamed.

"There's blood all over the floor."

"Jesus Christ," was his reply, and opened the door with a jolt.

He then blew his whistle very loudly and within seconds the area was swarming with screws. By this time the whole wing was in uproar and the screws bundled me out of the cell down to an empty room used for interviewing.

My cell mate wasn't dead but at first it appeared to the screws that I might have been responsible for his demise. Thankfully that notion was quickly put to bed but I had to wait five hours in that room while the cell could be thoroughly cleaned and disinfected ready for me to go back.

So that was my introduction to life in a borstal. It's an ill wind as they say as at least I had the cell to myself for a few days until a pickpocket from Bilton Grange was put in to share. At first I thought he was a relatively amiable type who I would be able get on with – that was until he told me he was a Rovers supporter! I think I would rather have had the wrist-slitter back.

I continued to keep my head well and truly down after that first night incident but I did notice one or two of the inmates looking at me a little suspiciously. One day while helping out in the laundry I saw someone I recognised from Hessle Rd, a known burglar and thoroughly bad lad who had been at our school.

I sort of sidled up to him and said: "Now then Pete, what are you doing in here?"

He gave me a disdainful look and, out of the corner of his mouth replied: "Fuck off and don't talk to me again." Charming.

After a couple of weeks I spotted someone else I had seen around the streets of Hull. I had played rugby against him in the under-17's and he was a big, strapping prop-forward who most of us kept out of his way when he came charging through like a raging bull. I did once foolhardily take my life in my hands and attempt to tackle him head-on but he hit me so hard I did a triple somersault and a back flip, ending up on the adjoining pitch. I played on the wing for the rest of the match.

He was far too good for us and signed professional forms with Hull FC and was playing regularly in the A team, which at his age was a big achievement. I had read in the Hull Daily Mail that he's been sent down for GBH outside of the Palace nightclub where he acted as a bouncer and here he was.

Once again I took the bull by the horns and casually walked up to him: "A bit different to playing against Halifax," was my attempt at witty conversation.

He obviously didn't know me, nor wanted to, but at least he did manage a reply of sorts.

"Look, he said.

"Whoever you are you're nothing in here.

"It's dog eat dog, you say nowt to anyone and do your best not to even look them in the eye."

"Yeah but it's different for you, I said.

"You're a well-known hard-nut and can take care of yourself."

"Hard-nut! was his contemptuous reply.

"Listen, there are 200 guys in here and I'm the 199th hardest," throwing me a look that left me in no doubt who was number 200 on the list.

The whole time spent there was completely soul destroying. Two hours in a morning working in the laundry and another three in the afternoon. An hour each day in the yard and the remainder of the time spent in the cell.

There was no way I was going to try out the recreational facilities. Darts, snooker and ping pong were OK in their place but I didn't want to offend anyone by beating them so I stayed well away.

Thankfully there was one saving grace that probably just about preserved my sanity. I had always enjoyed reading thanks to my grandma and the borstal had a reasonable library. Gran was an inspiration to me when I was very young, though in her own quiet way. She was my mother's mam and lived just a few doors away from us.

She had a piano in the front room and could play a little but it was books that were her great passion. She was originally from Norfolk and had followed the mass exodus out of the county in the late 1800's. Most had gone to London or Birmingham so it was strange how she'd ended up in Hull.

Thank God For Moby Dick

Gran was one of three sisters and two brothers from a small hamlet in the north of the county of Norfolk and their parents, like so many, were in service on the huge Sandringham Estate. They lived in a tiny cottage belonging to the Estate so it was no great surprise that one by one the children had to get out and make their own way in life.

Gran's elder sister, Bessie, had answered an advertisement in a local post office for someone to help in a big house in Hessle, which of course she'd never heard of but knew was somewhere near the Yorkshire coast. Travelling north was incredibly difficult in those days, especially from such a rural area, and involved a pony and trap to the local station, then a train to Kings Lynn, another to Lincoln; on to New Holland and finally the ferry across the Humber. But Bessie eventually made it, obviously impressed the owners, and was immediately offered the job.

She hadn't been there long when she realised there was plenty of work in similar positions in the area and asked her two younger sisters to join her, which they did almost immediately.

So here were three sisters from rural Norfolk thrust into life in Hull, a thriving fishing community and very, very different to what they had been used to. They all eventually found husbands and settled down but what an adventure it had been for them and such a massive upheaval.

I was a very fast reader so it was a real problem for me that I could only take out one book a week. I solved the problem by reading each book about four times – in fact I lost count of how many times I read Moby Dick. I loved all the great adventure stories and there were plenty of them in the library.

Treasure Island was, and still is, my favourite but Robinson Crusoe, Ivanhoe, Huckleberry Finn and The Great Gatsby all became part of my life and I was hugely indebted to the great authors who had created them. The latter novel, by F Scott Fitzgerald, wasn't very long and I could race through it in no time but learnt to savour every word and imagined myself in the rarefied atmosphere of Jay Gatsby's world, which was rather difficult from Cell Block F of Hull Borstal.

So, after four months, two weeks and a day I was finally let loose on society again. Nothing much had changed though I noticed people were very wary of me, even those I had counted on as mates. It's not surprising really as there's a huge stigma attached to being a 'borstal boy' but I knew I wasn't a bad lad and was convinced I would get over it quickly.

Referring back to Uncle Edgar, who had been the only black sheep in the family before me, what happened with him was a mystery to me until just recently, and even now it's all a bit of a blur and neither dad nor mother will talk about it.

Don't Mention Uncle Edgar

Edgar is one of my dad's brothers. Mother never made any secret of the fact that she detested him and dad didn't tolerate him for long when he came to the house. There was always that sort of embarrassed silence hanging around with lots of muttering and shuffling about and my sisters generally made their excuses and left.

I couldn't see what the problem was. He seems a decent enough bloke to me, always very clean and tidy and there's a hint of fancy cologne in the room whenever he's present. I suppose that might have given me a clue but I was completely unaware of homosexuality, which is what Uncle Edgar is – a puff!

He worked in a gent's outfitters in the city centre – under manager he always said though as there were only the two of them employed there it wasn't hard to be an under manager. I knew he was friendly with the man who owned the sweets and tobacconists shop down our street, or the 'goodie shop' as we called it, but would no more thought of him as being that way inclined than Rock Hudson. His name was Albert Hargreaves and he was a pillar of the local community, running the Sunday League soccer team and several other social events. Whenever there was to be a street party to organise Albert would be in the middle of it and none of it would ever have happened but for him.

I don't know anyone who ever thought of Albert as a puff – but it seems he and Uncle Edgar were more than just good pals and there was no doubt in anyone's mind where Edgar's preferences lay.

Anyway, why it should bother anyone I can't imagine but of course the law of the land thinks differently and so do most of the population. I got to know through Mrs Dosdale, the terrace gossip, who just happened to mention as I was walking home one day that: "Your Uncle Edgar's at your house, Ed, smelling like a Maltese brothel.

"I should watch your arse if I were you, the great big Nancy boy."

That shook me to the core though I pretended that it was all water off a duck's back to me. Within the few seconds from Mrs Dosdale delivering the news and me walking through the front door an awful lot of questions had been answered in my mind.

So that's why dad would never allow Edgar to be alone in the house with me and why mother and my sisters all treated him with such contempt. There was also the fact that he'd disappeared for over a year not long before and no-one ever said why.

One of dad's elder brothers, Victor, told me that Edgar wasn't like anyone in the family and always stood out like a sore thumb. They weren't Hessle Roaders, living in Pearson Avenue off Beverley Road, but Victor had a good job and a car and spent more time round at our house than anyone bar us.

"He'd never play rugby with us, or soccer, he said.

"In fact he seemed to spend most of his time cleaning the house – even the bloody windows!

"He'd borrow a ladder from the builder's yard round corner and do the upstairs. The other women in the terrace knew he was a soft touch so they got him to do theirs as well - all for nowt."

It's likely that the local women knew about Edgar before anyone else – they had an intuition for that sort of thing and would always take advantage whenever they could. His dad, my granddad, worked in the foundry at Ideal Standard. He once took me there and I couldn't have imagined a worse place to work – it was like the gates of hell.

He'd come home when his shift finished at 5.00, have his tea and a wash and shave then off to the pub just in time for opening. He'd be in there most night playing dominoes and could easily sup ten pints of ale.

How on earth had a man like that sired someone like Edgar! You wouldn't believe it was possible.

Anyway, Victor told me that Edgar had left school and gone straight into the gent's clothing department in Bladons and then to the shop where he currently works. There was still a complete silence surrounding his sexuality – it was never brought up – everyone knew he was just one of those 'strange' men with different tastes.

However, a bombshell of gigantic proportions occurred when Edgar, who had never been seen in the company of a girl, announced he was getting engaged to Margaret Chilton, a young lass who lived in Edinburgh Street and had worked with him at Bladons.

How on earth did that happen? Didn't Margaret know about Edgar?

Everyone was truly shocked but no-one was saying anything – there was never any question of granddad talking to him about the facts of life or any other such mysteries – and after a year's engagement the pair got married in the registry office in the city centre.

Neither of them was earning much money but at least Margaret, or Maggie as she was better known, kept working which was quite unusual as most women stopped work straight away once they were wed.

They rented a house near her mother and it wasn't too long before Maggie became pregnant. The whole thing was bizarre but to all intents and purposes they seemed happy enough and Edgar doted on little Sally. Not too long after another girl, Rita, came along then the family was completed when a boy, Philip, was born.

The strange thing was, according to Uncle Victor, Edgar was getting more and more feminine in his ways so how on earth could he equate that with his family life?

After Philip was born Edgar started going out much more on a night – not to the Club to play snooker or darts like most of the men in his family but to Albert Hargreaves shop where he said he was being taught to play chess. Who the hell plays chess?

In fact he was hardly ever home and Maggie, with the help of her mother, brought the three kids up virtually on her own. She must have known by now what was going on but never said anything to anyone – not even to Edgar – though her mother certainly did.

He denied any impropriety of course but then things took a turn very much the worse for him. He must have been enjoying his secret life as he began to frequent places where people of his kind would meet clandestinely. The majority of those that way inclined were extremely discreet as any show of public affection between males was asking for trouble. And trouble is exactly what Edgar got.

The police had been keeping an eye on a character, a local solicitor, who they knew for certain was a puff and pounced on them both while they were in the public toilets in Pickering Park one evening.

The pair of them were charged with an offence under the act that covered just about everything that deals with homosexuality. The solicitor got probation, despite it not being a first offence by any means, but Edgar got fifteen months in Wakefield Prison.

How a prison sentence is going to help matters is a mystery and when Edgar was eventually released after doing a year he was hardly about to return to the bosom of his wife and kids, who by this time had gone to live with Maggie's mother.

Edgar was a forlorn figure on his release though thankfully for him his employer was a kind and considerate man who took him back. Unfortunately though, kind and considerate people were in very short supply indeed in Hull and Edgar was not only shunned more or less wherever he went but was also the subject of much abuse, and on one occasion a violent attack – queer bashing as it was called - as he walked his little dog in Pickering Park.

Having already suffered being incarcerated myself, I was one of the few who had sympathy for Uncle Edgar and when I saw him at our house that day I greeted him warmly – never mind what Mrs Dosdale and their like may think.

Albert Hargreaves got on with his life despite no longer having Edgar as his 'chess companion.' He had lived with his mother until she died when he was in his mid-forties and I'd never realised what a lonely man he was despite his busy social life.

For all his numerous customers and acquaintances – for all his organising skills around the Sunday league football team – and for all the bonhomie when greeting people – Albert was a closed book regarding his private life. He must have decided long ago to keep himself strictly to himself and after Edgar's demise no-one ever saw anyone going to the shop after hours for lessons in chess.

Victor's Bombshell

Uncle Victor, who had been the one that informed me about his brother's predilections, had done very well during the war, starting off as a private and ending up as a tank commander and acting captain. On leaving the army he returned to his previous occupation as a draughtsman and was quickly put in charge of a full department.

Victor wasn't married but had a woman living with him though they had no children. That's why I thought he doted on us three – we were the family he didn't have. But in fact that wasn't the real reason and when we all found out what it was it hit us all like one of those bombs dropping from Hitler's 'planes.

Victor was always smartly dressed, as befits someone in his profession, and apparently when he was a young fella he was thought of as a good catch and always had plenty of female admirers. One of them was a girl called Lorna, a rather exotic-looking young woman who had something of a chaotic lifestyle. She lived with families of former fairground workers – that is when she was at home as she regularly left to follow the fairs around the country - only returning when it suited her or when she had run out of money.

She was friendly – very friendly - with many of the young men around town and soon caught Victor's eye. Some of his pals had warned him that she would be trouble but Victor said he knew what he was doing and could look after himself.

Anyway, they had a bit of a fling for a few days (and nights) before Lorna upped sticks and left to join a travelling circus which had pitched up on West Park but was now heading off to the midlands and beyond.

Victor was disappointed as they had been having a good time together but at least he didn't have to suffer the mocking of his mates anymore.

"Off round to the slag-house?" was one of the less intimidating jeers.

"Join the queue – roll up roll up" was another.

He didn't really expect to see Lorna again and of course knew there could never be a serious relationship with such a flighty piece though about eight weeks later she had turned up unexpectedly one tea-time at Victor's house.

She didn't get much joy when she knocked on the door.

"Who on earth's that at the door? grandma said to granddad, peering out of the front window.

"It looks like a Gypsy woman, buy some pegs or she'll put a curse on us all."

When granddad opened the door with a shilling in his hand for the pegs he was surprised to see a young woman there on her own with no obvious sign of any goods for sale.

"Are you Vic's dad?" she said.

"Yes, Victor's my son, he replied.

"Who wants to know?"

"Can I speak to him? said Lorna.

"It's something urgent."

"He's out, said granddad, and he won't be back for a week as he's been called up and on manoeuvres somewhere near Whitby."

Without saying a word, Lorna turned on her heels and was gone.

"Who was that? said grandma.

"She looked a bit of a tart."

As it happens, granddad didn't think she looked like a tart at all, just someone a bit more colourful than the norm.

"Just a young woman asking for our Victor, he relied.

"She's on her way now, we won't be seeing her again.

"Good riddance is what I say, said grandma, even though she'd only glimpsed Lorna through a front room window for a second.

Victor came back on weekend leave a few weeks later but no-one informed him of anyone turning up at the house looking for him.

However, about six months later, Lorna turned up at the house again – this time pushing a pram!

Once again he was out but grandma and granddad were in, as was my dad, who by this time was married to mother and living a few doors away. To say it was a bit of a shock to see that young woman again, this time with a baby in tow, is a serious understatement. The three of them had no option but to ask her into the house, particularly as the baby, a little girl, was crying and all the neighbours were peering from behind their front room curtains.

"Go get our Victor you Harry, he's round at Stella Massey's house," grandma said sternly to my dad.

"I suppose that's who you've come to see," she said to Lorna.

By now, Lorna was feeling more than a little annoyed at the reaction of the Doyle family. She was no shrinking violet and if grandma thought she could browbeat her just because she was a young woman she would have to think again.

"Who else do you think I've come to see? she said.

"It certainly isn't you, you old battleaxe."

Grandad then jumped in with his two pennorth's worth and all hell broke loose but before it got to blows dad and Victor came scuttling through the front door.

Victor's face when he saw Lorna was a picture and when the baby started crying again and he saw the pram his mouth dropped so low it almost touched his knees. You see by now Victor had taken a fancy to Stella Massey and was starting to think of engagement, marriage, kids and all that with her. This situation certainly looked as though it was going to put the boot into all those plans.

"Now then Lorna, nice to see you again, he said.

"What brings you to these parts?"

Lorna wasn't going to be derailed by Victor's attempt at niceties.

"What the hell do you think I've come for? She said, looking towards the pram as she spoke.

Whose do you think that is, Charlie Chaplin's?"

There was an embarrassed silence for what seemed like an eternity but surprisingly it was dad who spoke first.

"Mam, go put the kettle on, let's sit down and talk this through," he said, to the astonishment of all present.

So that's exactly what they did. The baby had been born in Nottingham a week earlier and had been named Kathleen.

Lorna had been working at the Goose Fair in the city almost up to the baby's birth and was rushed into the maternity hospital just in time. After the birth she had registered the little girl with the authorities when she got back to Hull and had with her a certificate which she claimed was the official birth certificate.

"There you are, she said, handing the document to Victor.

"It's all legal and binding, just read it."

The certificate certainly looked genuine enough. Nottingham was recorded as the place of the birth of a baby girl and she was called Kathleen. The mother's name was Lorna Tyson of no fixed abode; the father was recorded as Victor Doyle, a trainee draughtsman of Pearson Avenue in Hull.

Victor and dad studied the document for an age, looking for loopholes I suppose, but it was grandma who was to break this silence.

"Hang on a minute, she said.

"If you check the date of birth with the time our Victor said he was going out with you that's less than eight months, she said triumphantly.

"How can that be his? You're trying it on."

"Kathleen was early, replied Lorna.

"You can check with any doctor you like and they'll guarantee it was an early birth.

"I'd been working on the dodgems and it must have brought her on before her time."

"A likely story," said grandma, who was by now beginning to see a light at the end of the tunnel.

"Well, you can think what you like, Lorna said.

"There's the proof and I want to know what you're going to do about it."

Victor was in a state by now and dad had retreated into the scullery away from battle stations. As for granddad, he was in his potting shed, or his greenhouse area as he called it. That was the place he invariably skulked off too whenever grandma got into one of her tantrums and this looked a good time to absent himself.

Victor asked Lorna what her plans were as it was now beginning to dawn on him that he had responsibilities, however much it pained him.

Lorna then produced another shock.

"I can't provide for the baby and don't want anything more to do with you, she said.

"She's now your problem.

"I'll look after her for another month and then I'm off to America with the circus.

"You decide what you want to do after that as I have no family to look after her.

"If you decide you don't want her I'll put her up for adoption but you'll have to pay for all the legalities."

She then got out of her chair, took the pram and headed for the door.

"I'll be back a month today," was her parting shot and she was gone, leaving a completely shell-shocked family behind.

There was complete silence in the house. Grandad came back in when he saw Lorna pushing the pram at some speed out of the terrace but dad decided to go home to tell mother the sordid tale.

Victor was due back in camp in a couple of days so didn't have much time to discuss anything, not that he wanted to, he just wanted it all to go away.

The one thing that was niggling at him was the timing of the birth though he supposed it was all feasible enough as there's no doubt that Lorna led a chaotic lifestyle. He didn't see Stella Massey again before he went away, much to her disgust and disappointment, but really didn't have long to think about options as the month would surely fly by.

There was obviously no way he could look after a baby as he was in the army and neither grandma nor granddad was up to that sort of thing nowadays, even if they wanted to, which they didn't.

No, the only sensible option was for him to pay up and have his daughter adopted.

When dad told mother, who had the justified reputation of being straight-laced, he expected her to hit the roof and call Victor all the names under the sun. But she didn't. In fact what she did do, unbeknown to anyone, was find out where Lorna was living and went to see her and the child.

Our Molly once asked mother how she'd met dad and why she had married him. We had seen a few grainy photographs of the wedding but everyone looked so glum, a sign of things to come, maybe.

"Your dad was regarded as a bit of a catch when he was a young man, mother said.

"He was nice enough looking and had a reasonable job and I'd known him for such a long time.

"We'd met when I was in the girl guides and your dad was a scout. We went away to camp near Hornsea one weekend and just sort of liked each other.

"We started going out in our teens and never really thought about anyone else. Anyway, all my friends were getting married so it just seemed the right thing to do."

As you can no doubt gather, mother wasn't the emotional type as a young woman, more a rational sort, and she wanted to suss out this situation herself as she thought Lorna could be bluffing about the adoption, taking Victor's money and making a run for it.

She found Lorna in Rugby Street, living in a terraced house with another large family though they were obviously not related to her. The baby was a real bonny lass with a thick layer of black hair but she appeared to be crying a lot.

"Have you been feeding her properly? Mother asked.

"She's a bit on the small side and doesn't look very well nourished."

"There's nowt wrong with her, came the reply from a seemingly disinterested Lorna.

"I've had her at the clinic and they say she'll be OK though they've given me some vitamins to put in her milk."

Mother didn't like the sound of that one little bit. She knew some of the people running the clinic and they wouldn't have interfered unless they were a little concerned.

"Let's have a closer look," said mother, picking Kathleen out of her pram in the process.

Whatever happened in that moment when she picked up the little girl must have had a stupendous and life-changing affect on her.

After holding the baby for a few minutes, mother put her back into her pram; "I'm going to leave you for now, she said.

"I'll give you a couple of quid to make sure the baby gets fed properly and I'll be back within the next few days, I just need to speak to Victor."

Then she was gone, speeding up Rugby Street, onto the trolley bus into town then walking along Beverley Road to home.

Our Kathleen was a real livewire of a lass, always out and about enjoying herself, unlike my other sister Molly, who was rather quiet and reserved. In fact she wasn't like either of us in looks nor deeds, something that several people, not least the nosey Mrs Dosdale had pointed out on more than one occasion.

Molly was a bit of a sickly sort of girl though it wasn't her fault she was like that of course. She was the one who got every illness that was doing the rounds, some of them quite serious, and had lots of time off school. I remember when she got scarlet fever, a disease which meant she had to be isolated from the rest of the family for six weeks. Very inconvenient for all of us but it couldn't be helped and many young people who contracted it had to go into a sanatorium.

The day she went down with the illness is etched in my memory. She was obviously very feverish and, after much discussion, it was decided to send for the doctor. Than in itself was a massive ordeal – no-one sent for the doctor unless they were virtually at death's door. Our GP, Doctor Perkins, had been an army medic during the war like many of his kind and wasn't one for trivialities. He was more used to jabbing squaddies in the arse than treating girls and young women and his bedside manner with all of us likened him to Doctor Crippen.

Anyway, dad told me to run round to the surgery at the corner of Manchester Street and ask the receptionist to tell the quack to pay a home visit – and it was urgent. We could have used the telephone at the bottom of the street but the receptionist appeared to delight in not answering the 'phone and it was quicker just to run round there.

So off I went. The receptionist, a hatchet-faced old spinster called Mrs Gray, made me wait while she did some imaginary filing before she would even look up when I was at the desk. The surgery waiting room was full of wheezing people all looking as though they were ready to curl up and die and finally she managed to look up, giving me a contemptuous glance in the process.

"Yes, she enquired, what is it you want."

"My sister's ill and needs the doctor to come quickly, I replied, laying it on as thick as I could.

"My dad's very worried about her and wants the doc straight away."

That was like a red rag to a bull to Mrs Gray, who wasn't to be told what to do by a snotty-nosed Hessle Road kid. I could see her getting her dander up and it looked as though she was about to bite my head off so I had the presence of mind to turn round and shoot out of the waiting room as fast as I could, leaving Mrs Gray with my instructions ringing in her ears.

I told dad what had happened and he said I had done the right thing – we just had to sit and wait for 'Perky' to arrive, hopefully before Molly got any worse. What dad didn't realise, nor did I until I'd been home for some time, was that in my haste to get out of the surgery I'd completely forgotten to tell the haughty Mrs Gray who I was!

Oh God, I thought, what the hell do I do now. I thought about going to the 'phone box to put matters right but decided against that and sat there fretting until thankfully, about an hour after my visit, we saw the doctor's car pull up at the top of the terrace. Naturally curtains began twitching at just about every house as a home visit was virtually unheard of and not to be entered into lightly. The doc got out of his car slowly and began making his way down the terrace. He was a bolt upright sort of a man – I always remember him in a grey mac, a grey suit, and carrying a grey bag. I fact he was a grey sort of guy with a complexion to match.

He knocked on the door and walked in unannounced, which is fair enough as there would be many a house where the patient wouldn't have been able to get out of bed. He was also most unlikely to mention the fact that it was a neighbour who had been in the waiting room that had to explain to the receptionist who I was and where we lived.

He took one look at Molly and said nothing but started writing on a notepad he'd taken out of his bag. We thought it was a prescription for medicine but it wasn't – it was some sort of instruction to a higher health authority that Molly had scarlet fever and they were more competent to deal with it.

Thankfully, for all his faults, 'Perky' had identified the illness straight away and set her care into motion. He said he was leaving to make a telephone call and that someone would be coming to the house very shortly to examine Molly more carefully and determine whether or not she had to go into a sanatorium, which scared the life out of all of us.

Anyway, it didn't come to that and Molly convalesced at home and to give old 'Perky' his due he attended her regularly and even smiled on a couple of occasions, at least we think it was a smile though it could have been wind I suppose. The whole episode ensured that I, and probably everyone else for that matter, didn't take lightly to visiting the doctor's surgery for fear of bumping into the fearsome Mrs Gray though looking back on it nowadays I'm wondering whether that wasn't the whole point.

My 'Different' Sister

Kathleen and Molly never really hit it off as sisters though they were treated in exactly the same way by our parents. I was probably more like Molly and I must admit did look at Kathleen on occasions wondering how she could be so different to anyone in the family, though it never, ever entered my head that she actually was different, very different in fact.

She always had a way with words and could have sold an ice lolly to an Eskimo. She was a real flirt with the boys at school and also with the young men when she left school and went to work at the Metal Box Company in Gypsyville, though she was never going to remain there for long, it was just a way of making a living while she attended night classes.

She did well for herself and was soon working in the commercial office at Metal Box, earning a bit less money than on the shop floor but gaining valuable experience which she would put to good use later. Her ambition was to work abroad as she was always dreaming about far-off places and we used to say, prophetically as it turned out, that she had wanderlust.

When she was 19 she was asked if she wanted to go to Belgium with work. Several of the senior salesmen were going and they wanted a couple of girls with them to help with administration, or so they said. Kathleen could hardly contain herself when she went round to mother's house and told them, but I noticed they weren't anywhere near as enthusiastic as she, especially when she said she would have to get a passport.

Of course she would need her birth certificate for that. At first dad said they couldn't find it but I noticed mother giving him a resigned sort of look and she said she knew where it was but she couldn't get it until the next night so Kathleen would have to come back around tea-time.

Kathleen went off in a blur of activity – she could hardly contain her enthusiasm telling one and all she was going abroad for a few days – something that very few people were able to do.

Mother told me to be home the next night at tea-time and to make sure Molly was there as well – what was that all about? An official family gathering! That was unprecedented in our house.

I slept badly that night. I had a foreboding that something wasn't right and though I knew it was very unlikely to have anything to do with me I suddenly feared for Kathleen, who had left the house in such a euphoric state. To make matters worse it was one of those terrible 'North East' days, a gale blowing off the Humber, rain pelting down almost horizontally, and freezing cold that got into your bones.

The four of us minus Kathleen, were sat around the house when she waltzed in, still on cloud nine.

"Now then our Kathleen", said dad.

"We've got summat to show you so you'd better all come into the front room."

The front room was only ever used on very special occasions so what on earth was this about?

The five of us sat around the table. Mother pulled out a yellow envelope from a very old paper carrier bag she'd taken into the room. Slowly, very slowly, she took out what looked like a document and laid it on the table top.

"Kathleen, she said, this is your birth certificate.

"Me and your dad don't want you to be upset by it so take it and read it slowly."

Upset! Read it slowly! What the hell's going on, it's only a bloody birth certificate. I'd already seen mine and it's nothing to get upset about.

Mother slid the document across the table and Kathleen slowly picked it up. I could see the fear in her eyes. Her first reaction was puzzlement – there it is in black and white – Kathleen Doyle, correct age, born Nottingham!!

Nottingham, how did that come about I could hear her thinking. Then her eyes dropped further down the certificate. Mother – Lorna Tyson – WHO! – Father Victor Doyle – OH NO! – it can't be.

Her face was deathly pale by now and had a wild, tortured look which I'd never seen before. She was utterly speechless, probably for the first time in her entire existence, which until a minute ago had been as the daughter of Harry and Vera Doyle.

She was frozen solid. Molly snatched the certificate from her hand and let out a screech when she saw what was there.

"I knew it, she yelled.

"I knew she wasn't one of us, she screeched.

"I've always known it but nobody said anything."

With that she threw the certificate back on the table and ran out of the room.

Now it was my turn. It didn't take Sherlock Holmes to realise that something was dramatically wrong. I took my time digesting everything written on the document and, looking across at Kathleen, had an overwhelming sense of sympathy for her. What on earth must she be going through?

Dad and mother had said nothing by this time. The pair of them hadn't been getting along for a very long time but this appeared to bring them closer, as if a common crime had somehow bonded them.

"You need an explanation, mother said.

"So I'll tell you the whole story, right from the beginning."

She proceeded to tell us the story of Victor and Lorna – how they met and what happened between them – but that was only half the story.

"When I went round to see Lorna and the baby my only intention was to ensure that you were properly looked after and that your mother – Lorna that is- wasn't just trying to fleece Victor.

"But something happened to me that day which completely threw me and all my plans right out of the window.

"I picked you up and knew you were mine straight away.

"It was if a sudden peace had descended on me, I can't really describe it any other way."

After leaving Lorna's place, mother went home and, with her mind in a whirlwind, devised a plan that she thought would be best for everyone. Of course she needed to persuade dad and that would be difficult but not as difficult as pitching the idea at his mother.

Victor would be OK about it – it would cost him a few quid but it would anyway and at least he would know his daughter was safe and being properly looked after.

"I got everyone together, she said, and told them what I planned to do. They were all absolutely shocked of course, especially grandma, but it slowly dawned on them all that it could work."

"Your dad – I don't mean Victor of course – was wonderful about it and never offered any objections at all and he worked on his mother for a couple of days until she finally came round to the idea."

"Victor gave me £250, all of his savings and some he borrowed. I would need around £20 to pay the rent up on our house as we would need to move and also buy baby clothes and food. Another £20 was for rent on new premises and £30 was for Lorna to get a solicitor who would witness the conceding of all rights to Victor. She could have the rest to do with as she pleased."

Mother, dad and Victor went round to Lorna's to explain the plan and she agreed wholeheartedly, especially after doing the maths on the scullery table.

"That leaves £180 for me – wonderful," she said, and before the week was out had visited Smiley, Smales and Goldthorpe solicitors and signed away her daughter.

When dad and mother moved it had to be somewhere where no-one would no them or their circumstances and though Lorna had lived for a while on Hessle Rd she knew nobody in Westbourne Street and dad had heard through someone at work that there was a terraced house for rent there.

So that's how we all eventually came to be Hessle Roaders, mother and dad, Kathleen and the two later editions, Molly and me.

Mother said her and dad had agonised many, many times about telling her the truth but just kept putting it off, and off, and off. They always knew this day would come but could never find the courage to reveal the story. We'd been living a lie for 19 years.

Kathleen had sat and listened to the latter part of the tale without a flicker of emotion. She was obviously still in deep shock. To give our Molly credit she returned to the front room and put her arms around Kathleen, apologising profusely and crying her eyes out. We all assured her that it made no difference whatsoever to us and that she was still our daughter and sister but of course things were different – how could they not be?

Kathleen left the house in a daze. It would make no difference to getting a passport but she had a massive amount of thinking to do and was best left to her own devices.

She had a couple of days off work and though both myself and Molly went to see her she hardly spoke to either of us though of course after the trauma she had endured it was completely understandable.

We couldn't understand how our parents could have kept up the pretence for so long – they must have known the day would come when everything had to be revealed. Maybe they were trying to protect Victor – who knows? There was no point in asking either of them as it would be dragging them through the whole scenario again.

Victor was away at the time so it wasn't for a few days that he knew his cover had been blown – but by that time it was too late.

Kathleen had gone to Belgium with the company and apparently, from what I was told by a girl who accompanied her, she had made a big impression on the senior executives. She was asked if she would consider relocating to that country, learning languages and representing the company.

Considering what she had just been through it was a lifeline for her and within a month she was gone, not saying a word to anyone in the family. Not surprisingly it was a crushing blow to everyone.

That was a few years ago. The last we heard was that she was now living and working in France but all we had from her was a card one Christmas. I tried to get in touch with her on several occasions but was never successful and Molly even travelled to the place where she had posted the card, a small town near the Spanish border, but all to no avail.

After that the family unit more or less disintegrated – still in constant touch but all trust and honesty now lost for good.

Hanging Around The Fish House

As for me, there were bound to be consequences for my time in borstal and I wasn't likely to be offered a job in a hurry but it didn't matter as thankfully I was due my call-up shortly after being released.

However there was an unexpected and tragic consequence that no-one could possibly have seen coming. When the police first arrested me they were keen to find out how I had earned a living after leaving school, believing I might have been spending my time thieving and burgling.

I couldn't tell them about working in the club or at the dog track for fear of implicating Malloy, or even worse, Gallagher, but of course I had spent most of that time employed by Grubb Brothers fish merchants.

The police had passed that information on to other authorities and as a consequence Tommy Grubb's premises were visited one day and his accounting books, or what passed for them, taken away to be examined.

It turned out that Grubb's lease was due shortly and he had no funds to sign a new agreement. His two lorries were breaking down on a regular basis and he owed lots of money to the garage for repairs.

That was only the start of it. The business employed around a dozen regulars and a few casuals but it appeared that only two of the employees were actually registered as working there – and one of them was Tommy Grubb.

Some of the men had been there for years and Grubb had been stopping stamp money from their wages every week – but not actually purchasing the stamps. Consequently none of them had earned a single stamp in all the time they were working for Grubb.

Obviously when the men learned of the deception they were gunning for Grubb but before they could get to him his one old faithful pal – he whose card had been stamped every week - found him hanged in the fish house early one morning when opening up.

Some of the workers blamed me for a while believing it was I who had set the ball rolling but they soon realised that it was Grubb who had been betraying them and it could have gone on for much longer but for my totally innocent intervention

I spent most of my days after borstal just mooching around. It seemed impossible to get motivated to find work as I knew I would be going into the services before long. I still attended the dog track and found a job either clerking or doing tic-tac on most nights so I wasn't short of a bob or two.

Veronica's Timely Tonic

So far in my life I hadn't had much luck, or even contact, with girls, but that was all about to change. A school pal of mine, Pete Thomson, lived at the bottom of Albert Terrace on Hawthorn Ave. I called on him one Saturday as we were off to the Boulevard to see Hull play Featherstone. Pete's parents, who were elderly, had died when he was still at school and he lived with his elder sister Veronica in the family house.

Veronica was a nice looking girl of 20. When I had called for Pete in the past there was usually some guy or other hanging around – in recent times it had been the same one but Pete told me that his sister had blown him out.

I knocked on the door and Veronica answered. I must say she looked very attractive; the first time I had really taken any real notice of her. She must have latched on straight away to my sudden interest, or leering as it probably was.

"Come for Pete, have you? She said.

"He's round the back cleaning his soccer boots, I'll give him a shout, come on in."

Before she called for Pete she sort of looked me up and down before saying: "I've noticed you before when you've come for Pete. Why don't you come round tonight? Pete's got a date and I'm all on my own."

That flummoxed me no end but bravado got the better of me and I replied, trying not to stutter: "Yeh, OK, what time?"

"Come about 7.o'clock, she said.

"That'll give us plenty of time."

With that she shouted of Pete.

Plenty of time for what? I thought.

She must have something in mind and I think I know what it is!

Peter had told me that on several occasions he had come home to find Veronica and her last boyfriend in the bedroom and by the sounds they were making they weren't playing with Pete's Meccano set.

Pete came out from the back and we set off for the match.

What on earth had I said yes for? Can I get out of it? Did I want to?

I was in a blind panic and hardly noticed that Hull had won easily. Pete was jabbering on about what a great game Harry Markham had played but I couldn't remember any of it.

By teatime I had gathered my thoughts a little and then had to decide on a strategy. First of all I would need a French letter, or a packet of three. Where would I get them? I decided to go round to my cousin Syd's, he'd know what to do.

Syd was regarded as something of a lady's man, or that was the impression he gave everyone. According to him no young woman on Hessle Rd was safe while he was around, though in all honesty I'd never noticed the girls swooning over him.

I took the bull by the horns and went round to his place in Somerset Street.

"Now then our Syd, I said on entering the back kitchen.

"I need a bit of advice and you're just the man."

"Go on then, said my cousin.

"What's the problem? Don't tell me you've got some lass in trouble."

"Well, it's like this, I said.

"I've got a hot date tonight and haven't got any Johnnies, can you lend me some?"

I thought Syd was going to collapse; his mouth had opened so wide.

"Any Johnnies? Where the hell do you think I'm going to get them from?"

"You're always on about how many women you've had, I said.

"I thought for sure you'd have some spare and I didn't know where else to go."

"Listen, Ed, that's all a load of bollocks, I thought you of all people would have known that.

"It's just talk, I'm no more experienced with girls than you so I can't give you anything, or any advice for that matter."

What a bummer. Here was me, and half of Hessle Rd, believing our Syd was another Casanova when he was just as frightened of women as the rest of us.

"It's only half-past-five, Syd said.

"Harry Talbot's your barber, isn't he?

"He doesn't close until 6.30 on a Saturday 'cos he waits for customers on the way home from the rugby who are waiting for Miller's to open."

Before he'd got the last sentence out I was sprinting down Hawthorne Ave to Harry's barber's shop, praying that he'd still be open and that he had no customers.

I was in luck. One guy was just coming out and Harry was about to close.

"Can I have a packet of three, Harry? I said, making out as though I did this sort of thing all the time.

Harry gave me a sort of weary-eyed look.

"That'll be two bob, he said.

"Or you can have two packets for three and six."

"No, one'll do," I said, and gave him half-a-crown and told him to keep the change.

So, back home, washed and changed into something casual, and ready for the big occasion, if that's what it was to be.

Not wishing to appear over eager, I waited until just after seven before making the short journey to Albert Terrace, checking all along that no-one was watching though it was dark by now and deathly quiet.

I knocked quietly on the front door and Veronica quickly answered, greeting me in a pale blue housecoat that ended just above her knees.

"Come in, quickly," she said, grabbing my arm and ushering me into the front room where there was a big fire roaring in the grate.

"I've got us some beer," she said, producing a couple of glasses and a large bottle of Hull Brewery Mild. Bad start – I hated Hull Brewery Mild.

We sat on the large sofa with our drinks in our hands and for a few seconds there was an interminable silence. Veronica then took the glass from me and placed my hand on her very ample bosom, which she had by now revealed after unbuttoning her housecoat.

"Have you brought something, she said.

"I don't want to get pregnant."

"No problem, I said.

"It's all taken care of."

Before I knew it she had taken off her housecoat and her bra and pants and was laying there invitingly on the rug in front of the fire.

I'd never seen a naked woman before. I'd seen my sisters floating around the house with little on but that was different – very different!

"Come on then, she said invitingly.

"Don't be shy."

It wasn't shyness I was suffering but fear – mortal fear.

"I'll just go check the front door's locked." I said - anything to delay the inevitable.

"Don't worry about the door, she replied.

"No-one will be coming in, let's just get on with it."

By this stage sweat was pouring from me and I removed my shirt and trousers, getting down on the rug with Veronica, who by now had a lustful look in her eyes, at least I think it was lust – I'd never seen it before.

Well, in all honesty I cannot say doing the deed was a great success. In fact it was a bit of a failure. No, let's be honest, it was a disaster.

I had no idea what I was doing and it was all over in a few seconds. Veronica was brilliant about it though.

"I didn't realise it was your first time, she said.

"You should have said, I would have done things differently."

She didn't laugh at me or show contempt but, after we finished our drinks, got changed and sat on the sofa holding hands for a while, told me to come back the following night when she promised things would be very different.

"Are you sure, I said.

"I'm really sorry about tonight though."

"Don't worry, I'll give Pete ten-bob to take his girl to pictures and we'll do the job properly.

"What do you do when you're learning to ride a bike and you fall off?

"You get right back on again of course otherwise you'd never be able to ride a bike."

I was a bag of nerves all Sunday, part of me hoping that Pete wouldn't take up the offer and have a night at home. Still, when I saw him in the afternoon and he said he was going out that evening I started to get excited.

This time I couldn't wait for 7.00 o'clock and got there half-an-hour earlier.

"You're eager, Veronica said as she opened the door.

"Not too eager like last night I hope."

Thankfully I wasn't and things were much more successful – not perfect but better – and even better later in the evening when the last of my packet of three was put to good use.

The bike-riding comparison was true. I would never have won the Tour De France but at least would be confident enough to get to Withernsea and back.

Veronica was absolutely wonderful and I was so pleased to get that part of my life out of the way. We saw each other a few more times and it was always fine and I wasn't remotely concerned when she took up again with the bloke she had dumped before I came along.

After all he would be better at it than me – he'd had a lot more practice!

Saved By The Army

It wasn't long before a saviour came to rescue me from the streets – the good old British Army. My release had coincided with my call-up papers being issued and it was the making of me. I could get away from the environment I had grown up with and see a different aspect of life. The police wouldn't be on my back and no-one would know or be interested in me as long as I did what I was told and got on with life in the forces.

After being served my papers and issued with an ill-fitting uniform, I was sent to Wenlock Barracks on Anlaby Road for a haircut and a fierce injection. We had to stand in a long line for the latter and several guys in front of me fainted when they saw the size of the needle but it didn't bother me, I just got to the head of the queue quicker.

None of us had any idea where we were to be sent but hoped it wouldn't be too far away and I was one of the fortunate ones as I was put on a train to North Yorkshire and ended up at Catterick camp.

Whilst doing my duty, which mainly consisted of marching up and down the parade square or charging about the local forests pretending to be soldiers, I quickly graduated to taking bets on all manner of events and regular visits to Catterick, Wetherby and Ripon racecourses cemented my love affair with the horses.

I was a great boxing fan and though later in life I was always reluctant to bet on the fights I had a far greater knowledge of the sport than most and was able to take advantage when the British heavyweight champion Don Cockell went to the USA to fight Rocky Marciano for the world title.

Everyone in camp was rooting for the popular Cockell and wanted to back him but patriotism must have blurred their judgement. They thought he was invincible and that he could take Marciano when he liked, but I knew otherwise and was certain the American would knock him out.

I decided to take all bets on Cockell and stood to win a lot of money if Marciano could end the fight within the 15 rounds but faced a big payout if my judgement was proved wrong.

Thankfully for me Marciano did what I expected and knocked the gutsy but limited challenger out in round nine, much to the disgust of my fellow squaddies. I must have been the only Briton cheering for the champion early that morning as we all crowded round the radio to listen to the BBC's live broadcast.

How I would have paid them all out if I had lost is another matter – probably by polishing their boots, buckles and rifles for the next two years though of course I didn't tell them that.

I became an expert at the racing formbook and by the time I had left the army I was convinced my future lay not in any old working-man's job but using my racing and betting knowledge to its best effect.

Elvis Changes Everything

When not spending time playing and watching sport, like millions of youngsters our outlets were the local dance halls and the 'pictures' and I had a particular interest in the music of the day, which in the mid 1950's was just emerging out of the dark ages. Until then, we youngsters had to listen to the same music as our parents but then along came Elvis with That's All Right Momma in 1954 and the world changed forever, though it took a little time to reach our particular part of it.

OK, there had been attempts made by the likes of Bill Haley to introduce pop and rock but they weren't much different from our parents – very much the safe option. Every home had a radio and most a record player. The vinyl records of the day came in LP's, EP's and singles and were sold in their millions.

LP's would have around a dozen tracks; EP's four and singles just one, often with equally popular tracks on the 'flip' side. Cleveland's record store near St George's Road was the main outlet on Hessle Road but we would often go into town to Gough and Davey to buy our records.

They had three or four record booths where we could listen to the singles before buying – sometimes of course we didn't have the money but listened anyway. It's absolutely incredible how the music scene changed in the space of a couple of years.

We spent our childhood's listening to our parent's favourites like Frank Sinatra, Nat King Cole, the wonderful soprano Kathleen Ferrier, who was mother's favourite, and Bing Crosby, who was dad's. Brilliant artists of course though not necessarily to the taste of the youngster generation, but we also had to endure Gracie Fields, Bud Flanagan and his Crazy Gang and even worse, George Formby and his little ukulele! Thankfully for us along came Elvis, Ray Charles, Little Richard, Jerry Lee Lewis, Buddy Holly, Chuck Berry, Gene Vincent, Eddie Cochran, Roy Orbison and numerous others who were speaking to the younger generation, probably for the first time in musical history.

All those greats were of course American and our home grown versions were not in the same class. Cliff Richard, Marty Wilde, Vince Eager and Billy Fury were just a few who attempted to imitate Elvis with limited success. Of the four of them I quite liked Billy Fury and if any of them are to survive long-term I reckon it will be him.

Tuning in to Radio Luxembourg instead of the staid BBC, we were able to access pop music from all over the world and Jimmy Savile's voice has became as familiar to us as any BBC Radio newsreader was to our parents.

The man credited with changing the lives of millions of us youngsters is of course Elvis, and quite rightly so, but it was Carl Perkins, who wrote and recorded Blue Suede Shoes in 1955, who really started the revolution.

That song later became a massive hit for Elvis and once Heartbreak Hotel and Jailhouse Rock burst onto the scene there was no stopping us. Like the new 'teenagers' of the era I bought into pop music in a big way and it was a great distraction from the seemingly endless attempts at making my fortune, through fair means or often foul.

Perks Of The Job

After leaving the confines of the Army I had a few quid in my pocket – though hardly a fortune – and a demob suit that quickly went onto a bonfire. I had to find a way of earning a living and tried a few things which didn't work out for one reason or another then appeared to find a more settled role in a thriving newsagents/toyshop near Division Road.

The pay wasn't much but there were several perks attached, not least its position right next door to a pub. Not that I was a drinker, far from it, I reckoned every pint of Hull Brewery Bitter cost the same as a forecast double at Kings Heath dog track and I knew where I would rather put my money.

No, the pub had a much greater attraction for me and many others. The rear door of the snug led to an illegal gambling parlour which had a commentary and starting price service piped in. The landlord was a great racing fan himself and had a minor share in a leg of a horse in training with Pat Rohan at Beverley and had a couple of well-known investors in the operation, one of them Gerry Malloy, who were content to let him run the business.

He had seen how some of the proprietor's Clubs operated a betting wire service and decided to enhance his pub business with this illegal operation. Naturally it was invitation only but the business was run very professionally and had hundreds of regular customers.

After my demob I had decided I was to become a professional gambler – an idea and career move that lasted a week – or as long as it took for my operations fund to run out. It seemed a lot easier taking money off recruits at Catterick than it did attempting to back winners but like all gamblers a big pay-day was just around the corner – it was just a matter of patience.

I regularly nipped out next door during the afternoon and the manager didn't mind too much as she also regularly nipped out to visit her man-friend across the street – and sometimes never came back – and when she did she wasn't always in a fit state to do much work.

One particular afternoon, when down to the last three quid I had to my name, I went next door to look at the day's dog results as I had had a few forecast doubles in the hope of making a killing. On seeing the results from Park Royal dog track I cursed my bad luck – again.

I had reasoned that recent rain would make the going sticky on the inside and that wide runners would have the call so put my faith in 6-5 combinations. Not for the first time I was to be proved totally wrong and it was traps 1-2 which had a field day.

Now, almost totally skint and nothing more to bet on, I remembered that 'old Aggie', a daily punter who lived down Division Road, always went for traps 1-2 at Park Royal and would be in the money. So in my desperation I hatched what I thought would be a plot to replenish my little pot.

I walked the few yards to Aggie's house and, after knocking lightly, went inside where the old dear was sitting at a linoleum clad table drinking a mug of tea and knitting a pink cardigan for her great-granddaughter.

"Had a bet today Aggie? I said, already knowing what the answer would be.

"Yeah but I don't think I've won 'owt," she replied, which was music to my ears.

"Tell you what, I said, I'm going back to the bookies and I reckon you want a couple of quid so I'll give you that if you give me your ticket."

Aggie appeared perfectly happy with that arrangement so I parted with almost all of the money I had left and gratefully accepted the betting slip.

The dim-wit, I thought, she must have at least ten quid to come, that'll set me up nicely for a trip to the 51 Club Casino tonight for a game of poker. I hurried as best as I could to the bookies before closing and got there just as the manager, a surly Scot called Adam, was shutting up, and handed him the betting slip.

"Aggie asked me to pick this up for her, I said as nonchalantly as possible.

"She's got her sister coming and was treating her to bingo tonight with her winnings."

"What winnings? said the Jock.

"There's nothing to come off this slip."

"Don't be stupid, I said.

"She always does combination forecasts 1-2 at Park Royal and five have come in so there must be plenty to come."

"Don't call me stupid", the surly one replied.

"Anyway, she changed her mind at the last minute at went for 6-5 as some fool told everyone in the place that the inside traps had no chance."

He passed the said betting slip back to me and sure enough the daft old bat had taken the advice of 'some fool' and changed the habits of a lifetime, in doing so costing her ten quid and me my last hope of solvency for the day.

Adam's (and shelves) Downfall

One of the things I always did do well was form a grudge and the Scot Adam was now definitely a figure of hate after he told just about all of regulars what an idiot I was for not checking the betting slip. His demise was on my 'to do' list though how I was to manage his downfall wasn't apparent at the time.

In fact it didn't take too long for revenge to come my way, though in a wholly unexpected manner. The Jock was well known for having a terrible temper and was regularly seen hurling small objects around behind the counter on a bad day.

One evening just as the last race had been run, he completely lost the plot after a string of favourites had won, costing the company plenty and damaging his bonus as a result. The few punters who were in at the time witnessed him picking up a large metal stool and hurling it at the wall which divided the premises from the newsagents where I worked.

Under normal circumstances this would have been seen as just another fit of pique by the bad-tempered manager but these turned out to be far from normal circumstances.

On the newsagent's side of the wall stood a row of six glass shelves, which not surprisingly came crashing down when the offending article slammed into the wall. Glass figures, Dinky toys, Coronation mugs and assorted bric-a-brac, all worth very little but quite good sellers, were scattered all over the shop floor with the broken glass an obvious threat to life and limb.

Naturally head office was informed straight away and they contacted the bookie who owned the illegal joint. Poor Adam the Jock lost a week's pay as well as any bonus due and was totally crestfallen.

I should mention at this point that the shelves had been erected by myself, whose attempts at DIY inevitably ended in disaster. It's more than likely that they were ready to fall anyway as they were always hovering on the brink and the Jock's fiery temper ensured they came down earlier than expected.

That particular illegal parlour, which for some reason never had its collar felt by the local constabulary, was the only one of its kind on Hessle Road and had an extremely varied clientele. Most were working men having a few bob on the horses every day and doing little damage to their pockets but inevitably there were a few addicts who took things much too far.

One of the heaviest of them, and certainly the biggest loser, was a local solicitor who came into the place every lunch time and gambled away more money than most of us had seen. Of course he had the occasional success but generally ploughed the lot back into the bookies' till and in a few months he must have lost a fortune.

He never spoke to anyone, never cursed his bad luck or the jockey riding his horses as was the general rule, but just walked out as if nothing had happened and drove away in his shiny new car.

He suddenly stopped coming in and it was no great shock when we read in the Hull Daily Mail that he'd been sent to prison for 'misappropriating' client's funds. I bet he was popular in the nick.

Another regular was a doctor, a GP, who spent hour upon hour playing the fruit machines, or 'one-armed bandits' as they were known. He would plough at least £5 per day on the machines, usually paying for his change by cheque, and I know for a fact that a couple of them bounced though they were quickly sorted out by the bank and the bookie wasn't going to press charges against one of his best customers.

Nicko the Eye-Tie was another regular. He was a mechanic with his own repair business and always appeared in oily overalls and black hands. Nicko was a really popular guy and if he had a good win would treat some of the older punters to an ice-cream.

Unfortunately he met a sad end. He had his own workshop close to Smith And Nephews in Neptune Street and one night, well past midnight, he was trying to earn a few quid extra by welding two car chassis together when an oxy-acetylene tank caught fire and blew poor Nicko, and the premises, to smithereens.

Adam the Scot was crestfallen when he heard the news – another good customer lost.

You're Called What? – Humorist!

A family of former fairground workers were daily punters. They were descended from gypsy's but had given up the travelling way of life long ago and lived in terraced houses down Manchester Street.

They always seemed to have money in their pockets though no-one had a clue what they did and whatever it was it certainly didn't include the daily grind. But they were always very polite and well mannered and often, during a lull in the racing, would have stories to tell of their days at the fairgrounds.

One of them we all called 'Humie', a strange name which no-one took much notice of until one day I said to him: "That's a weird old name, Humie, how the hell did you come by it."

He said he was born on the first Wednesday in June in 1921 and his place of birth is the reason for his name. His parents were fairground people and his mother gave birth in a caravan on the famous Epsom Downs the day Humorist, ridden by the immortal Steve Donoghue, won the Derby.

So Humie was actually christened Humorist and it's not surprising that he didn't use his full name. As my mate Billy said on hearing the story: "Just as well it wasn't the year St Paddy won."

One example of my long memory for a grudge came about in a strange way. I was travelling along Hessle Road one sunny afternoon as a passenger in my pal Les's car. We came to a stop at the corner of

Boulevard as there were some Gas Board men digging a trench and a guy with the stop-go sign was in front of us.

I didn't take a lot of notice at first but then recognised him as Baz Shorthouse, the lorry driver who had given me such a hard time in the fish house. I hadn't seen him since those days but knew his firm had gone out of business and that he was now labouring for the gas board.

Shorthouse had been a big, strong-looking guy when lumping fish boxes and driving the lorry but he'd gone to seed and didn't look anything like as ferocious.

A sort of red mist descended on me and, without saying a word to Les, got quickly out of the car, marched towards the stop-go man who had turned around to look at the traffic coming the other way.

By the time I had reached him he had just turned back again and saw me at the last minute. I could see that he recognised me and that he realised what was coming but before he could even think about defending himself I planted a right hook firmly on his chin.

"Take that Shithouse", I said, and Shorthouse and his 'lollipop stick' were sent flying into one of the holes dug by his colleagues and ended up in a pile of mud. I like to think it was the blow that did the damage but it was probably a combination of that and him losing his balance as he attempted to escape.

I then walked calmly back to the car and Les, thinking I must have gone crazy, sped off down Constable Street at a rate of knots screaming at me to explain what had just occurred.

Once I explained to him that I hadn't gone crazy but was just getting revenge for something that had occurred in my youth, it took me all my time to prevent Les going back and hitting Shorthouse again.

I never heard another word about my actions so presumably Shorthouse was well aware of why it had happened and kept his mouth shut.

It was a tough period for everyone and we all had to make our way in life through whatever means we could. It wasn't always pretty and there are things I look back on and don't feel proud of but sometimes you just did what you had to do to survive.

The Fading Beauty

Like so many inveterate gamblers, I always managed to find funds to start another day though I'm sorry to say the ways and means were rarely attractive and more often than not downright nasty.

We always began the day with great hopes only to be flailing around in the mire by teatime, wondering how on earth we were going to worm our way out of another calamity.

As I said, I had a regular job in a thriving newsagent's where ready cash was never in short supply. My manager, Dorothy, a fading beauty in her late thirties, not only had her bit on the side but was also in the habit of 'borrowing' a few quid from the till when things got tight, as they invariably did with her husband away at sea for three weeks at a time.

Dorothy thought no-one was aware of her unofficial fiscal activities and to be fair to her she always put back what she owed on payday each Friday. I had found out purely by mistake as she left herself a little note in a drawer with an I.O.U. and kept the information purely to myself for possible future reference.

I too was dipping into the till on a regular basis, only very small amounts at first but then, when things got really tough, more than was prudent and I was very fortunate not to get caught on a couple of occasions. None of it helped of course, what I stole I lost in the bookies so all it was doing was giving me more and more grief.

One day, disaster struck when a company inspector, who hadn't been sighted for over a year, made an unexpected visit. It was a Wednesday afternoon around two-o-clock and Dorothy had been on an extended lunch over at her boyfriend's house.

I was currently owing the till twelve pounds, not a fortune but this eagle-eyed inspector had quickly determined the money was short and I could see a spell in Gordon Street police station and possibly prison staring me in the face as the company had a policy of prosecuting thieving employees and of course I had 'previous'.

This was the time to think on my feet – not my finest hour ethically but at that stage a flash of inspiration came to me.

"I can't understand it, I said.

"The till's never wrong, there must be some mistake."

"There's no mistake, the inspector replied.

"Someone's for the high-jump here and with your record it's likely to be you."

Realising Dorothy often left her I.O.U's in the secret drawer, I began 'assisting' the inspector to look for any lost money.

"Is this anything"? I enquired, managing to open the said drawer, which thankfully for me though not for Dorothy, contained not one or two but a small bundle of I.O.U's totalling more than the twelve quid that was missing.

The idiot had failed to tear them up when she paid them back the previous weeks therefore incriminating herself in the fraud.

The inspector examined the slips of paper and a look of triumph came across his face.

Dorothy arrived back in the shop looking hot and flustered, which was hardly a surprise as her boyfriend was a professional rugby player about a dozen years younger than her, though she was totally unconcerned about the inspector's presence as she believed she hadn't 'borrowed' this week so the till should balance correctly.

The inspector presented her with a bombshell, triumphantly showing her the bundle of I.O.U's.

"What's the explanation for these? He said in his most authoritative manner.

"The till's twelve pounds short."

That question floored her completely and she began attempting to bluster her way out of trouble.

The inspector was by this time in his element – he was loving every minute as he's now justified his exalted position in the company with what would certainly be a 'pinch'. All it needed was a confession and he'd get that soon having presented the manager with the fait accompli – the I.O.U's.

Dorothy was too stressed to think straight and began apologising for her wrongdoings though neglecting to mention that in fact she didn't owe the till a bean. None of her grovelling impressed the inspector nor did my slightly constrained though heartfelt pleas for leniency.

The inspector told Dorothy to leave the premises immediately and by a stroke of good fortune instantly promoted me, a loyal servant of the company, to manager with a nice increase in salary.

Thankfully the firm didn't prosecute Dorothy but stopped her wages and bonus and of course a reference was out of the question. I regularly saw her on Hessle Road after that – she didn't have the brains to figure what really happened and never had any idea I had been the architect of her downfall.

Still, it wasn't all bad for her, she left her AWOL husband for a greengrocer and as far as I know benefited from the wholly corrupt, yet for me, strangely satisfying episode.

Council workers clearing the 'oss-muck from Hessle Rd

Early shot of Gillette St/ St Georges Rd where the Walk begins

A salubrious early betting shop in Harrow St

The iron bridge at Dairycoates - the walkers jostled for position here.

Raich Carter - the 'King of Boothferry Park'

The great 'Gentleman Johnny Whiteley

Ernie Parker's 'open all hours newsagents'

The Eureka 'flea-pit'

Bomb damage in Manchester St

Three formidable ladies of the terrace

Caravan holidays at Withernsea

The author - not Elvis

The annual Club Wembley outing

Flinton St Coronation party

Joe Davis And The Betting Scam

That was a huge wake-up call. I regularly woke up in the night in a cold sweat having dreamt of a couple of years eating porridge at Her Majesty's Pleasure again. If you can't learn something from an incident like that there's no hope and my heavy gambling and 'borrowing' days were most definitely a thing of the past, especially as the firm now sent inspectors round at regular and unannounced intervals, which made it suicide to be even a few pence short in the till.

Not that I was ever going to stay as the manager of a newsagents for long, I had other things on my mind. I was still a regular at the dog track and had long ago learnt to tic-tac while my maths skills meant that I could stand in as a bookies' clerk when needed and earned a few quid on the side for doing both jobs.

I could think on my feet and the regular bookmakers knew I was an asset so I began to get more and more work. On a couple of occasions I stood in for a bookie who had gone on holiday, shouting the odds and taking bets from the punters. I loved every minute and was determined that this was the game for me – no more getting up at 6.00am to do the daily newspapers.

The majority of people went about their daily business just glad to earn enough to get by, with a packet of Woodbines and a couple of pints of Hull Brewery Bitter on a night as luxuries. Plenty of people had a bet of course - the illegal parlour and street bookmakers were always busy - and most of us accepted that betting was a mugs game but still came back for more.

When I became a bookie myself things changed. I never told any punter this – I didn't want to kill the goose that laid the golden egg - but if they walked into any betting shop, legal or otherwise, the first thing that should have struck them is that there are three windows for placing bets and one for paying out! Shouldn't that tell them something?

There were always the odd punter looking for a scam but Adam the Scot ran a tight ship and very little got past him. He had a regular till-girl, Tina, paid cash in hand of course and on a Saturday was helped by his wife's brother Frank Castle, a filleter on the dock who was earning a few quid on the side to fund his not unsubstantial drinking habit.

Adam didn't like Castle, nor did many of the punters for that matter, but he employed him to keep the peace with his wife and as long as he stayed mainly out of the way he was tolerated. The business on a Saturday not only revolved around horses and dogs but soccer as the fixed odds coupons were extremely popular and generated lots of income.

Castle was handed the task of taking the coupons and filing them for later reference.

The soccer results wouldn't be known until late Saturday evening and the shop was often closed by the time the results of the last games filtered through so more often than not it was Monday before they were checked.

One particularly busy Saturday after racing had finished, Castle went outside for a smoke and some fresh air. He returned to finish sweeping the floor and left around 6.00pm. The following Monday Adam went in early to check the soccer coupons.

As usual most of the punters had gone for two selections in each of the five divisions, four English and the Scottish first. Adam went carefully through the huge pile, mainly crossing off losers, which wasn't a surprise as there had been some real shocks in the Third Division North and South.

There were a couple of minor winners then he came upon a coupon with an incredible four selections in all five divisions.

"What a nutter, thought the Scot.

"Here's some lunatic attempting to pick twenty winners."

Adam was almost inclined to throw the coupon straight into the loser's tray but began checking and was amazed that the punter had picked eight correct selections in the first two divisions, including three aways and one draw. He continued going through the games and couldn't believe his eyes when both Third Divisions were correctly forecast.

This was now getting extremely serious as the odds had mounted up by now and a massive payout was a possibility. Onto the Scottish First Division and unbelievably the first three selections, including two draws, were also correct.

Everything now hinged on the final game, East Fife v Aidrie which the punter had selected as an away win. Adam checked the score in the Daily Pink, East Fife 2, Aidrie 3. DISASTER!

All twenty selections had been correct. Adam checked every game three times just to see if he had been imagining things but no, there they were, all present and correct. The stake was ten shillings, a not inconsequential amount and the total odds for twenty correct results were out of the stratosphere.

Adam began the task of calculating the winnings and it came to an astonishing £2,256,20, probably more money than the business was worth and certainly more than could be collected from the shop's owners.

Adam then remembered that there was a limit on winnings of £1,000 which was of some relief but it was still a sum of money virtually unheard of at the time.

He certainly wasn't looking forward to informing the landlord or his investors as pulling a grand out of back pockets wasn't on the business plan but it had to be done and the landlord was soon on hand to oversee proceedings.

He quickly called Gerry Malloy, the major investor, and he was in the shop almost before the landlord put the 'phone down.

Malloy could scarcely believe what he was seeing. He began asking Adam questions about when the coupon was taken, whose was it and who took it. Every coupon had to be signed by the punter who had a counterfoil. Malloy smelt a rat when the signature on the coupon was that of Joe Davis.

Joe Davis had been world snooker champion for 20 years and was still one of the most famous sportsmen in the country. It would be intriguing to find out who this 'Joe Davis' was and how he came to pick twenty winners.

They didn't have long to find out. About 11.30am the door opened and a little man in clogs smelling of fish sidled up to the counter. He presented a well-worn coupon to Adam and said: "I had a bit of luck on Saturday didn't I?"

Adam had never seen the guy before which seemed odd.

Malloy said to him: "What time did you put the coupon on?"

"12.47 exactly" said 'Joe Davis', by now looking a little uncomfortable.

That was exactly the time stamped on the coupon and was well before the kick-off of any of the games involved.

"There's a limit of £1,000 and I'm going to pay you with a banker's order, said Malloy, bluffing.

"I'll need you to sign your name."

By this time 'Davis' was starting to sweat and was most reluctant to put pen to paper. Eventually though he bit the bullet and signed Joe Davis on a blank cheque that Malloy had produced. The signature was nothing like that on the coupon, just as Malloy had known it wouldn't be.

"Tell me how this was done and I won't call the cops," Malloy said.

Davis attempted to bluff and bluster his way out of it but he'd been caught red-handed and worse was to come for him as the door opened and another fish dock worker walked in.

"Now then Charlie, haven't seen you in here before," he said.

And 'Joe Davis' shot out of the shop as fast as his clogs would take him.

Malloy quickly worked out that Frank Castle had stamped the coupon at 12.47, gone outside for some fresh air at 5.30 when his pal Charlie gave him the soccer results he'd just heard on the radio. Castle then filled in the coupon and signed it Joe Davies but was so stupid he hadn't reckoned on twenty selections busting the bank.

If he'd been a little more careful and just tried to win £60 -£70 he may have got away with it but once more greed came to the rescue of the bookie, who ended up ten bob richer instead of £1,000 poorer.

Three-piece Suites For Nowt

Tina the till-girl was regarded by all as completely trustworthy. Unlike Frank Castle she was always smart and presentable but hadn't had much luck with boyfriends, until now that is. She was shacked up with a local character called Dave Preston, who had been involved in numerous failed ventures and was mainly regarded as one of life's losers but suddenly appeared to be well and truly flying.

Preston had rented a huge, cavernous warehouse on Bankside at the back of Smith and Nephews and was selling three-piece suites as fast as hot cakes. Preston was a punter, though not a massive gambler, and owed me a few quid which I went to collect one day.

As I arrived a large removal van was being unloaded by a couple of Asian guys. There were dozens of suites of all sizes, colours and material. All were piled on top of one another in Preston's warehouse and I had to climb over most of them to reach his office at the back of the building.

Preston was waiting for me with an envelope. I never had any problems with his gambling debts so didn't bother to check. He was strictly a cash only man and I saw him give a very large envelope to the Asian men.

The reason for Preston's success was an incredible advertising campaign in the local newspaper. The suites, which were very reasonably priced anyway, if not the best quality, not by a long way, were offered with a 'money back guarantee' which gave the buyer the option of returning the suite in three years time and getting half their money back.

And believe it or not, hundreds fell for it!

Preston was selling suites on this basis almost before they could be made and to say he was cash rich is an understatement. Nothing but the best for Dave, who was driving around in an imported Cadillac, wearing ill-fitting but hand-made Italian suits, smoking specially imported Havana cigars and having a very large detached house built in the Anlaby Park area.

It's amazing just how many gullible people there are around. Preston had already gone bankrupt or been liquidated on at least three earlier occasions yet kept bouncing back. He always looked a plausible character which is why, I suppose, people kept falling over themselves to put money in his coffers. There was hardly ever any chance of getting it back but they just kept the cash rolling in.

Preston had absolutely no scruples whatsoever. He delighted in conning folk and never blinked an eyelid. He'd been abused, spat on, threatened with castration and evicted from houses but it never bothered him in the least, he just kept on finding new ways to relieve people of their hard-earned. I'd never met anyone with such a thick skin in my life but it couldn't last forever and it was about two years before the bubble burst. Preston believed that tax was what the lino was nailed down with and hadn't paid a penny to the Inland Revenue; no National Insurance; no advertising costs in the Hull Daily Mail; no anything else for that matter, including the Asians, who weren't the sort of people to fall foul of.

The only thing he had paid for was a ticket to Spain which had no repatriation agreement in place. However, it wasn't too long before the pesetas ran out and he was on his way back to Hull and Tina, though she was now shacked up with a guy selling Ringtons Tea from a van.

Wrong Side Of The Tracks

By this time I was renting a two-bed terrace house in Hawthorn Avenue at the Dairycoates end of Hessle Road. I was on my own most of the time but our Molly came round regularly and kept me well fed and the house was always clean and tidy thanks to regular visits from Jane, who I had met at a City Hall dance

Jane was a nice girl from a decent hard-working family but unfortunately she came from the wrong side of the track - East Hull. Her dad, Len, was a docker who had played a few games for Rovers when they were desperate and mum Irene worked in a grocery. An elder sister had married an accountant so though they lived in a council house they were regarded as almost middle class in that sort of environment, unlike us vagabonds from across the river.

It was of course impossible for Jane to move in with me but she visited whenever she could. Her dad, who was incredibly protective of his 'little girl, questioned her regularly about any prospective boyfriends and what they might be up too. After a few months courting, Jane decided to let the cat out of the bag.

"Dad, I've got something to tell you and you may not like it", she said.

"Oh no, groaned Len.

"Don't tell me you're pregnant, please not that, think of what the neighbours will say and it'll kill your Grandma.

"No dad, nothing like that, Jane replied.

"But I've had a steady boyfriend for a while and thought you might want to know about him."

"Well what might I not like about him? Len enquired quizzically.

"He's not, er, a blackie is he?

"It's not that I'm prejudiced or anything, and if he is then fine, I'm only asking so to speak", he said awkwardly.

"No it's not that" said Jane and before she could explain Len was at her again.

"Don't tell me he's been in jail, he said.

"I'd rather not have a jailbird in the family but if you're happy with him I suppose I would have to get used to that."

Jane told a little white lie. Of course I'd been in borstal but that wasn't prison was it?

"Definitely not dad, she said.

"It's nothing like that at all".

"Is he a Scot? Len asked, or from Liverpool?

"Oh no, he's not a ginger-headed Glaswegian is he?

"I've seen a few of them knocking about the streets and pubs. They're mostly bad news but still I suppose there could be a few decent ones amongst them."

No dad, he's not a Scot, in fact his family are Irish and quite respectable."

"So what is it that I'm not to like then? Len said, by now exasperated by proceedings.

"Well dad, I don't know how to tell you this but you'll probably get to know anyway.

"He's from Hessle Road and he's a season pass holder at Hull FC."

Jane thought her dad was about to explode. His face turned the colour of a beetroot and steam was coming out of his ears.

"Hull FC, he screamed.

"A pass holder, are you crazy?

"Don't think you can ever bring him into this house, he yelled.

"And don't let me see you with him again. I fact I forbid you ever to see him."

Thankfully she defied him but she wasn't at all happy when I handed my notice in at the newsagents and our relationship petered out though I wasn't to be deterred and my only objective was to secure a regular position at the dog track and to find myself a decent pitch and act as an illegal bookie.

Gerry Molloy - Mr Big!

There was certainly no place for shrinking violets making a book on the streets of Hessle Road, nor anywhere else in the city for that matter. No-one was going to give a young upstart like me a pitch so I had to pay my dues, and a hefty tribute, to Gerry Malloy. Malloy, who had been the unintended instigator when mother attacked dad with that poker, was by now a money lender, Club proprietor, property owner, an investor in the illegal betting parlour and all-round business man who lived in one of the better areas on the south side of Coltman Street.

As a youngster I had impressed Malloy with my intuition when I got him to give up the twenty quid that dad owed but now had to ingratiate myself on him in the hope that he would back me in my street bookie venture. Just about every street on the road, and every other road in the city, already had a bookie but one or two hadn't been doing so well and were into Malloy for big money so there were often pitches available at the right price.

Malloy generally favoured catholics like himself – the streets were teeming with second generation Irish who tended to stick together - and though christened into the faith I had decided long ago that I was agnostic, even though I hadn't an earthly what one was. But Malloy knew that I had built up a nice pot by now and he could always be tempted by readies.

The punters needed to know that if they had a decent win on the horses they were certain to get paid out. Few of them would have known me from Charlie Chaplin but with Malloy's backing there would never be any doubt about them receiving their winnings in the unlikely event of them getting lucky.

Malloy decided that it would be worth his while taking a chance on me and his own pitch in Liverpool Street, which had been operated by one of his lackies, Sam Sawdon, hadn't been doing as well as expected so he decided to ditch the unfortunate Sawdon and set me up in his place.

Naturally, Sawdon wasn't best pleased and when I went down Liverpool Street for the first time to take up my new pitch he was waiting for me with what looked like a gang of relatives - and they weren't there to give me a round of applause!

Thankfully Malloy was well aware of what might happen and the sight of his big black saloon car inching its way slowly down the street was enough to send Sawdon and his motley crew on their way.

Malloy is the most interesting and complex character I have ever met. He could be absolutely charming one minute, handing out sweets to kiddies and generally behaving like everyone's favourite uncle; and utterly ruthless the next, bollocking everyone for the most minor of misdemeanours. If anyone was from the school of hard knocks it was he but overall he was generally respected, not for the aggression or bad-mouthing, but because he had a certain aura about him that's impossible to define, plus of course he had the back-up of that oaf 'Gormless Gordon' Spradbury, who could crush someone's neck in his huge hairy hands if Malloy were to order it.

Spradbury was a simpleton who spent his life at the beck and call of Malloy, feeding off the few scraps he left him. It's said that human beings are descended from Neanderthalls and looking at Spradbury confirms that view. I suppose we shouldn't be too hard on him – it's not really his fault – I'm not certain he actually enjoys playing the villain but his size and general demeanour are suited to little else.

He's expected to ferry Malloy around in his big car but whether he's ever passed a driving test is debatable. He reckons he passed his test in the army and there are hundreds like him driving around though there's never been any sign of a test certificate. He also acts as a bouncer on the door of the Club and there's no doubt his intimidating presence is a deterrent.

Some bright spark once thought they could make a boxer out of him and managed to get him a professional license. I once saw a fight of his at Madeley Street Baths and it was an embarrassment. He was up against a brute from Pontefract, himself a no-hoper who could hardly string two punches together. The Ponty fighter just circled around poor Spradbury and smacked him a few left-handers and the poor guy had no answer.

His big problem was that he couldn't move his feet so he ended up with a record of eleven fights; no wins; no draws; eleven defeats. Even his hapless manager/promoter gave up on him after his last fight where he lost all five rounds and never laid a glove on his opponent.

I suppose the best that can be said about Spradbury is that he's very kind to his mother, who he still lives with in Rugby Street, and though Malloy pays him peanuts it's difficult to imagine where he would find another job. At least he's not sponging off society.

I have got to know Malloy very well, which is quite amazing as according to his wife Joyce he is normally very reticent to speak about personal matters to anyone – even her! He often invited me round to Coltman Street for breakfast, which the ever-faithful Joyce always prepared with loving care – eggs, bacon, sausage, mushrooms, black pudding, fried bread, tomatoes etc etc – it never varied and I looked forward to those breakfasts with eager anticipation, sometimes I didn't need to eat until the next day so great was the feast.

Tough Start In Life

Occasionally Malloy, whose thriving and diverse business interests now included the St George Club where the great Walking Race was to set off from, would sit and tell me stories about his upbringing, his youth and on one occasion his time in the army at the start of the Second World War, which I can tell you had me almost in tears.

He was born right at the end of 1918, just as the Great War was ending. He was the last of ten kids born to an Irish immigrant James and a Hessle Roader named Peggy. The reason he was the tenth and last became plainly obvious when he told me about his father, who had come over from Dublin with no skills whatsoever and had somehow been inducted into fishing and worked his way up to chief engineer on trawlers.

With his crewmates on board Steam Trawler Scotland, he was fishing off Flamborough Head when the ship sank, presumably after hitting a mine, and all hands were lost. That was in March 1919, just a few months after the war had finished, but Malloy told me that hundreds of ships of all nationalities were sunk in that year and the following year including three Scarborough vessels, and thousands of men were lost in that short period, the vast majority due to hitting mines.

So Malloy never knew his father and Peggy was left with numerous mouths to feed.

The only consolation, if there could have been one, was that the trawler had been requisitioned into the Fishery Reserve during the war and had not yet been decommissioned, which meant a navy pension on top of the widow's pension she was due. Small comfort but at least it meant destitution was kept at bay.

That was probably the most inauspicious start in life possible and to make matters worse the family were living literally on top of each other – six boys and two girls at home with the two elder boys already having flown the nest, which is just as well as their house was a two-up and two-down!

In many respects all of them were like the youngest in that they were very strong characters who always spoke their minds, whether anyone wanted to hear them or not, which naturally didn't make for harmonious living in the Malloy household and fights, verbal and physical, were a daily and accepted part of growing up.

Church was the salvation for a few of them - the Catholic Church of course as Malloy senior had insisted they were all baptised at St Wilfred's in The Boulevard. Many of them, including Gerry, went to the school attached to the church though a couple of them hardly attended lessons at all despite being persecuted relentlessly by the authorities.

Being taught by nuns and priests meant an extremely tough regime but like my own experiences at Westbourne Street they hammered reading, writing and arithmetic into their pupils and it was only the very thick or long-term absentees who didn't leave at least with a basic education.

In fact the much maligned priests performed a great service to their 'flock'. Malloy and his siblings were visited regularly at home by the priests who were able to provide them with clothes that had been donated to the church by wealthier catholic organisations.

One of Malloy's elder brothers, John, was 20 years older than him and had long flown the nest. He was a much respected bookmaker at the Boulevard dog track and also owned a few greyhounds himself, which not only ran at the Hessle Road venue but also at the recently opened Craven Park Stadium on Holderness Road.

Gerry Malloy told me that one night, when he was still at school, he was told to wait at the rear gates of the Boulevard track in Gordon Street until after the first race when one of his brother's dogs, a bitch named East Lynne, was engaged to run. When the race was over, his brother led the dog out, handed the younger Malloy the lead, who then walked her to Hessle Road, took her on a tram to the town centre, then another to Craven Park, where she won the last race in the name of Bonny Bird.

Humber Street

On leaving school (with no qualifications, naturally), Malloy did something a little bit different to the majority of his schoolmates – he went to work in Humber Street rather than the fish dock. Humber Street was a truly incredible place, the hub of the fruit trade not just in the city but the whole of the north of England. It was the recipient of fruit, vegetables, flowers and nuts from all over the globe. In a 24-hour operation, they will have been landed at the nearby Albert Dock and transported by railway on the short journey to the dozens of warehouses in Humber Street and the surrounding area where the merchants stored them.

Amongst the numerous merchants in the area the names of Kamstra, Nellist and Jack Johnson, or 'JJ' as he was universally known, resonated with customers not just in the north of England but all over the country and also in Ireland where 'JJ' had a thriving export business.

The Riverside Quay, on the South side of the Albert Dock, had been constructed for the sole purpose of a quick turnaround, ideal for perishable goods like fruit and vegetables. Fruit and veg merchants from all over the north came to Hull every day to purchase goods and much of it was transported via the old Hull and Barnsley Railway Company, by now part of North Eastern Railways, to major destinations in Leeds, Manchester and Sheffield, from where it made its way to every corner of the country.

Malloy was employed as a barrow boy by one of the biggest importers in the area and he told me that his time spent with the company was the most informative of his young life. He was one of the first there early in the morning, worked very hard and very quickly caught the attention of the boss, a bluff and tough character called Eric Shipley.

One of his very first tasks was to take a barrow loaded with fruit and vegetables to the Victoria Pier, from where he would catch a ferry across to New Holland and wait there until the cases were unloaded on the quayside. He would then make his way back on the 30-minute journey with his empty barrow.

Although he had only just left school, Malloy was quickly learning the way of the world and would attempt to slow down the transaction as best he could as he didn't want to catch the return ferry and go straight back to work.

Most days he would hang around for an hour or so while the barrow was unloaded and he got himself well known amongst the ferrymen, who were all employed by the railway company that owned the ferry, and occasionally slipped them a few bananas, oranges and peaches without the recipients of the load noticing.

In turn the ferrymen would invite him into the ticket room on the quayside for a quick cup of tea and biscuits while he waited for the goods to be unloaded, even more of an incentive to slow things down so he didn't have to catch the same ferry back.

The Pier, which had been constructed in 1887 and opened on the day of Queen Victoria's Jubilee, had witnessed several tragedies including in 1921 the destruction of an R38 class airship which broke up while making a sharp turn in full view of spectators on the jetty.

The ship exploded and burst into flames, eventually crashing into the River Humber killing 45 of the 49 on board. How on earth anyone actually survived that disaster is a miracle.

Malloy quickly made his mark in the business and after five years at the age of nineteen he was made a foreman in charge of a dozen men, much to the displeasure of those who had worked for Shipley for many years. But that situation wasn't to last.

Here's A Rifle - Go Stop The Germans!

The year was 1938 and Malloy, like all young men apart from those in 'reserved occupation', like my dad, a railwayman, joined the forces. He was enlisted in the East Yorkshire Regiment and so began a boring year doing very little, though of course the threat of war had been coming for a very long time.

As the year went on training got tougher though equipment was mostly cobbled together and bore little resemblance to what would be required in the now almost inevitable eventuality of going into battle.

After several false dawns, the Second World War was declared in 1939 and Malloy, along with his regiment, was sent to France to halt the German invasion of that country. It really does seem incredible now: "Now then lads, 'ere's a rifle, just pop over to France and stop the Panzer Divisions overrunning the Low Countries and France."

Of course by now we now all know the story of the humiliating defeat of the British Expeditionary Force and the subsequent triumph of the evacuation by the little ships though Malloy's experience, like that of so many others, was anything but triumphant.

Badly injured by a bullet that fragmented after hitting his helmet and passing dozens of pieces of shrapnel into his body, he lay on a stretcher with hundreds of other wounded comrades waiting to be evacuated. The Royal Navy carried tens of thousands of troops, British and French, away from the beaches but initially the order was only for able-bodied men to be evacuated; the wounded were left to fend for themselves with a few brave officers in charge as the German army poured through the meagre defences.

Thankfully the armada of little ships saved the day and the BEF salvaged some much needed pride from the action though thousands of men and almost all of their equipment was lost.

That, of course, was the end of Malloy's war and he spent much of the coming few years recuperating in army hospitals.

He never said too much, to me or anyone else apparently, about his experiences, apart from saying that the soldier stood next to him when he got hit was killed by a single shot, but it was obviously a hugely traumatic time for him and for his new wife Joyce.

The vast majority of men who returned from the war rarely spoke about their experiences, though there was the odd exception. One man in particular, Lenny Cowen, never stopped regaling one and all about the time he parachuted into Arnhem in the ultimately futile attempt to capture the infamous bridge of the same name, though whether he had done so was always a matter of conjecture.

In fact that's just about all he ever talked about for years. One day he came into the newsagents where I worked and I said to the manager, Dorothy:

"I bet I can get him to talk about the bridge at Arnhem before he says anything else." She didn't believe me so I said to Lenny:

"It's a lovely day Lenny, isn't it?"

Lenny replied: "Beautiful, just like the day we parachuted into Arnhem."

Like I said, most men rarely spoke about their war time experiences. For most it was a traumatic period and there was a general consensus among the population to put it all behind them. Just occasionally a few things would emerge, piece by piece, but on the whole if anyone really wanted to know anything they would have to drag it out of the returning servicemen. They certainly didn't all have a 'good war' and one man from our terrace had been a prisoner for almost all of the duration, somehow ending up on the Polish border with Russia despite being captured in Tobruk when his vehicle got stuck in the sand.

Another, a fine man who ran errands for me around the streets for the occasional packet of fags, was in the Royal Navy and his ship had been torpedoed. He was one of the few who had managed to get off into a lifeboat but when they eventually sighted land it was an island occupied by the Japanese!

He worked on the notorious Burma railroad for almost three years. He was fifteen stone when torpedoed and less than half that when finally released. Most men have a story to tell but prising it out of them before they all eventually slip off this mortal coil, will be very difficult – few are like Lenny Cowen.

Where There's A Will

Malloy gradually built up enough strength to think about earning a living again as his meagre army pension wouldn't go far. Any physical work was totally out of the question so when he went back to Humber Street to speak to Eric Shipley about a job he wasn't given the slightest encouragement. Shipley had done quite well out of the war and was still employing plenty of labour but Malloy's condition was of no concern to him and if he couldn't lift a sack of spuds he was no good, and he told him in no uncertain terms.

Malloy didn't expect charity from anyone, nor would he get it, but Shipley's rejection and the manner in which he dished it out was a real hammer blow and he vowed to get his own back one day, though at this stage that day looked a very long way off.

So, how does a man like Malloy, uneducated, seriously wounded and virtually unemployable, go from the very dregs of the earth to running a series of thriving operations? One thing's for sure, he didn't do it by bowing and scraping to the likes of Eric Shipley. He had to use every thread of ingenuity just to survive, never mind thrive, though the old saying 'where there's a will there's a way' was never truer than in Gerry Malloy.

Having a large constantly warring family had been a big hindrance in his early home life but it was a positive aid when faced with total destitution. His brothers and sisters rallied round as best they could though most of them were almost as skint as he was.

One brother, Al, had a job as a pit-prop carrier on the docks. 'A pit-prop carrier on the docks!' It sounds a bit strange for someone in Hull to be associated with pit-props but huge vessels from the Baltic ports arrived in Hull every day to disgorge timber at the Victoria Dock and many of them were carrying pit-props which had been manufactured exclusively for the Yorkshire mines.

Once unloaded by gangs of men like Al, they were transported via the Hull and Barnsley Railway to the West Riding and goods such as coal and textiles were sent the other way to be shipped to the continent. It's a matter of record that Hull has more lines of railway than any other place in the country and to say it's thriving is a huge understatement.

Al was a tough and rough little man – completely the opposite to Malloy – who was tall and had a certain composure about him. Al got into more scrapes than was good for him and didn't always come off best but he was to become instrumental in setting Malloy on his way up the ladder.

The docks were absolutely heaving with goods of every shape and size and it was inevitable that some of those commodities managed to get 'lost in transit' occasionally. There was an acceptable loss factor in all transactions and as long as that code wasn't abused everyone seemed to get along fine.

One of Al's best mates was a foreman working on the ships coming in from the continent with every variety of tinned fruit, something that was a standing dish in most households at that time. There were no refrigerators until the late '50's so canned pears, peaches and a concoction of fruit salads were greatly in demand and were almost a staple diet, especially as a treat after Sunday lunch. Like everyone else, we always had a tin of mandarin oranges in the pantry. Tins of biscuits and chocolates also came in from Belgium and Holland and they too were eagerly sought after by housewives.

Grocery shops all around the city would purchase cases of these commodities from merchants but some had a direct line into dock workers and would pay them to supply the odd case that had 'fallen off the back of a lorry.'

Malloy saw an opportunity to act as a middle-man in these transactions and would pay Al's foreman friend a fee for every case he could pass on without arousing suspicion. The system worked perfectly for a couple of years, long enough for Malloy to earn himself a few extra pound notes in his pocket and a reputation as someone who could get a job done quickly and efficiently.

On A Hand Cart

Malloy didn't have a car – hardly anyone did in the early days after the war – and he could hardly take cases of fruit salad and cream crackers on the trolley bus, nor would it have been practical to carry them on a bike. The best option was to put them on a hand cart, which was a common means of carrying goods. Malloy would turn up at a designated meeting place in East Hull, invariably a pub, pick up the goods and push the cart with its supplies all the way back to Hessle Road where he had several customers amongst the grocers.

He did, of course, ensure the goods were disguised just in case any inquisitive policemen were around but he never got stopped and all was going swimmingly until someone just got a little too greedy, which nine times out of ten is the way this kind of 'scam' is ended.

One of Malloy's biggest customers was a general grocery and fruit store run by two brothers, Ernie and Benny Benfield. 'Benfield's Emporium' was the grandly titled sign above the shop doorway and it was undoubtedly one of the most successful of its kind in the area, always packed to the rafters with every conceivable item. Working your way from the front door to the back of the store was an art in itself and usually included climbing over cardboard boxes and giant tins stuffed with cream crackers. At Christmas time it was a nightmare as boxes of dates, walnuts, figs and chocolates were added to the mix.

The brothers would pay Malloy in cash for whatever he could supply and were making a nice profit on the goods. Not surprisingly many of their competitors were getting envious and some of them were very eager to discover how they could undercut them is such popular commodities like cans of fruit and tins of biscuits.

It wasn't too long before one of them tipped off the local bobbies that something was amiss and, after a undercover enquiry, the brothers were arrested for receiving stolen goods. Ernie, the youngest of the brothers, kept his mouth shut and denied everything but Benny squealed louder than one of Hughie Rawson's pigs and Malloy was quickly hunted down and charged with theft.

He had little option but to plead guilty for which he received a small fine and a suspended sentence but that wasn't the end of the matter. Benny Benfield also 'shopped' Malloy's supplier, the foreman docker, and he didn't get off so lightly being at the forefront of the scam. He was sent to jail for two years and also received a huge fine, which he couldn't pay having spent most of it in the pub with his mates so another six months were added.

Not surprisingly he was rather displeased with Benfield senior and let it be known that turning Queen's Evidence against him had not been in the best interest of the perpetrator and that he, his family, and his business would be in for a very rude awakening when he had done his time in Strangeways.

Investing In 'A Sure Thing'

Malloy was very grateful to get away so lightly and wasn't about to make the same mistake again. From that day on he stayed within the law, sometimes bending it a little but never doing anything reckless enough to see the possibility of being incarcerated at Her Majesty's Pleasure.

His early days in Humber Street and recent dealings in the fruit trade via the stolen goods gave him a taste for the business and he set about investing his money.

My mother's brother, Gordon Gibson, had a stall in the nearby covered market. Like so many in the fruit business he had been left the stall by his father, my grandfather, who had been killed in an accident while working part-time on the docks.

Uncle Gordon was a bit of a playboy who thought himself better than a fruit stall trader and consequently didn't put his heart and soul into the business. He had a huge advantage over many of the traders in the market as his father had left much goodwill as well as a very prominent position near the entrance.

Gordon was the eldest brother and, as such, became the sole recipient of the business, much to the disgust of the rest of the family. Mother in particular was very bitter that her brother had taken over the business without paying any due to the remainder of the clan which is probably one of the reasons she was always so embittered against the world. We hadn't seen anything of him for a very long time.

Gordon preferred living it up to working and could be seen out most nights around town, usually with a new girl on his arm. He went away most weekends, again with a girl in tow, drove a fancy car and his spending appeared well out of control for someone who ran a market stall. It was a mystery to us all where the money came from, that is until Malloy came along. He'd been keeping a close watch on several market stalls for some time as he was desperate to get involved in the business.

He'd noticed with some surprise how Gordon's customers were mainly of a much younger age to those of similar businesses around him. It was incredible how many youngsters came to the stall, usually buying just a banana or an apple but also receiving from Gordon, rather furtively, a small paper bag, which contained who knows what.

Malloy could see that the market was thriving and Gordon should have been coining it in but he was bone idle and often left the stall at lunchtime to have a pint and something to eat in the George. So how was he making his money? It certainly wasn't from selling apples and pears and he didn't have a second income. Malloy was very intrigued to find out exactly it was that Gordon had in the small bags he handed out to the youngsters. So he laid a trap!

He asked me to find him a young guy who frequented the local dance halls and said he would pay him a few quid for information supplied. I grabbed my chance as Uncle Gordon hadn't seen me for years and wouldn't know me from Adam so I joined Malloy as he waited in the market, hidden behind another stall, until we noticed a youngster at Gordon's stall. As Gordon handed him the paper bag I stepped in behind him and said I would like one of the same.

Gordon looked very suspicious for a while and for a split-second I thought the game was up but greed got the better of him and he handed over a small paper bag in exchange for a ten bob note. I then handed the bag over to Malloy and waited until he opened the bag - he got the shock of his life – it contained four lumps of cannabis!

Cannabis had been banned in this country since 1928 when an Egyptian delegate at an international drugs conference convinced everyone that it was a threat to society. It didn't really take off here until the influx of migrants from the Caribbean after the war and the first-ever drug bust was in Soho in 1952.

It was popular in the local coffee bars and dance halls and there were always plenty of people willing to try it though it wasn't cheap. Gordon, who got his supplies from Holland, was not only using the drug himself but supplying it and making a nice living in the process.

Malloy wasn't remotely interested in illicit drug dealing but, with his mind racing he could now see a way of buying into Gordon's business – and at a knock-down price thanks to the information he had in his possession. He went to him with a proposal – well more an ultimatum if the truth be known. He told Gordon he knew all about his illicit dealings and he wanted to purchase half of the business and work it himself. Gordon need only do the occasional half-day when Malloy was unavailable with one major proviso – no more cannabis!

Gordon realised he had been rumbled and had little option so Malloy paid him a lump sum in cash before setting about revitalising the business. Malloy reckoned, probably correctly, that he'd done

Gordon a big favour as he was beginning to attract attention to himself and it was only a matter of time before the bobbies came knocking. I also came up smelling of roses as Malloy was so pleased with the transaction and my part in the process that he handed me a crisp five-pound note.

It wasn't too long before customers – proper fruit and veg customers that is - were flocking to the stall. Malloy was a natural and after just a year he had built up enough of a bankroll to totally buy out Uncle Gordon, who was glad to get out.

Uncle Gordon took the money and ran. Through a business contact he had become friendly with a fruit exporter who lived in Rhodesia. The last time we heard from him he had moved there and bought a farm which he insists will be a great investment for the future.

Malloy was on good terms with many of the bigger traders on Humber Street, though not Shipley of course, and most had enough faith in him to give him credit for goods, which he always paid back as promptly as he could.

He quickly expanded into a shop near Eastbourne Street, from where he sold every conceivable perishable item. That too made a tidy profit in its first year and Malloy had the foresight to buy the property on a mortgage rather than pay rent.

He also bought the house he currently lives in and in a few short years had gone from nothing to successful businessman with several fingers in many pies including a fish and chip shop and, incredibly, Benfield's Emporium as Benny Benfield had taken those threats very seriously indeed and decided to get out of the grocery business and head back to Leeds, where many of his family lived.

Whitfield The 'Singing Sailor'

Malloy was by now very much part of the Hessle Road social club scene and had his eyes on purchasing such an establishment, which by a quirk of local licensing laws was possible in the city. The Albert Club in Somerset Street was one of the most successful of these members' clubs and its proprietor, Cyril Wheeler, had become the first of a new breed of owners who had bought the premises from the brewery.

There were numerous clubs all around the city and most were packing them in every night, especially weekends where artists from all over the north appeared, sometimes 'doing the double' by performing at around 8.30 at one venue then rushing off to do their act at another from 10.00 onwards.

Hull was very much at the centre of the entertainment business in the early 1950's. Two of the countries leading recording artists, David Whitfield and Ronnie Hilton, had been born in the city. The former, always a popular figure in and around clubland, was originally known as 'the singing sailor' and struggled to make a living after leaving the navy.

He earned himself a few extra quid playing the clubs and pubs in the area to supplement his job as a coalman but made a breakthrough in 1953 with a couple of minor recording hits before moving into the big time a year later with Cara Mia. Whitfield, in fact, had claim to being the top artist in the country up to the mid 1950's and was only the third UK artist, and the first male singer, to receive a Golden

Disc. The previous recipients were Vera Lynn and the trumpeter Eddie Calvert.

Whitfield was also the first UK artist to sell a million records in the USA but like so many of his kind was swamped when rock 'n roll hit the streets.

The city and its clubland played host to top acts from around the country. Laurel And Hardy, the world's most famous double act, appeared at The Palace and I remember going to see a young local comic called Norman Collier starting his career in clubland, entertaining packed houses with his brilliant farmyard animal impressions, and he was on the under bill when Jimmy Young topped the bill at the Tivoli in 1952.

The Tivoli Theatre had played a huge part in the city's nightlife and it was a massive blow to all of us when it closed in 1954, the same year that the famous Arthur Lucan, or Old Mother Riley as he was better known, collapsed and died in the wings while waiting to go on stage.

Clubs such as Dee Street, where clubland legend Harry Hemingway ruled the roost, Empress, Cholmley, South Newington and many more were doing a roaring trade on Hessle Road and the likes of West Park, which actually staged big band concerts most weekends, Ambassador, Trinity, The Dockers Club, known as The Willows, and Humber St Andrews also had massive memberships and played to full houses every weekend and made local stars of artists such as Sammy Walsham and Al Gilyon.

I remember when very young we all crowded round the radio to listen to Top Town Quiz from Leeds, presented by Barney Colehan.

That night a group of local entertainers led by Norman Collier, Harry Hemingway, Marion Campbell and Roy Longbottom won a heat of the quiz and then went on to win the Final a few weeks later.

The clubland scene throughout the north was bursting with talent and many a young entertainer learnt their trade in the working men's clubs and the social clubs of the area.

New Club Owner

Malloy had noted Wheeler's success at the Albert Club which had its own racing wire service piped in every day and was a regular there. Most of Hessle Road's illegal bookies went to the club every afternoon to do their business and Malloy wanted to be a part of that enterprise. With his now thriving businesses he had the credibility to start taking bets and quickly established himself as someone the street bookies' could hedge with, and he never failed to pay out even when taking a big hit.

The Hull Brewery owned the St George Club in St George's Road and though the club had been doing reasonably well it wasn't well enough for the brewery bosses, who could see others in their portfolio taking much more money, therefore buying more of their products, not just beer but wines, spirits, furnishings and fittings, glasses etc etc.

Malloy went to the brewery headquarters in Bond Street and put forward a proposition which they eagerly accepted and he became a proprietor's club owner once he received a license.

Not surprisingly, being a man now of considerable fortune and a gregarious one at that, Malloy had acquired a string of friends and acquaintances along the way though he was never in any doubt who is real friends were. He entertained them on a regular basis at the St George Club where afternoon snooker and drinking sessions - after hours of course with the doors firmly locked - were the norm.

These new 'fair weather friends' included local soccer and rugby professionals who had little else to do after training finished at lunchtime, but mainly fish 'bobbers', who worked nights landing the fish from trawlers. But there was also an invitee who was there for a particular purpose.

Martin Shipley was the only son of Eric, who had treated Malloy with such contempt when he attempted to go back to work after his injury. Martin wasn't anything like his old man, he was a feckless character, weak in many things but particularly the three great sins, wine, women and song, though he was never seen doing much of the latter.

He had never been a betting man until Malloy gently, but assuredly, tempted him into having a small wager or two on the outcome of their snooker games. Being such an easily led individual, Shipley soon became addicted to gambling and after less than a year owed Malloy a staggering sum of money, which he was in no way able to pay back, well not in cash anyway.

Malloy's plan had always been to ingratiate himself into Shipley's world and he had become very much a confidante. He had learnt that on his 21st birthday the old man had given his son half of the shares in his thriving business in the expectation that he would one day take over.

As it happens the younger Shipley had absolutely no interest whatsoever in the fruit and veg trade and only turned up to work when it suited him, which was hardly at all. His father was in despair and many times had begged the son to buckle down but it was to no avail. Young Shipley's ambition was to be a playboy and he was well on the way – at least in his own mind.

Malloy was now at the stage where his plan was to come to fruition – and this is where his dark side appeared. He confronted Martin Shipley with his debts and told him he would be a ruined man in the city if it came out that he owed so much money to a bookie. Gambling debts are not recoverable by law so Malloy was treading on thin ice but Shipley was so terrified of losing his reputation that he had to listen to Malloy's proposals.

Malloy would tear up the debts and pay Shipley a substantial sum for his half of the Shipley Fruit And Vegetable Company. Shipley was of course mortified by such an arrangement but it quickly dawned on him that his father wouldn't, or couldn't, pay anything like what Malloy had offered (including wiping out the debts of course) and he was very much inclined to go with the offer.

The legalities of the sale of half of the business were quickly concluded, Shipley received a bundle of cash to do whatever pleased him, and Malloy tore up the I.O.U's in front of the seller, thus becoming a joint partner with his despised former boss in his lucrative business.

And what was the reaction of Shipley senior when told that Malloy was his equal partner? He no longer wanted anything to do with either his son, Malloy or the business and sold his half to a rival company, who Malloy quickly offered a profit on the transaction which was accepted.

No Laughing Matter For Comics

Once installed at the St George Club, Malloy began his quest to turn the establishment around. It had once thrived but thanks mainly to a typical working man's committee ethic had been allowed to sink into a depression that it would never have got out of without someone of vision to invest their time and energy. Malloy was certainly the man for the job.

With the backing of the brewery bosses, who to their credit had seen that they were onto a winner right from that first meeting, Malloy began a programme of rebuilding, not just in the structure but in the whole system of management. Out went the old committee men and a new influx came in, naturally hand-picked to do exactly as they were told by Malloy.

The main income from most proprietary clubs came from beer sales, and they were mostly generated from concert nights on weekends. Friday and Saturday evenings were incredibly busy, as long as the right artists were booked, and though Sunday could be a little trickier it was still a very good earner for the club given the right circumstances.

Malloy had employed a new concert secretary from the ranks of members and he was in charge of booking the artists for the coming weeks and months. Friday and Saturday nights could be filled by any artist, either local or out of town, and they invariably put on a good show and everyone went home satisfied.

However, Sunday was best left to local comics. The reasoning is that on Friday and Saturday night everyone was in a good mood with no work the following morning but Sunday the atmosphere was always different as work next day, and for the following week, was rarely a laughing matter for the normal working man, and woman.

The local comics knew the situation and reacted accordingly, getting a few grudging laughs from their routine was a real bonus but as long as there was no real problems and they got paid at the end of the performance they were always willing to take the risk.

Booking the artists was a fairly simple task as every Monday night the Ambassador Club on Holderness Road would put on an artists night where the locals would showcase their talents. The regular and well known artists had their agents make their bookings but club proprietors and their concert secretary's viewed these showcase evening as extremely important for their business and most were regulars at the concerts.

The One And Only Juanita DeMarx

One Sunday night in the Saint George, Malloy wandered into the small and very cramped area at the back of the stage where the evening's artist was getting changed. He hadn't spoken to the concert secretary and wasn't aware who would be performing so was rather alarmed to see a middle-aged lady in her very best frock putting her not inconsiderable make-up on.

Malloy was very perturbed about the situation as the evening audience appeared to be in an even worse state than normal. One particular group, a dozen-strong family called O'Malley, had been arguing amongst themselves for the whole time they were in the Club, and probably for most of the day as they had certainly been in and out of the pubs at lunchtime.

They had taken up their usual position at the nearest two tables to the stage and God help any new member who inadvertently wandered into their seats by mistake.

"Haven't seen you before, where are you from?" Malloy asked as politely as he could.

"Leeds, replied the artist.

"I'm Juanita DeMarx, I've been on the circuit for years and have worked most of the top clubs in the West Riding."

"The crowd are a bit restless tonight, said Malloy.

"I hope you can handle them."

"That's no problem to me at all, said Miss DeMarx, who appeared to resent the slur on her professionalism.

"I'll soon have them eating out of my hand."

Malloy wasn't really reassured but didn't have much option at that stage. He went back downstairs to the bar area and struck up a conversation with a few regulars.

The artist was to be backed by the club's own trio, the Westerners, a pianist, base and drummer. The artist had sent them copies of her music when she heard of the booking and they had put in a few minutes rehearsal though the music was familiar to them as it was a repertoire performed by many of the locals.

The Westerners had originally been a quartet until an unfortunate incident at the club one Friday evening when their leader was almost electrocuted while plugging in his guitar. It was only thanks to a quick-thinking customer, who just happened to have a pair of rubber gloves on him, that saved the day though any thoughts of the musician making another appearance on that stage were very quickly dispelled.

Malloy faintly heard the trio strike up and the pianist, who had taken over the reigns as leader, introduce the artist with as big a build-up as he could muster.

"Now for tonight's star turn, he shouted, which was something of a misnomer as she was in fact the only turn.

"Ladies and gentlemen, introducing to the St George, someone new to the club who has been entertaining audiences at venues all over the north for many years.

"The one and only Miss Juanita DeMarx."

The artist, whose real name was in fact Ruth Shoebottom from Pudsey, swept onto the stage to the tune of 'I Like To Be In America' from the original Broadway production of West Side Story but wasn't given the rapturous welcome she had expected. In fact she wasn't given a welcome at all, there were a few ripples of applause from the back of the club but it was generally silent.

The O'Malley's, seeing Miss DeMarx in her silk ball gown and with back-combed hair standing on end, began laughing and one of their number, the chief protagonist Lena O'Malley, started heckling before the artist had even sung a note.

"Juanita DeMarx, she screamed.

"She looks more like Groucho DeMarx."

The O'Malley's were cracked up laughing by this time but Miss DeMarx made a fatal mistake – she had a go back.

"Groucho DeMarx is still better looking than you, dear, and twice as funny" she said, expecting the audience to cheer with laughter at her quick wit and repartee.

Unfortunately for her, wit and repartee don't come easily to audiences in Hull's clubland, not the least this one where the O'Malley's ruled the roost.

For an instant, the audience were stunned into silence, then all mayhem broke loose. Lena O'Malley, who had the sharpest elbows on Hessle Road and by this time had downed at least four pints of Hull Brewery Bitter, got out of her seat, stood on the table scattering a dozen empty glasses in her wake, and launched herself onto the hapless and helpless Miss DeMarx.

The artist cowered on the stage floor praying for an unlikely rescue as she fended off O'Malley's blows but of course no-one in the vicinity was likely to come to her aid, including the trio, who by now had struck up into their own theme tune, 'Happy Days Are Here Again.'

Thankfully for Miss DeMarx, Malloy had heard the commotion, rushed up the stairs and dragged the kicking and screaming O'Malley off her victim. Some of the O'Malley men were deciding whether to risk attacking Malloy but thought better of it and he ushered the artist down the stairs where safety beckoned.

At first she was insistent that the police were called but Malloy, fearing a scandal not long after taking over the license, gently calmed her down and, with a very lucrative cash incentive, persuaded her that the best thing she could do was get out of town as quickly as possible. Not surprisingly, neither Juanita DeMarx nor Ruth Shoebottom ever put in an appearance in the city again.

Malloy then had the dilemma of how to handle the situation with the O'Malley's, who were by far and away his best customers. It was obvious that Lena O'Malley had to be banned; even the most hard-bitten of the members agreed with that decision, but there had to be a way of admonishing the rest of the family without losing their custom.

He was in luck when he went back to the concert room as Lena O'Malley had fled the scene of the crime along with a couple of others but the bulk of the family were sat drinking their beer as if nothing had happened.

Malloy sat down at their table, bought them all a drink, and gently warned them about their future behaviour. He never had any problems with them after that.

Major Sporting Venue

As well as extending and redecorating the concert room, Malloy's main plan for the club was to turn it into a big sporting venue. The Walking Race was the only high-profile event at the club and Malloy wanted to expand into soccer, darts, dominoes, snooker, billiards and particularly rugby.

He already had a soccer team playing in Division 16 of Hull's Sunday League, said to be the biggest amateur league in Europe at the time, but quickly put together another side to play in the Thursday League. That league was made up of teams who had Thursday afternoon's off work, which meant all of the main shops in the city, and others such as Police, the Fire Brigade, dock workers, railwaymen, NHS workers and may more who were able to play on that mid-week afternoon.

Malloy's team was made up of fish dock workers, mainly bobbers, and he ensured they were very well catered for with facilities, equipment and refreshments. The word quickly got around that the club looked after its teams and soon there were dozens of darts, snooker and domino players in leagues every night of the week.

One of the soccer team's best players was a big centre-half called Bobby Hall and for the first half of the season he was in outstanding form – but then he disappeared not to return. Hall was a bobber who had a thriving sideline selling fish around the villages in the East Riding from the back of a van. Of course how he acquired the fish in the first place was common knowledge. Most of the fish dock workers were allowed a few perks and a fry of fish was used in all kinds of barter. But as ever there were always some that went too far and Hall was certainly one of those.

He had been stocking up with supplies at regular intervals, concealing them in the back of his van and driving off the dock past the police box close to the tunnel at the bottom of Subway Street. It was only very occasionally that the police stopped and searched anyone coming off the dock with fish and never had any problems if someone just had their normal quota.

One morning, after an evening spent mainly loading his van with haddock, skate and halibut, Hall was driving off as usual when a policeman walked slowly out of his box and put his arm out for him to stop. Realising the game would be up for him if the van was searched, Hall put his foot on the accelerator and sped off.

Unfortunately for him, the policeman attempted to prevent his escape by jumping on to the bonnet of the van and he was clinging onto the windscreen wipers for dear life until Hall came to an abrupt halt, throwing the policeman onto the pavement in the process, thankfully doing only minimal damage.

Hall sped off into the distance but not surprisingly the long arm of the law was soon on his trail and that was the end of his career as a bobber, fish merchant, and centre-half as they didn't have a team in Wakefield prison at the time.

Scandal At The Darts

The rugby team was to be Malloy's own project and he was determined to turn out a side bearing the club's name that would do it proud. He recruited a former professional player as coach and he quickly put together a group of players who could challenge for top honours in the amateur league.

The team had a deserved reputation for having real characters and many of them were involved in other activities at the club. Some of them played for the Wednesday Night darts team and caused a scandal one night when playing a match in the Trinity Club.

There were four players to a team, all named, and on this particular night six made the journey across the town - two were supposed to be supporters. The first pair of players took their turn as did the first two from Trinity, who took the game very seriously indeed. Then it was the turn of the third St George player.

That's when the commotion began. One of the so-called supporters, Ernie Clough, had been kitted out in a long white raincoat, dark glasses and a white stick, and was led to the dart board by the team's skipper Alan Gower. Clough was of course supposed to be blind and stood on the okey while Gower called "left a bit; down a bit; up a bit" and so on and on.

The St George lads were all taking this stitch up very seriously but it didn't go down well with the Trinity team, or committee, who promptly threw them all out and reported them to the League.

When Malloy heard of the incident he was delighted. The club attracted more publicity than he could have imagined and membership enrolment went through the roof.

It's true of course that people make their own luck but there are some who just have that bit extra of what betting people call 'mazzle.' Malloy may have had a rough start in life but when it came to betting there was no-one with anything like his good fortune and he was renown for 'getting out of jail' when all looked lost.

In 1956, the betting public decided almost to a man (and woman) that Devon Loch would win that year's Grand National and backed the horse accordingly. He was a real punter's favourite being owned by the Queen Mother and ridden by the popular novelist Dick Francis.

Malloy, like just about every other street bookie in the land, was inundated with bets on the nag and faced a heavy loss if it was successful as the bookies he tried to lay the bet off with were also heavily into the horse. So he had to sit and suffer as Devon Loch jumped superbly around the giant Aintree fences and stormed away from the last fence to certain victory.

But that's where Malloy's 'mazzle' came into play. As everyone knows by now poor Devon Loch, with the race at his mercy, somehow managed to spreadeagle himself within sight of the winning line and the unconsidered ESB shot past for the most fortuitous of victories. We should have known better than to doubt the Malloy factor.

So that was the man I had come to for funding and backing in my new venture on the streets of Hessle Road. And though I was never to regret the action for one minute by now I was beginning to have aspirations of my own. In fact my main target was Malloy himself as I never really forgot the part he played in my dad's demise.

Extra Expenses

One of the big advantages of betting in the streets was the lack of expenses. I had to pay a tribute to Malloy each week and a small fee for renting my pitch but overall what I earned I mostly kept though there was one occasional 'expense' I hadn't counted on and to be honest, absolutely loathed paying.

Every now and then the coppers would have to nick someone for illegal betting. The experienced bookies all knew this and accepted it as part and parcel of their trade. The local bobby would alert them that they were coming and not to have too many betting slips on them and once nicked they would march them to Gordon Street police station to be charged.

A £5 fine at the Magistrates Court was the order of the day but the bookies also had to pay-off the bobby for information received about the raid and for not bothering them too much. Some of the coppers were receiving backhanders from several bookmaker sources and it was one of the main reasons why the 1961 Betting and Gaming Act came into being. Once betting became legal there were no more 'sweeteners' for the coppers and I was delighted about that.

My pitch was in the next street to that of George Mooney, whose brothers John, Alf and Wilf had pitches on Hessle Road for many years as did the likes of Arthur Grimwood, Leo (Cloggy) Brown, Truss Wells, Tim Brown, Roy Bangs, Arthur 'Conk' Bullock and Tommy Trushell.

Tommy had a brilliant pitch in Gillette Street where he took advantage of the hundreds if not thousands of workmen and women passing by on their way to work on the dock. He would have a bagful of betting slips every day and was one of the wealthiest of the illegals. He was also amongst the most generous and many a customer facing real hardship were given a helping hand by Tommy though he also had to pay out plenty to the local coppers on the take.

East Hull also had its stalwarts with great characters such as Len Young, Wilf 'Tiger' Pepper and Ambrose Brown all providing a service for which they had the backing of almost every citizen in the land though not at that time the law.

Of course giving the bobby a sweetener was seen as police corruption which undoubtedly it was and though it wasn't right, most were happy with the arrangement and few saw it as anything but a happy marriage, that was until a new chief constable or station sergeant decided to get tough though in the vast majority of cases that soon fizzled out and the status quo was back.

Every street in every city in the country had its 'illegals' as did thousands of pubs and Clubs and it wasn't until the Betting And Gaming Act of 1961 that betting became legal and the street bookies were legitimised, though many decided that betting shops were too expensive to run and carried on as normal, though admittedly to a shrinking clientele.

One Last Throw

So there I was, in my twenties, a fully-fledged illegal bookie on the mean streets of Hessle Road, heading I hoped for a life of luxury from my ill-gotten gains. Little did I know!

But back to my dilemma - to cheat or not to cheat. The Walking Race had looked like being a disaster for me and it was impossible to see a way out – that is until an opportunity presented itself right at the last minute and I wasn't about to turn it down.

Many of the participants in the event were my regular clients and even those who weren't came to me for a wager as I was deemed to be the local bookie who would stand a good bet from anyone. Consequently I had taken an enormous amount of money on the race and though always priding myself on a sound business plan this time, for some unknown reason, I was left with an unbalanced book which could have cost me dearly.

There were other bookies taking money on the event including Malloy but all were reluctant to help me out with 'hedging bets', which wasn't a surprise as it's definitely a dog eat dog business and it's very unlikely that I would have done the same for them.

I had been taking bets on the race since the last one finished a year ago – it's amazing how many of the beaten competitors think they can do better the following year.

They would ask for a price and back themselves accordingly so a couple of them had got on at bigger prices than they should have as there was always the chance they couldn't take part as with any ante-post bet it was definitely a case of losing your stake if you didn't turn up.

The race always took place on a Sunday in the spring and on this particular day I entered the fray in very good spirits after an unusually profitable night at the dogs the previous evening.

Tommy Bowes was the Secretary and Treasurer at the St George Club had been entrusted with the weekly collection of the Wembley outing subs but when the time came to access the Hull Savings Bank account for the Final, there was nothing there.

Just about every club and pub in Hull had a 'Wembley outing didlum' and there was a mass exodus from the city when the Rugby League Challenge Cup came around. Special trains were put on from Paragon Station to Kings Cross, many of them leaving on a Thursday so as to give the outing members a full weekend in London but there were also some that went at around midnight on Friday evening.

All of these trains were booked exclusively for Wembley trips and carried not just members but dozens of cases of ale, spirits and bags of crisps and pork scratchings, in fact everything a supporter needs to get through a gruelling weekend.

The Friday night special would take around eight hours to chug its way to Kings Cross where the fans would alight, having been drinking and singing for most of the journey. It was then a traditional visit to Covent Garden for breakfast before the journey on the tube to Wembley for the big match.

Most people knew that Bowes liked a bet but only one, yours truly, knew he gambled more than he could afford. He had already blown a sizeable amount with me and though I had a very good idea where the money was coming from I was hardly likely to go blabbing and lose my best source of income.

When Wembley was rapidly approaching, Bowes had one last throw of the dice, coming to me and putting his last £50, a huge sum, on the unnamed third favourite in the first race at Craven Park on Saturday.

When the race was over it looked very much like the third favourite, Tom Mix, had won at 4/1 which would have all but cleared Bowes' debts and allowed him to purchase the match tickets, train tickets and hotel rooms. However, he hadn't reckoned with the fact that the starting price returner at the track, Syd Grummit, was another client of mine and owed me a few quid.

After Tom Mix had won I quickly asked Grummit what price he was returning the winner and said it was third favourite.

I said it would be very much in his best interests, re the money he owed me, to return the winner second favourite rather than third.

He was happy to oblige, of course, with most of his debt to me wiped out. Of course there were suspicions of skullduggery but no-one could prove a thing and the starting price return was sacrosanct so there was never any possibility of an enquiry.

Poor Bowes was bereft and, fearing a lynching from the members, handed himself into the safe custody of the police at the first opportunity leaving his poor wife and children to bear the brunt of the member's hostility.

It certainly wasn't the first time that the Wembley outing money, so diligently paid by club and pub members all over the city on a weekly basis, went missing and it most definitely won't be the last.

The Great Day

At last the great day dawned and there couldn't have been a soul who was more eager than me to see the event finally under way.

"Who the hell is that? said Col Barker, stood with his mates outside the Club.

"He's not from round here – there's no way he can be entered."

"I've heard he's a cousin of Slaughterman Sam, his mate Tony replied.

"Under this year's Rules he's as much right to take part as the next man, even though he looks as though he's from Timbuctoo not Tadman Street."

The stranger did indeed look an unfamiliar sight 'round here', amid the swarming and deeply insular fishing community of West Hull. We had all seen plenty of black men before, along with numerous Scandanavians, Russians, Chinese and other nationalities washed up by the trawlers and timber boats at the area's massive docks complex. But this guy was different – and he was here for a specific purpose.

This was The Annual St George Club Walking Race - Hessle Road's social highlight of the year in the 1950's and early '60's - not the sporting highlight – that was thrashing Hull KR at the Boulevard every Christmas Day or Good Friday – but an event looked forward to more than Christmas Day, New Year's Eve, Bonfire Night and St Patrick's Day put together.

Hessle Road is a village within a city. The whole area covering the top of Osborne Street to the railway crossing at Dairycoates is only a couple of miles long but has dozens of streets along the route, and several of those have streets running off them. There are even 'streets off streets off streets' if you get my meaning, each containing dozens of individual terraces which are packed with houses and people.

Many of the streets, especially on the western side including Manchester Street, Liverpool Street and Havelock Street, have fish curing houses mainly populated by women workers. To be frank they're not a pretty sight with their white wellies and gowns stained yellow by the curing process and hair tied into bunches underneath blue hairnets.

But they work long and unsociable hours to keep the plants open 24 hours a day and the money earned keeps many a family from abject poverty.

One of Hessle Road's great landmarks is Boyes, or 'Boysiz' as everyone called it. 'Boysiz' was always a nightmare for us kids as that's where our mothers took us to get kitted out for a new school year. They could manage a pair of shoes, a shirt and jumper for about ten bob but to be honest you wouldn't call us stylish though everyone was wearing the same gear so it didn't really matter.

Still it was better than going to the Army and Navy Stores like some did – who'd want to come to school dressed as a marine commando or merchant navy seaman?

Off To The Seaside

The only decent green area is a good mile or so away at Pickering Park so just about all the local kids played in the streets and on the bombed building sites which litter the area.

The one relief for most of us was the annual holiday trip to Withernsea. Every year, much of Hessle Road decamps to the seaside and 'With', being the nearest and undoubtedly cheapest, was the chosen spot. Most of us didn't realise there were any alternative resorts though a few people went to Hornsea but hardly any as far as such exotic locations as Bridlington or especially Scarborough, though I did once manage a trip to the Cricket Festival with my dad one year and the Co-op took around 1800 people on annual excursions to the town, though I never got invited.

We would take the trolley bus to Paragon Station and there alight a steam train for the journey. Once on our way the train would call in at several stations en-route. First came Botanic Gardens, a rather grand name for Spring Bank corner, then Stepney which served Beverley Road. Next came Wilmington in smoky Cleveland Street then Southcoates followed by Marfleet. The last two stations served East Hull then it was on the way to South Holderness with Hedon the next stop. After Hedon we were really into the countryside with Ryehill and Burstwick followed by Keyingham.

There were many youngsters on that train, especially those who were travelling for the first time, who had never seen a cow or a sheep in their lives, apart from in picture books at school. I had an advantage in that respect as when I was very young I was riding my bike along Woodcock Street and suddenly there was a bullock heading in my direction in the middle of the road being chased at a good distance by several men in very bloody white coats and wellies, screaming their heads off.

The poor demented animal had made a bid for freedom from the abattoir at the very top of Hessle Road, somehow got itself onto Goulton Street, then turned right in a frenzy down Boulevard. It crossed the main road and went helter skelter towards Gordon Street, knocking into the few cars that were parked on the side of the road in the process and sending poor Jimmy Logan's fruit and veg cart scattering all over the road.

On hearing the commotion the neighbourhood suddenly erupted with people all willing to help Jimmy collect his apples, oranges, caulies and cabbages, along with the dish containing the morning's takings. He reckons he got about half his commodities back and less than half his half-crowns, two-bobs and shillings.

The bullock continued its mad dash, turning left into Gordon Street and then into Woodcock Street which is where I saw it hurtling towards me. Thankfully it veered off towards one of the terraces where there lives a whole bunch of 'tatters' or rag and bone men. By this time the chasing employees of the abattoir had turned into Woodcock Street but there was no sign of the bullock. They began searching the terraces and back yards of the area but to no avail and the bobbies in Gordon Street police station weren't interested in going into the area. The bullock had mysteriously disappeared. Over the next few days the 'tatters' began knocking on doors in the area asking if anyone wanted to buy cheap cuts of beef – it was the first time we'd had steak in our house for many a day.

There's a twist to the story, however. Paddy O'Riley, who worked at the abbatoir where the animal got loose, told me a while later that the bullock had actually been found alive a few days later on waste land at the bottom of Haltemprice Street. So what were the tatters selling? Is it a coincidence that the old nag who pulled the rag and bone cart disappeared around the same time?

By now we would be getting very excited as Ottringham and then the penultimate stop at Patrington came and went. Finally, every youngster in every carriage would be straining to be the first to view the lighthouse, the main feature of our destination.

On arrival at Withernsea, hundreds of people alighted with suitcases to be greeted by a gaggle of local youngsters with home-made wheelbarrows. They were touting for the business of carrying the heavy cases to the various caravan sites around the town. These young entrepreneurs would earn themselves pocket money every Saturday during the summer months and many would be working from early morning until the last train left for Hull late in the evening.

Most of us would take advantage of these porters and walk along with them to the sites. Amongst the major camps were Colleys Field, Nettleton's, Moon's, Stephenson's and Highfield, with its large fishing pond as a major feature. Dad would hire a caravan for a week from a local woman for a few pounds – on a couple of occasions when he must have been flush, we even went for a fortnight.

The caravans were wooden structures, almost all painted green or brown, generally far enough apart to offer a degree of privacy though that was something that never bothered anyone as we were obviously used to living on top of each other. The one structure that offered no privacy at all was the lavatory, a shed-like contraption that stood beside each caravan. Never the most fragrant of places, I always had a great deal of sympathy for the council workman who had the job of emptying them once a week – probably the worst job imaginable.

The vans were lit by paraffin lamps and whole feasts were produced by mothers everywhere using ancient equipment and primus stoves, which were often temperamental and burst into flames on many occasions though thankfully I don't recall any real damage, apart from a few singed eyebrows.

We spent our days playing cricket on the beach or if the tide was in on the nearest spare piece of ground. Everyone joined in, mothers, fathers, boys and girls from every neighbourhood and friendships were formed there that stood the test of time.

My recollection is that the sun was always shining but that's obviously not the case and when it rained we listened to Test Match cricket on the radio, played cards, Monopoly or snakes and ladders, and generally amused ourselves before a trip into the town centre each night to play in the amusement arcades or a ride in the boating lake if funds would allow.

Of course Sunday was always very different. Many people went to church but the main occupation of the day was listening to the radio. Millions of us tuned in to Forces Favourites, or Two-Way Family Favourites as it later became and presenters Jean Metcalf and Cliff

Michelmore were household names, as were Wlfred Pickles, Peter Brough and Archie Andrews.

Brough was a ventriloquist and Andrews his dummy – that's right – millions of us have sat and listened to a ventriloquist on the radio. The long-running gag was that 'you couldn't hear his lips move.'

The Goon Show started in 1951 and has only just finished. It's made stars of Peter Sellers, Harry Secombe, Spike Milligan and Michael Bentine but wasn't to everyone's taste – mother always said: "It's too daft to laugh at" but it's been certainly hugely popular as has been the Billy Cotton Band Show.

It's a simple pleasure for thousands of families and a massive diversion from the daily grind of normal existence.

Later, when in my teens, we would catch the train on a Saturday night for the weekly dance at the Grand Pavilion. The last train home was packed with teenagers, many who had been drinking most of the night in the Spread Eagle or some other of the numerous popular watering holes in the town. Not surprisingly there were plenty of fights but the transport police usually had a couple of vicious looking Alsatian dogs with them and quickly diffused the situation.

Yes, Withernsea held a great resonance for me and my dream had always been to make enough money, by fair means if possible but not exclusively, to buy myself a place beside the seaside.

Even Women Can Enter

Hessle Road differed from the rest of Hull by its proximity to the fishing docks. Holderness Road was always very busy and had the advantage of the superb East Park with its water chute, newly opened Lido and excellent bandstand while the Beverley Road area, though having many more large and expensive properties, had a good community spirit through its proximity to the superb Pearson Park.

But Hessle Roaders thought themselves different, definitely not better but somehow different to their neighbours from other parts of the city and nowhere else was there anything remotely like the great St George Club Walking Race to bring everyone together, if only for one day a year.

After that series of incidents concerning bribery and corruption just after the war, the Rules of the Race had been relaxed somewhat to allow cousins, nephews, grandchildren, and God forbid, and over the dead bodies of several committee members, even women, to take part, not that any had ever entered.

The stranger was indeed related to Slaughterman Sam, and though originating from West Africa he had been in the country for many years and was a private in the army, based at Aldershot. He regularly visited Sam and his family and hearing of the great event had decided to enter.

Sam had told anyone who was interested that his cousin Jake had represented the army in the Combined Services Walking Race at

Cardiff the previous year, which certainly got the bookies interested and I had installed him as 6/1 third favourite. Sam and his family had a few quid on and there were other backers reckoning that anyone with his pedigree should be taken very seriously indeed. In fact at one stage there was a flood of money for Jake and he had been promoted to favourite for a while.

"It's not fair, declared my mate Les.

"Where he comes from they have to walk 20 miles over a mountain to post a letter."

Jake's participation was serious enough but what no-one knew, not even cousin Sam, was that the army private was a serial 'enterer' who would do anything to get out of his army duties which mainly consisted of cleaning latrines and spud bashing.

He did indeed represent his battalion at Cardiff but finished 84th out of the 86 who had entered. The guy in 85th had disappeared for an hour and a half as the walkers went through the city's Red Light district yet even he was only five minutes behind Jake at the finish, and very much blowing for a tug!

As for the soldier who finished last – there wasn't one. Private Syd Morrell of the East Yorks Regiment based at Catterick disappeared completely during the walk and was marked down as a deserter.

So while Jake's participation had attracted attention he wasn't a serious player, though only he knew it at the time.

'Scumbag-Murderer'

The crowd were beginning to gather along the route by now, a pleasant sunny Sunday morning in late-May, and several had joined the throng at the club entrance to see some of the more serious competitors going through their exercises. Among the spectators were a few women with their numerous offspring, there to support their menfolk as well as hurl vitriol, bile and obscenities at others who they had fallen out with in the passing of time – and there were plenty in that category.

One of the main recipients, who for some unknown reason had decided to enter the contest, was Charlie Dudgeon, who had only been released from Wakefield prison the previous December after serving 7 years of a 10-year sentence for manslaughter.

"Scumbag! Murderer! Jailbird" were just a few of the invectives hurled at the unfortunate Charlie, though the term unfortunate doesn't immediately spring to mind when thinking of him.

Dudgeon's tale was a very sad one, even though his demise was very much self inflicted. The son of hard-working parents who lived in small house on Hessle High Road, he had a very good education and was bright enough to get a good job in the local housing department's financial division where he was doing well. His parents doted on him and he never married or as far as anyone knew had a girlfriend. His one great passion was gambling and he prided himself on being a good judge of horses and greyhounds leading to many a skirmish with us bookies in the streets, clubs and at the dog track.

His father, an insurance salesman and a pillar of the Methodist church, was not one to throw money about so when he died suddenly he left Dudgeon with a nice few quid in the bank. His mother, who worked part-time in the local post office, followed him to the grave not too long after so he decided to give up work and concentrate on his gambling.

Dudgeon had an extremely high opinion of himself, probably due to the fact that he could never do any wrong in the eyes of his parents. He was quite successful at betting without causing too many sleepless nights for the bookies but his general arrogance made him few friends and many more enemies than was good for him.

One bookie who had a good reason to despise Dudgeon was Ben Leeman, who had a pitch at the dog track. Leeman was a well-liked character who had stood at the track for many years and was regarded as a straight as a die bookie who always played strictly by the rules. Dudgeon was a regular punter with Leeman and like many would have his wager 'with a ring' meaning on credit and either pay up or be paid at the end of the night's racing depending on how successful he'd been.

Dudgeon had never failed to pay his debts when losing until one night when he had considered himself so hard done by that he refused to acknowledge his losses. He had placed quite a large wager on Trap 4 in the main race on the card, believing it to be a certainty after studying the form. The dog had duly won the race by a very narrow margin but the stewards at the track had decided that it had 'turned', meaning it had attacked the dog in Trap 2 who was challenging it for the lead in the closing stages.

They then disqualified the dog and placed it last, leaving Trap 2 as the winner. Dudgeon was absolutely mortified and demanded that the stewards rescind the verdict but there was absolutely no chance of that happening. He then began to bet more recklessly than was good for him to get his losses back but had no luck whatsoever which found him well down at the end of the night.

Dudgeon went to Leeman and asked how much he owed. The bookie knew exactly how much it was and told Dudgeon who handed over a sum but didn't include the losses incurred on the disqualified dog. Leeman of course told him in no uncertain terms that all gambling debts had to be paid whatever the circumstances but Dudgeon said that he would never pay as he believed himself to have been cheated by the stewards.

What made matters worse for Leeman was that he had hedged half of the bet with another bookie and of course had to pay out. So he was a double loser and he knew there was no way under law he could make Dudgeon pay his debt.

The rest of the track's bookmakers were very sympathetic to Leeman's case but it really is a dog eat dog world in the bookmaking industry and it didn't prevent a single one of them taking Dudgeon's bets at subsequent meetings.

Now in his late thirties, Dudgeon decided, for some reason known only to himself, to befriend some of the less than salubrious characters who frequented the gambling world and fell in with a really bad crowd which included a couple of local prostitutes. Not surprisingly they saw him as a meal ticket for life and took advantage of him in many more ways than one.

Dudgeon had never been anywhere near a woman in the past and was desperately uneasy with members of the opposite sex but of course his new found female friends were extremely adept at making him realise what he had been missing all those years.

Being very naïve in the ways of the world, he fell madly in love with one of the girls and was soon treating her and her friend to fancy jewellery, expensive holidays, and a not inconsequential amount of drugs. Having never previously been involved with anything remotely as sordid as this dalliance with his two 'ladies of the night', Dudgeon found himself is some highly dangerous situations.

One of the girls came from a big family who weren't concerned where she got her funds. Illicit drugs were a rarity and could generally only be found in seedy bars or on ships, brought into the docks by foreign seamen. Dudgeon, whose upbringing had mainly resolved around the Brighton Street Methodist Church, was placed in situations that he could never had envisaged including trailing around the dock entrance with one of the girl's brothers looking for someone to sell him drugs. He also began to frequent some of the less than salubrious late-night coffee bars in the city where the substances could quite easily be obtained.

Not surprisingly the money soon ran out – as did his girlfriend and Dudgeon, realising all too late that he had been taken for a ride, planned a final showdown with her which resulted in tragedy for both.

Having tricked her into a meeting at his house on the premise that he had landed a very large bet at the dog track the previous night, Dudgeon pleaded with her to return to him but when she refused he attacked her so savagely that she bled to death. Neighbours who heard the commotion called the police but by the time they reached the house the lady of the night was no more.

Perhaps the biggest surprise to many was the fact that he wasn't charged with murder, which carried the death penalty. Someone, somewhere must have decided on leniency as there is no doubt he had been lured into a world that was totally alien to him but the fact is that he took a life and was probably very fortunate to get away with manslaughter on the grounds of 'diminished responsibility.'

So Dudgeon served 7 years of his sentence and hadn't been out long when he decided to attempt integration back into the community. But no-one wanted to know. He hadn't been well liked before going off the rails and was more or less snubbed wherever he went. It didn't help that he was skint so why he decided to enter the race is anyone's guess but the reaction of the women waiting around the club entrance suggested he shouldn't have bothered.

Bookie's Favourite

All shapes and sizes were now appearing in the throng gathering at the entry to the club where some of the the contestants were paying their £2 entry fees. The new favourite for the race was Denis Batte, a 30-year-old cheeky Charlie, who had backed himself to win a lot of money and told the few of his mates that were left to avail themselves of the odds as he was a certainty to win.

Denis didn't have a 'proper' job as far as anyone knew. He was, in his words, a 'mover and a fixer' though what he moved and fixed is anyone's guess. According to him he was an importer of commodities; a jockey's agent; a part-time financial advisor and a member of the elite Marine Commandos, all in his spare time of course.

He could also tell a good yarn. He regaled everyone with a story of how he'd carried Bobby Locke's bag when the South African won the second of his British Open golf championships; advised Lester Piggott how to ride Never Say Die in the Derby; was in Freddie Mills' corner when he won the World Light-Heavyweight title; and became understudy for Robert Taylor on the set of the film The Adventures Of Quentin Durward, a job he got through his friendship with the Withernsea-born Kay Kendall, who also starred.

Batte was bright and as sharp as a new pin despite the fact he left school long before his fifteenth birthday. As far as any official knew he'd never done a day's work in his life as he certainly wasn't on any payroll and had never paid a penny in tax. Having said that he wasn't a scrounger either and never claimed a penny in dole so how did he live?

I had known him for a long time and had to admire his cheek even if he hated all bookmakers. On leaving school he earned himself a few quid doing little errands for people; a bit of painting here and there; cutting someone's grass in Hessle and generally keeping busy. He obviously didn't need much to live on though he claimed he ate the very best food and drank wine from France, which would have put him in a minority of one on Hessle Road.

Jack Wallis said that Batte was "The biggest holy friar in Hull" and he wouldn't have been far off but he certainly enriched lives that would have been much more mundane without him.

Denis was never lacking in confidence and would regularly issue challenges for money to all and sundry. He would take on anyone for cash at a huge variety of things including poker, tennis, chess, snooker, billiards, sports questions, darts, in fact anything where he thought he could earn himself a few quid.

He almost always came out on top but there was one famous occasion when he was 'had over' in a big way.

Lawrie Rubens was a local bookmaker who stood alongside myself at the dog track and took bets in one of the many social clubs on Hessle Road. Lawrie, a great guy who helped me out on a few occasions when I'd had a bad night, was a very good sportsman though his rotund figure suggested otherwise.

He regularly played badminton, table tennis and cricket, the latter being a particular favourite as he was a successful opening batsman for the local Judeans side.

Like many of his peers in the betting game, Lawrie had a quick wit and an exceptional sense of humour. The repartee he built up with his clients was an integral part of his business and he was one of the most successful bookies in the city.

Denis Batte was a regular client and the pair of them produced many examples of the cut and thrust of betting, often to the entertainment of the crown who gathered around Lawrie's pitch. One night when Denis was doing his dough, he made a remark about Lawrie's ample figure and suggested he could beat him in a race any time, any place, anywhere, and could even give him start over 60 yards.

Lawrie seized his chance and told him he would race him over 60 yards with five yards start as long as he could choose the venue.

After a split second to think about it Denis took up the cudgel and a wager was made for the not inconsequential sum of £50 each, Lawrie with five yards start at a place of his choosing.

The following Tuesday evening after racing and at the top of Westbourne Street, Lawrie, Denis and a crowd of interested onlookers, gathered to witness the event. The stake-money was held by Jack Taylor, a committee member of the club, and Denis was very eager to get started and win his fifty quid.

"Come on then, let's get it on, he said.

"Where's the venue?"

Lawrie didn't reply but pointed down the street and began walking slowly.

The crowd believed he was leading them to the bombed school building at the bottom of the street but about halfway down he suddenly stopped.

"It's here," he said.

"Where?" replied Denis, just as bemused as all who were in attendance.

"Here, down this passage" relied Lawrie, pointing to a long narrow stretch in-between two rows of houses that were probably only a yard apart.

Denis turned a whiter shade of pale. He'd been well and truly had over. The passage was just wide enough for two normal sized people to pass but of course Lawrie's ample girth would make it impossible for anyone to get past him, especially with £50 involved.

To Denis's eternal credit he conceded defeat before a yard was even attempted and Jack Taylor duly handed the £100 over to Lawrie who then invited everyone there to attend the club where he bought them all a drink.

The Jewish community of Hull has contributed massively to the business, cultural and social activities of the city and there is hardly a sporting activity that doesn't include at least one Judeans team. They are particularly strong at cricket, table tennis and snooker and games against them are invariably played in a genial manner as there are some great characters amongst the fraternity.

I once stood in for a friend of mine who played cricket for the Judeans and was unavailable. The match was on the side pitch at the

Anlaby Road Cricket Circle and I stepped in to bowl when the opposition openers were at 24-0. After three overs I had taken four wickets – most of them flukes – and the team's skipper suggested I have the 'snip' and become an honorary member! Not likely.

Jewish businesses thrive on Hessle Road with one in particular, Geoff Levy's Clothing House, always doing a roaring trade as it's just about the busiest shop in the area as fishermen and their families are always assured of a warm welcome, and with a bit of bargaining some discount, from the ever-popular Geoff.

By now Hessle Road was thronging with hundreds of people gathering along the route to gain the best vantage point. The finishing line was almost outside the club doors and the committee had placed tape around the final 100 yards so there was no interference from supporters. That area was already full as was the next 500 yards or so but the whole route was filling up quickly.

In the early days of course there was very little traffic with Corporation trolley buses, East Yorkshire Motor Services, Stipetic's ice cream cart, the occasional rag and bone man and the coalman's horse and rulley providing the main hindrance to the walkers. But they were basically of little consequence while the organisers had the foresight to send the contestants over the iron bridge that straddled the railway crossing at Dairycoates as one year a steam train had interrupted the race to a great extent and half the walkers had to go via the bridge while the others managed to get through.

Vicar's Tea And Bacon Sandwiches

The route took the participants from the top of St George's Road to the Dairycoates crossing, past Gypsyville towards Pickering Park, then along Hessle High Road towards Hessle Square where they turned round and came back again. The crowd were almost all gathered at the side of the road from the club to Gypsyville as the few people who resided on Hessle High Road and Hessle itself didn't necessarily want to be associated with Hessle Roaders. There were a few in the Square offering encouragement but they were almost exclusively supporters of the walkers and not general well-wishers from the town.

The best vantage points were difficult to find but the enterprising vicar of St Mary's and St Peter's opposite Hawthorne Avenue in Dairycoates had a novel idea of adding to his coffers. He was serving tea and bacon sandwiches at a shilling a time on the flat roof of the parish hall which offered a fantastic view over much of the route and like many previous years he was doing spectacular business.

With just an hour to go to the noon start time, the crowd had swelled into thousands and the starting area was beginning to get seriously jammed with competitors and spectators alike. Some of the early walkers were outside warming up but many more were inside the club, some taking advantage of the early opening time to avail themselves of the pleasures of the bar.

It was rumoured that Gordon 'The Bounder' had already downed three pints of Hull Brewery Bitter though thankfully for him well out of the sight of 'Mrs Bounder' who was still anticipating at least a place in the first three from her hero.

Those gathered around the start were mainly in a boisterous mood but suddenly, without warning, a hushed silence fell over the gathering. Riding up to the club entrance on his bike was the glowering figure of Arthur Bullen, a huge man with a girth so wide in took two belts sewn together to keep his trousers up.

Ginger Tom's Demise

Bullen had that effect on people. He had a fearsome reputation. A labourer in a local scrap yard, his feats of strength were legendary. It was said that he could lift a bus engine out of its housing without breaking sweat and he was never invited to participate in the numerous arm-wrestling contests that took place in the area as it would have been a one-horse event.

Unmarried and never kissed according to local legend, he had just two hobbies – pigeons and drinking. He had his own table in the corner of the club and sat alone there almost every night of the week, never joining in any of the activities - not even the Bingo or raffle.

He would occasionally grunt at work colleagues or others he knew but basically he just sat there all night – brooding!

Arthur lived in a two-up, two-down in terrace down Wellsted Street with a backyard where he kept his beloved flock of pigeons, which he occasionally took to Hessle foreshore in a wicker carrier on his bike and let loose. He belonged to the Chalk Lane Pigeon Fanciers Club but very rarely got involved in their activities as he had never had a bird good enough to take on the other members.

That was until about six months previously when a young bird he had reared himself began coming home from his Hessle jaunts much quicker than anything he'd previously released. This was the one he thought would help establish him as a pigeon breeder of distinction.

Tragically, what happened next went down into Hessle Road folklore and is the main reason why Arthur's malevolent presence scared so many people.

New neighbours had moved in a few doors away – not uncommon in an area where doing a moonlight flit to avoid the rent man was a regular occurrence. They were a boisterous lot with a load of kids and several animals including a large and fearsome looking Ginger Tom cat. The said moggy immediately began roaming the neighbourhood looking for trouble – and soon found it!

One evening just after his usual tea of sausages, mash and baked beans, Arthur heard an unholy screeching coming from his backyard. Moving with the speed of Billy Boston, he crashed through the back door and reached his pigeon loft just in time to see the Ginger Tom holding his beloved young pigeon by its scraggy neck, blood pouring out of a gaping hole and obviously already gone to the great pigeon loft in the sky.

Arthur grabbed the moggy by the throat and shook it so severely that the pigeon dropped onto the floor. What happened next is not for the squeamish but the story goes that Arthur dispatched the Tom with one blow before walking calmly back to his small tool store.

Most of the neighbours had heard the commotion but decided discretion was the better part of valour as Arthur was definitely not someone to make small talk with, even at the best of times, and this didn't sound like the best of times.

A few minutes later a quick burst of hammering was heard before all went quiet. The new, boisterous neighbours, decided to go out into the backyard and investigate. Nothing untoward appeared to have happened until the lady of the house, a small shrewish looking woman who hailed from Dewsbury, opened the wooden back door to find the Ginger Tom nailed to it by its neck.

All hell then broke loose with the woman and her husband, a scruffy foul-smelling local who worked at the tannery, charging through Arthur's backyard door to confront the 'murderer'. Arthur stood there saying nothing. The woman picked up a yardbrush and attempted to hit him but he snapped the offensive object with his fingers. Her husband, on seeing this exhibition of raw power, beat a hasty retreat followed by the wife who was hurling foul-mouthed insults but had quickly decided that a full frontal assault wasn't in their best interests.

The police were called but did anyone see the said incident? Case closed.

Of course Arthur was an unlikely competitor in the Race but had decided to take advantage of the club's early opening time and was soon to be seen sitting at his usual table drinking a pint of Hull Brewery bitter and reading this week's edition of the Pigeon Weekly.

A Spanner In The Works

The Race committee was made up entirely of club members and their word was final. They appointed the stewards who stood at regular intervals along the road checking that none of the competitors broke into a trot.

The competitors had been handed a Rule book when the entered that laid down the regulations though the majority hardly bothered to read them as they all believed they knew the difference between walking and running.

The Chairman, Terry Walker, was also the club's MC on concert night and fancied himself as a cross between Frank Sinatra, Johnny Mathis and Danny Kaye. He also thought himself a bit of a ladies man though it was only he who thought so and the women of the club mainly treated him with contempt, if not pity.

In truth he wasn't the best MC in clubland - probably not even the best in his own club - but Malloy knew how to get value and not only did he come cheap he doubled up cleaning the toilets after closing time. This was Terry's big day of the year, the one time when he was in sole command of all he surveyed, and he lapped it all up. He had come outside to oversee the starting preparations and had already designated an area for each of the stewards to position themselves so all was going exactly according to plan.

Then along came a spanner in the works!

Tottering down the club stairs to the starting post in a skimpy vest and shorts so short they looked more like briefs was none other than Jo Jones, the barmaid with the long blonde hair, ample bosom and spindly legs.

"What the hell do you think you're doing? The shocked Terry asked.

"Get back behind the bar were you belong, there's customers waiting to be served."

Jo looked at the Chairman with the disdain she normally reserved for the young trawlermen who fancied their chances with her.

"I'm taking part in the walk, what do you think I'm doing? Jo replied.

"I signed up like everyone else and paid my entry fee so my money's as good as theirs."

To be fair to Walker, it's not too surprising that he hadn't noticed the entry. Jo had placed her form in the cardboard box behind the bar when no-one was looking and registered under J Jones. With over 100 entries in the event her name hadn't rung any bells and there was nothing Walker or anyone else could do to prevent her taking part.

Why she would have wanted to is anyone's guess but there was a definite method in her perceived madness and thankfully it was me who was to be a major beneficiary, though I certainly didn't know it at the time. She had watched the previous year's walk and the presentation of a big cheque to the winner and decided that she was as fit as just about everyone taking part.

Jo had been one of the instigators in getting the Rules altered to allow women to compete and, unbeknown to anyone, even her husband, she had been training in Pickering Park for months.

She came to me one night and said: "What price will you quote me to win the race?

"I think I've got an each-way chance and want to win a few quid."

Of course I was taken aback by the request as I hadn't even dreamt she would be in the race never mind have a chance of winning it.

"You can have 50/1, I said.

"I think that's fair enough seeing as how you appear to believe in yourself."

"I'll take it, she said.

"I'll have £3 each-way at 50/1."

She then took me through her training regime which seemed extremely vigorous and I was beginning to think I may have made a mistake in offering such big odds. If she was willing to risk £6, I reckoned, she must be very confident as that amount of money would have taken a lot of saving from her barmaids tips.

I thought about it for a while and decided to take the bull well and truly by the horns. The only bookie willing to lay me a decent bet was of course Gerry Malloy so I approached him at the club.

"I see Jo Jones is entered in the race, I said as nonchalantly as I could.

"She reckons she's in with a chance so I think I'll have a few bob on her."

"Have you gone barmy? Malloy replied.

"A woman! - winning the Walking Race – impossible."

"What price is she then? I enquired.

"You obviously don't think she can win so she must be at big odds."

"You can have 100/1 with me, said Malloy, looking at me as though I had completely lost my marbles.

"But only to win, I'm not taking each-way bets at such big odds."

That put me in a slight dilemma as I really wanted to back Jo to finish in the first three but I could hardly resist the massive odds on offer.

"OK, I'll have £10 to win at 100/1" I said.

"That shook Malloy a little but his pride wouldn't allow him to show it and he duly accepted the bet, handing me a receipt that said I would draw £1000 plus my £10 stake back if, by some miracle, Jo Jones were to win the great St George Club Walking Race.

The Interview

Jo was having an affair with trawler skipper George Unwin and it was the talk of the club. Everyone appeared to know about it apart from her hapless husband Ronnie, though it's just possible he knew but turned a blind eye as Jo was regarded as quite a catch for someone as nondescript as he.

Jo was rightly now regarded as one of the best barmaids in the business but she hadn't always been in clubland; far from it, and the way she got the job was a major talking point in the area for years. The club advertised in the Hull Daily Mail for an evening barmaid, 'preferably with experience', and Terry Walker was put in charge of interviews. To be blunt, it wasn't the best paid job in the business and there weren't too many applications but Terry had already seen half-a-dozen women before arriving at the final interviewee, a Mrs J Jones.

Jo walked up the stairs to the concert room where Terry was waiting, already fed up with the poor quality of candidates and ready for home. When I say walked I really meant staggered as she had the largest pair of stiletto heels on that anyone had seen.

She also had a very large pair of something else that Terry could hardly miss and, coupled with a skirt halfway up her backside and a low-cut blouse she was a fair sight to someone who believed he was god's gift to women.

"I've come about the job." said Jo.

"OK, said Terry, eyes bulging.

"Have you had any experience?

"Of barmaiding I mean," he added with a snigger.

"No, none at all," said Jo, and Terry's face dropped a little.

"Where do you work now," said the Chairman.

"As a pattie slapper in the fish factory," replied Jo.

"Have you ever worked with money or on a till," Terry asked hopefully.

"No, never," said Jo, much to Terry's obvious disappointment.

Terry was now beginning to look desperate.

"Are you any good at figures," asked the Chairman.

"Well, I got an F in my GCE exams," replied Jo.

Gleaning a ray of hope from the last reply Terry had one last throw of the dice.

"What's 9 times 7," he asked

"Er, 9 times 7, that's, er, let me see, 58," said Jo triumphantly.

"That's near enough, said the Chairman,

"Can you start on Monday?"

And that's how Jo Jones became an evening barmaid at St George Club and quickly added weekend shifts to her rota as she was a very hard worker and was extremely popular, especially with the male members.

She also came under the wing of Flo Hemingway, Hessle Road's best known and best loved barmaid, who quickly befriended Jo as she recognised a good worker when she saw one. Flo is a legend on Hessle Road and it's been said she can serve half-a-dozen trawlermen, make a plate of ham sandwiches, and throw a couple of drunken deckie learners out while holding a conversation with all of them at the same time.

However, life hadn't always been that kind to Josephine Jones, or Josephine Barton as she was christened, not by a very long way.

Jo's Story

Jo's father, Stan Barton, was a repulsive character, roundly despised by all who knew him. He had worked on the railways from leaving school and had somehow managed to avoid doing his duty in the war, though how that came about was anyone's guess as that was by no means an easy thing to do and he was never in what could be regarded as a reserved occupation on the railway.

Jo's mother Doreen or 'Do' as everyone called her, was a timid little woman and very private. She kept herself strictly to herself, was never seen in pubs or clubs and walked around with her head down most of the time. Not surprisingly she didn't endear herself to her neighbours but there were probably extenuating circumstances, not the least of them being married to an ogre like Barton.

Jo had a sister, Freda, who came along not long after Jo was born. The two girls were generally well dressed and behaved and attended school in Westbourne Street, which was very close to their home in Welton Crescent, Hawthorne Avenue.

The sisters were devoted to each other and rarely needed the company of other girls and were regarded as a little bit strange by their schoolmates.

Stan Barton was a bully who regularly took a stick to the girls, and it was rumoured, to his wife. He rather fancied himself as a bit of a hard nut though he came badly unstuck one day.

Jimmy McKeown, a Scot who lived at the top of Welton Crescent with his wife and five daughters, saw Barton slap Freda in the terrace and admonished him in no uncertain terms. Barton wasn't to be told what to do by anyone and had a go back which from his point of view turned out to be a bad move.

McKeown attacked him with venom and the pair of them went at it hammer and tongs with just about all the neighbourhood watching. They must have fought for at least 10 minutes with McKeown always having the upper hand and seemingly toying with Barton. He handed out a real beating and the neighbours, to a man and woman, were on his side.

After what seemed an eternity, Barton finally called it a day and limped home battered and bruised but unfortunately, being the type of person he was, he took his revenge on his wife and daughters who were subsequently on the end of violent beatings.

On hearing what Barton had done, McKeown went round to the house and threatened him with more of the same if he ever laid a finger on any of his family again. That was enough for Barton who left his wife and girls and went to live with his brother, an equally disagreeable sort, in a seedy terraced house in Madeley Street, and never came back.

Jo, her sister and mother perked up no end once the scumbag had left and her mother became a completely different person, spending more and more of her time in the local pubs and clubs where she quickly got herself something of a reputation. Of course the rent needed paying and there was no relying on Barton for that so how the mother managed is another matter but suffice to say Jo had a lot of 'uncles' while she and her sister were growing up.

By the time she entered her teenage years, Jo had developed physically rather more than the majority of her schoolmates and not surprisingly the boys of the school started taking notice. Her mother's reputation didn't help of course but Jo was an innocent of the period, just like most of the youngsters growing up in the early1950's.

The main interest for young girls at the time wasn't boys of their own age, who only had football, rugby and cricket on their minds, but music and the cinema. Going to the pictures was by far the most popular form of entertainment and venues like Eureka, Langham, Regis, Priory and Carlton were close by and even a venture into town to the ABC was sometimes on the agenda as it featured all the best films from America on a weekly basis.

Film stars were Gods and there were dozens of major stars who could sell a film just by their name, in particular heart throbs such as Cary Grant, James Dean, Kirk Douglas, Clark Gable and Errol Flynn were guaranteed to fill box offices all around the country with cinemagoers eager to put their mundane existences away for a few hours each week. Any film starring Humphrey Bogart was certain to be a hit while Bette Davis could easily carry a movie on her own and did so at regular intervals.

The slow death of cinemas started from around the mid '50's with the advent of television into most homes. One by one they started closing due to lack of patronage and by the end of the decade the West Park cinema had shut its doors along with the Londsborough, Berkeley, Eureka, Priory, Regis and Waterloo.

The only venue to buck the trend was the Cecil which had opened its doors for the first time in 1955 showing the Marilyn Monroe film The Seven Year Itch. The cinema was complemented by a massive organ and often staged concerts featuring many major recording artists.

Anyway, Jo loved her weekly trips to the cinema, usually with her sister but sometimes, if the film was a little more of the grown up variety, with her friend Janet McKeown, whose father had been instrumental in getting rid of her brutal dad. The pair of them, whose favourite singers were Petula Clark, Pat Boone, Bill Haley and Frankie Lymon and the Teenagers, would sometimes go dancing at a local church hall where they could mingle with the boys, most of who the pair knew from school but occasionally with others from more exotic places like Francis Askew School in Gypsyville.

Ronnie The Rocker

And that's where Jo first came across Ronnie Jones, a couple of years older than her at sixteen. Ronnie was a rocker, which meant he favoured motor bikes rather than scooters and wouldn't be seen out without his leather jacket (fake leather in his case as he couldn't afford the real thing) and tight jeans.

He hung around with a group of like-minded friends who all had bikes, a couple of them top-line BSA's but most had Norton's like Ronnie, very much the second and third-hand version but at least it got them around. Ronnie had already left school and had a job at a local painters and decorators store on Anlaby Road, not a taxing occupation and the downside that he had to work Saturday's but at least he finished at five o'clock every night and was soon out on his beloved bike.

He soon found himself attracted to the young girl from Westbourne Street School and occasionally took her for a ride on his bike around the streets though always carefully avoiding Hawthorne Avenue in case Jo's mother happened to be in the vicinity. Jo quite liked him in a giggling sort of way but really, at that stage, didn't know what fancying someone meant. Anyway, she was much more comfortable in the company of Ronnie's friend Andy, who was better looking and wasn't full of himself like his pal.

Andy Glossop grew up with Ronnie Jones and they went to the same school until the age of eleven, then he passed his exams and went to Kingston High in Pickering Road. On leaving school with good GCE results he quickly got a job in the drawing department of a local architect's office and, with a day off each week to attend college along with two evening classes he was establishing himself as a young man going places.

While a very different character to his pal Ronnie, the two had one major interest in common which bound them together like brothers; motor-bikes. Ronnie, with little education and even less ambition, was the mechanic of the pair and could take a bike apart and put it back together again in no time at all while Andy was the brains of the outfit and organised all of their many biking outings, often requiring a stopover at a youth hostel or a camp site.

Ronnie wasn't at all confident around girls but plucked up enough courage to ask Jo if she would go to the pictures with him. There was a new film showing in the town, the first ever to be shown in something new called Cinemascope. It was called The Robe and starred Jean Simmons and Richard Burton and Ronnie asked Jo if she would like to go with him.

Jo was rather taken aback by this request as she'd never even thought about going out with anyone apart from Janet but couldn't find an excuse in time and said she would go with him. To be fair, the pair of them fretted and worried about this first date for the next few days until Saturday night when them met at a pre-arranged meeting place on the corner of West Dock Avenue.

Naturally, Ronnie paid for both as Jo wouldn't have had any money and the evening went pleasantly enough despite ending with Ronnie attempting an embarrassing kiss as he walked Jo home.

Ronnie must have read something more in the date than Jo as he asked her out again the next time they met at the parish hall dance. This time Jo was anticipating the request and gave out the time-honoured excuse of 'washing her hair'.

Ronnie was completely crestfallen by this knock-back and went into his shell for a few weeks before gritting his teeth and asking her again. Once more Jo found an excuse and Ronnie took the hint and sulked for another few weeks.

Jo liked Ronnie enough but by now, and with the encouragement of Janet, had begun taking more notice of the opposite sex, though certainly not boys of her own age but like Ronnie and Andy, a couple of years older. Janet was very much the more forward of the pair and though just turned fifteen had been going out with her second cousin Brian, who was almost twenty.

Brian Pinder was a sleazy character from Scarborough Street, who as far as anyone knew, never had a proper job but somehow managed to always have money in his pocket. He was Janet's mother's nephew on her brother's wife's side, or something like that, and was one of those people who never seemed to fit in wherever he went.

Pinder left school early – not that he'd spent too much time there anyway – and did a few shifts labouring for a firm who made some kind of greenhouses out of metal. He may have been bone idle but he certainly wasn't stupid and quickly picked up the complicated procedure of putting these frames together.

How he did it no-one knows but before too long he'd left the firm and started putting these frames together himself, with the help of a couple of like-minded layabouts. He'd obviously got hold of the firm's client list as before long he was selling the frames to them at a reduced price.

Within six months he's rented a yard in West Dock Avenue and had around twenty men working all hours to put the greenhouses together. Pinder was now very cash-rich and was driving around in a flash car and gambling in ten pound notes rather than the half-crowns he previously bet with. Not surprisingly the bubble burst when he sacked one of his workers for stealing and he reported Pinder to the authorities. The whole enterprise was completely illegal and though he got away with a caution Pinder was quickly back where he started. The sad part is that Pinder could quite easily have done things properly and built up a lucrative business giving mass employment but he was just one of those characters who would rather do something wrong than right.

For some reason Janet had become very close to her cousin – much too close as it turns out because Jim McKeown got to know of the liaison and all hell broke loose. McKeown, who had been the architect in the downfall of Jo's father, beat the living daylights out of Pinder, who was never seen in the vicinity again.

Janet took some time to get over the scandal but it didn't prevent her from persuading Jo to make a beeline for Andy Glossop, who she had by now taken a real shine to. Glossop generally had plenty of girls for company and Jo didn't think she stood a chance but with Janet's help she started looking more like an attractive young woman than a schoolgirl and, as she had now turned fifteen and started work at the local fish factory, she had money in her pocket to buy nice clothes and make-up.

Andy didn't take too much encouraging and the pair quickly became an 'item'. Poor Ronnie was even more downbeat now that his best friend had stolen his sweetheart but there was nothing he could do about it and didn't want to lose Andy's friendship so kept his thoughts to himself.

Andy was approaching his eighteenth birthday and Jo was just short of sixteen when a bombshell hit the couple – Jo was pregnant! What an unmitigated disaster. How on earth had that happened and what were they to do?

Jo of course had to tell her mother and that wasn't something she was looking forward to doing while Andy's parents, both pillars of the local Methodist church, were certain to be absolutely devastated, especially as they never approved of their son going out with Jo, whose mother had such a risqué reputation in the neighbourhood.

After much discussion Jo decided she would tell her mother by herself while Andy went home to break the news to his parents. Mrs Barton not surprisingly hit the roof and though hardly a paragon of virtue herself had wanted more for her daughters. She had put her hat and coat on ready to go round to Andy's house but was persuaded by Jo to leave it until the following day when everyone had time to digest what had happened and what should be the outcome.

If the news of her pregnancy was a blow to Jo it was nothing compared to what happened next. At seven o'clock the following morning Jo was woken up by a banging on the front door and along with her mother went downstairs in their dressing gowns to be greeted by a wailing and hysterical Mrs Glossop. Jo had realised that the news would be upsetting but didn't reckon on such a reaction.

Jo's mother was also taken aback and began scolding Mrs Glossop for her insensitivity but was stopped in her tracks by another woman who was accompanying Andy's mother.

"Andy's dead," she shouted hysterically.

"He had an accident on his motor-bike last night and was killed outright."

What started out as a disaster had turned into a tragedy. Andy had been travelling home to tell his parents the shocking news of Jo's pregnancy when his bike skidded on a wet patch of road propelling him head first into a telegraph pole, killing him instantly.

Both Jo and her mother at once realised that Mrs Glossop nor anyone else knew that Jo was pregnant and she had taken it upon herself, despite being overcome with grief, to inform her beloved son's girlfriend of his death.

The pair were now in a terrible dilemma. Do they inform Mrs Glossop that their dead son would have an heir in a few months time or keep the news to themselves? They decided, almost telepathically as there was no means of communication , to say nothing for the moment and attempt to work out what was best for all of them.

As far as they knew only Jo and her mother were aware that Jo was having Andy's baby, even Jo's sister hadn't been informed at this stage. However, what they didn't know was that someone else was in the loop.

It shouldn't have been a surprise that Andy had stormed off in a confused state from Jo's house as telling his parents would be a nightmare. He decided to make a detour on his way and called at Ronnie's house. As ever Ronnie was busy taking a bike apart and though always pleased to see his mate he had been brooding for such a long time over him taking away the one girl he had ever really wanted.

"Now then how are yer? said Ronnie.

"And how's that lass of yours?

"I hope you're treating her right."

Andy then broke the news to Ronnie. It was of course a devastating shock to him, even more so as he'd always secretly hoped that Jo would come to her senses one day and take up with him.

"What the hell are you going to do? Ronnie said.

"You'll have to marry her when she turns sixteen in a couple of weeks."

That scenario had already occurred to Andy but what a situation to be in, he thought. Where on earth would they live and how could they possibly manage financially?

Still, it did appear to be the only realistic option and though he was dreading telling his parents that was the most likely outcome.

So, buoyed up with a couple of bottles of Carlsberg Special Brew, which had been provided by Ronnie, he set off for home only to have that tragic accident which not only decided his own fate but that of those closest to him.

A couple of days passed with Jo and her mother keeping their own countenance about the pregnancy. They were still no clearer about the most suitable outcome though several options had been scrutinised, all as bad as each other. Abortion, which was illegal, was quickly put aside as Mrs Barton had witnessed some terrible sights in her time with women and young girls attempting a back-street abortion.

Mrs Barton had a cousin who had moved to Pontefract and married a miner and she wondered if Jo could go and stay with them for the duration of the pregnancy. Unfortunately her cousin's husband wouldn't hear of it which wasn't really too surprising as they already had four kids of their own and the house wasn't big enough even for them.

So that was out, as was adoption as Jo wouldn't hear of giving up her baby to strangers, however well meaning. Jo reached her sixteenth birthday and her sister and friends, especially Janet, understood when she couldn't celebrate as she was still in mourning for Andy, the love of her life.

A Solution Of Sorts

The day after her birthday another bombshell hit the family, though this time it offered a solution to most of their problem. Ronnie visited the Barton house for the first time since Andy's funeral. He was obviously still in a state of shock but had gathered enough of his thoughts to make an incredible offer.

He would marry Jo at the registry office in a few weeks time. Everyone would assume it was a shotgun wedding, not uncommon in the era, and he would bring Andy's baby up as his own. Mrs Barton was beside herself with joy. While this wasn't the answer to all her prayers it was the next best thing and would go a long way to solving the predicament.

Not surprisingly Jo wasn't quite as enthusiastic but with realistic options closing all around her she succumbed to her mother's persuasion, bit the bullet and said yes to Ronnie.

Ronnie's family were not best pleased either and the whole neighbourhood thought it rather strange that Jo was marrying her boyfriend's best pal so soon after he had died but nonetheless the wedding went ahead and, after a reception at the Barrel Tavern in Tadman Street attended by a few relatives and friends, the couple settled down to married life in a rented two-up and two-down house at the bottom of our terrace, owned by another neighbour called Mrs Cook.

When the baby girl was born they decided to call her Andrea after her real father. The story was kept quiet for a long time after the birth with only Jo, her mother and Ronnie knowing the true identity of the baby's father. However, Mrs Barton confided in Freda one night after a few drinks and it wasn't long before everyone knew, including Andy Glossop's parents.

It was a very sad tale but it made Jo incredibly strong and she was determined, one way or another, to make a better life for herself and her family though that was very much easier said than done.

Before the baby was born, the neighbours, including my family, didn't pay much attention to Ronnie or Jo and there certainly didn't appear to be too much of that so-called community spirit about. Everyone knew about the situation and more or less left them to get on with their own lives but what a difference when little Andrea came onto the scene.

The three great events of life, birth marriage and death, were always treated with the greatest reverence by everyone. No bride ever left her house, however humble, without a parade of neighbours throwing confetti and if a funeral came down the street it was hat's off and heads bowed whether we knew the deceased or not.

I remember vividly when Mr Baxter the coalman from Haddon Street died and the hearse inched its way slowly up Hawthorne Avenue. People from every terrace made their way to the main street and stood quietly while the cortege passed by. A mark of respect for a well-liked man even if he did sometimes give us kids a belting if we tried to pinch a bag of coal from his yard to sell to one of the neighbours.

Jo had been home from the maternity hospital for less than an hour when a knock came on the front door.

"It's only me, came a voice that neither Jo nor Ronnie recognised.

"I've just come to see if you could do with this."

The voice belonged to Mrs O'Farrell from number two. Ronnie and Jo had spoken a few words while they were moving in but hadn't seen or heard of her since. She walked in, opened a brown paper carrier and pulled out the most beautiful knitted baby coat imaginable.

"I've done it in white as I didn't know then whether it was a boy or girl, she said.

"Now, where is she?" and proceeded to pick Andrea up and hold her close.

Jo was astounded. She had never seen such a beautiful coat and Andrea would be the best dressed baby in the street when wearing it. But amazingly there was more to come.

Another knock on the door and another voice said: "Can I come in?

"I wondered if you would like this?"

Jo went to the passage where Mrs Dixon from number five was stood. She couldn't believe what she was seeing.

"I know it's not the most modern of prams but it's done me proud and hopefully I'm finished with it now."

Stood in the passage was a rather scruffy but very serviceable pram.

"Just get your hubby to polish it up a bit and it will do you fine until you can afford a new one" said Mrs Dixon.

Again Jo was lost for words. While the pram wouldn't have been what she would have picked herself the fact is she hadn't bought one as most of her money had gone on a cot and clothes for Andrea. Ronnie could certainly do it up and she would be proud to walk the baby out in it.

Another neighbour, Mrs Bellamy from number nine, also came round. She'd crocheted some socks and tiny mittens and they were pink so either she was psychic or she'd done a pair in blue as well just in case.

The house quickly filled up with neighbours, a couple of them with their own babies, and Jo had found that the women of the community pulled together when needs arise and she wouldn't forget their generosity in a hurry.

The aforementioned Mrs Cook lived in the one house in the terrace that was always immaculate, the reason being that she owned the house and two more in the terrace. Mrs Cook was a mystery woman to me and all the other kids. She invariably dressed all in black, lived on her own and no man every appeared at the door though women were regular visitors. She rarely went out, just to the Co-op for her groceries and to church on a Sunday and hardly ever spoke to the kids.

I later found out that she was regarded as a 'mystic' or fortune teller which is why there were always groups of women at the house. She would hold regular sessions and I've seen many a woman run out of the house in terror after being told something she didn't want to hear.

To be honest she frightened the life out of me and my pals but she certainly wasn't all bad as we were to find out later. When the King died in February 1952 everyone knew the Coronation of Queen Elizabeth II wouldn't be for at least another year. Every street would be holding a party and many, like ours, had more than one.

The women of our terrace and Frederick's Grove across the street decided to form a committee and join forces for the party. They met in the Parish Hall at the top of Carlton Street and appointed Mrs Dixon as chairwoman assisted by Mrs James from across the road. Their task was to collect a shilling a week from everyone in the two terraces so that by the time of the Coronation there would be a nice sum of money to put on the best street party on Hessle Road.

Everyone agreed, apart from one. Mrs Donovan at number 14 had seven kids and a husband who always appeared to be at death's door. She simply could not afford a shilling a week and wasn't too proud to let the committee know why.

Anyway, all of the neighbours had some sort of hand in the organisation and no-one blamed Mrs Donovan but when the actual great day dawned there was a huge surprise for her and her children. Mrs Cook had been secretly putting money away for her every week and the day before the big event Mrs Dixon told Mrs Donovan that her and her family would be warmly welcomed with nothing more said about the matter.

What was most surprising was the way the event brought everyone together – even neighbourhood warring parties – and there were always plenty of those. The aforementioned Mrs Dixon was a formidable woman with a load of kids, a dog and a cat, and a

263

husband who earnt very little working in a clothes shop. The house was always untidy, unkept and not particularly clean, as were the offspring, and it was that which led to a confrontation with Mrs Widdup from number 16.

Mrs Widdup was a different kettle of fish altogether. She had just two children, Mary and Robert, who were both kept sparkling clean and always shone with good health – a bit like their shoes. Robert was a regular playmate of one of Mrs Dixon's brood, Peter, but one day Mrs Dixon told the surprised and disappointed Robert not to play with Peter any more.

"You Robert", she said.

"Don't you dare bring that Peter Dixon back home with you and I don't want you going to his house anymore.

"Everytime you go there you come back with fleas and nits so you're banned from that house from now on."

Poor Robert was as miserable as sin. Peter was easily his best pal and he didn't know what he was going to do without him. Not surprisingly he relayed the orders to him and when he told his mother all hell broke loose. Mrs Dixon stormed round to the Widdup's house and started banging on the door and screaming blue murder. Naturally all the neighbours could hear what was going on, including yours truly, though I wasn't very old myself and didn't understand half what was being talked about though I did know the swear words.

"Think you're posh do yer, Mrs Dixon screamed when Mrs Widdup opened the door.

"We all know why your lot are well fed don't we?

"It's cos yer 'avin it off with the Co-op butcher and getting your extras that's why."

Even innocent me worked out that Mrs Dixon was accusing Mrs Widdup of being more than just good pals with Arnold Pashley, the butchery manager at the Co-op who lived down the next street.

"Don't be bloody ridiculous, said Mrs Widdup, attempting to keep her cool in the face of the onslaught.

"Myself and Mr Pashley are just good friends, that's all.

"I thank you to keep your gossip to yourself."

"It's more than gossip, Mrs Dixon yelled back.

"I've seen you going into the store room with him and I'll bet it's not to taste his sausages.

"Then again it might just be that."

By this time the whole terrace was screaming with laughing though the two combatants were deadly serious.

Mrs Widdup was obviously dumbfounded to think that anyone believed she was getting more than her fair share of rations from Arnold Pashley but she quickly realised that any further arguments on the front door step weren't in her interests and slammed the door in Mrs Dixon's face.

Believing she had won the battle, if not the war, Mrs Dixon retreated to her hovel and the pair of them kept their distance from then on so it was a massive shock to all when they began talking as if nothing had ever happened when the Coronation came round.

The street party went brilliantly. There were magicians, a donkey ride and a Punch and Judy show though the highlight was the three-legged race for dads when even Mr Donovan managed to get off his sick bed and take part.

Jo didn't love Ronnie but he had enough for the pair of them for the first few years, that was until Jo began to get restless and then Skipper Unwin came along.

George Unwin was also taking part in the Walking Race, his ship having landed the previous evening, but he wasn't a likely winner having spent an exacting afternoon at Jo's house while Ronnie was at work.

Silver Cod Trophy

Unwin himself was married with two children. His wife, a real glamour girl type, had a string of men friends around the town and, as long as her errant husband was sending home barrow-loads of cash, as just about all skippers were at the time, she couldn't care less that he was having an affair with a barmaid, a stripper, or anyone else for that matter.

It was true to say that trawler skippers, on the whole, were earning vast amounts of money for themselves and the trawler owners. Most of them lived prudently and many of the big houses that were being built in the suburbs of Kirk Ella, West Ella, North Ferriby and Swanland were for the owners and skippers and their families.

Some of them were legends and were far better known in the area than most footballers and rugby players. A great number of people relied on them for a living and the skipper who landed the most fish in a calendar year was presented with the Silver Cod Trophy, a hugely prestigious prize and greatly valued by the trawlermen of Hull.

The first Silver Cod was presented by the British Trawlers' Federation in 1954 and won by the Beverley-built Arctic Warrior.

Of course not all fishermen could become skippers, or first-mates or bosuns for that matter. Most were deck-hands and the youngsters were 'deckie-learners' and, as in all forms of maritime transport, there was a strictly observed hierarchy and the rules and regulations regarding seniority were exactly the same as in a Royal Navy vessel.

In the final year of school, boys were visited by representatives of the trawler owners and asked if they wished to go on what was euphemistically termed pleasure boating, which meant a trip on a trawler during the school summer holidays.

Many boys took up the option and most went on to become trawler hands and the Nautical School in Trinity Lane also provided boys for such trips. I most certainly wasn't one of them as just the thought of travelling across the River Humber on the Tattersalls Castle was enough to make me sea-sick.

Great Tragedy

My schoolmate Jackie O'Dowd, who was in a couple of classes above me, was one of those who did go and it didn't take much to persuade him that being a deep sea fisherman was how he planned to spend his life, which in every aspect was one of the great tragedies of my formative years.

Jackie was one of those people that lit up life. A natural sportsman, he captained Westbourne Street soccer and cricket teams and could have turned his hand to any other sport had he wished. Sports such as golf and tennis were never an option but if he picked up a table tennis bat or a pair of boxing gloves then Jackie would effortlessly thrash whoever was placed in front of him, all done with massive grace and good humour.

He had the ability to make everyone around him smile, even the teachers, though academically he never really tried to push himself as he always had just one ambition – trawlers. He was also good looking and charming which not surprisingly led to him getting all the best girls including my elder sister Kathleen and the school netball captain Margaret Mason, her of the legs up to her armpits, who awoke the developing urges of the older lads in the school.

None of them stood a chance while Jackie was around and he just appeared to glide through life on a bed of roses, gifted beyond belief and surely heading for much grander things.

Unfortunately things rarely turn out the way we expect. From the moment Jackie went on the pleasure trip he was smitten. The life of a deep-sea fisherman is one of the toughest imaginable but that suited Jackie's personality to a tee. He threw himself into life on board and had no qualms whatsoever about taking up fishing once leaving school at fifteen.

That was in effect the end of Jackie O'Dowd's career as a budding sportsman as three weeks away at sea and three days at home was hardly conducive to playing sports. He had always enjoyed the occasional cigarette but quickly turned into a chain-smoker with the fags being easily available and very cheap. Booze also reared its ugly head and despite his tender years Jackie could hold his own with even the most hard-bitten of drinkers, something that endeared him to his colleagues on board ship and in the boozers when on leave.

After a few years of this life, Jackie was no further on than he had been at fifteen, still a deck hand and unlikely to be offered promotion at any time soon. And that seemed to suit him fine. His family and friends loved him to bits and were always supportive but were beginning to despair of a lifestyle that saw him absent sailing for most of the year, and in the pub for the remainder.

He rented a house in Rugby Street, not too far from his sister, who collected his wages every week and did his washing when he came home. However, her husband was never a fan of Jackie, especially when he came rolling to the house drunk, as he so often did, and to say relationships were strained is an understatement.

Jackie once told me that he had been half-asleep in his bunk one stormy night and got the scare of his life. The ship as always was rolling with the huge waves – up, down, up down, and that went on for hours at a time. Everyone was so used to the monotony of it that it didn't really register until that particular night the ship went: up, down, up, down, DOWN and Jackie's hair stood on end until, after what seemed like an eternity but in fact was a split second, it came back up to continue on its monotonous way.

He said that incident scared the life out of him but by now his drinking had become a real problem. All of the money he earned from fishing went straight into the pub. He had his own regular taxi driver who would meet his ship whatever time it docked and drive him from pub to pub to Club for a full three days before it was time to sign on again for another trip. On board he was still as popular as ever though his shipmates began to notice a change in attitude brought on entirely by the amounts he was drinking.

He also began making minor mistakes which of course in the confines of a ship can lead to major problems and twice had to have emergency treatment after slicing off tops of fingers. The first-mate had a quiet word with him on one trip then it was the turn of the skipper on another and very soon he had become a liability who had to be sorted out one way or another.

Still just in his mid-twenties, Jackie now found himself out of a ship and no trawler company would give him a job. He had to make a living somehow and got a job filleting fish on the dock but his heart was always at sea and he hated the life.

He continued to drink excessively and was admitted to the Hull Royal Infirmary on several occasions with liver problems. He spent most of his time in The Half Way opposite Scarborough Street and had to be dragged out of there on numerous occasions by his sister.

It wasn't long after that he finally succumbed to sclerosis of the liver aged just 26. A brilliant young man in every respect the lifestyle was just too much for him to handle, showing just what an incredibly challenging and hazardous job fishing in the Arctic waters is, a fact horribly emphasised earlier that year when the trawlers Lorello and Roderigo went down off Iceland's North Cape due to black frost with the loss of all hands.

The same year also saw nine men lost when the Prince Charles ran aground off the Norwegian coast making it a terrible period not just for Jackie O'Dowd's family but for so many other relatives and friends of the men who put their lives at risk in such a hazardous occupation. *Jackie's younger brother Rodney had decided to enter the Walk in memory of him and though unlikely to win there were many old friends of his brother who hoped he would honour his memory and do well.*

My sister Kathleen always had a soft spot for Jackie O'Dowd and tried her very best on numerous occasions to turn his life around though, to be honest, she was one of the many who would go out drinking with him when he first went to sea obviously not having a clue as to how things would turn out.

I know she always deeply regretted the way things got out of hand with Jackie and if things had been different for the pair of them they would undoubtedly have made a brilliant couple.

Fit As A Butcher's Dog

Anyway, there was Jo Jones, warming up in front of a flabbergasted Committee with the male members of the crowd gawping and the females looking daggers.

With just a few minutes to go to the start, the favourite for the race, Alan Wilkes, had yet to make an appearance but as ever he was playing things cagey. Alan was as fit as the proverbial butcher's dog having worked as a drayman at the local brewery for the past seven years. Still only 25, he had finished runner-up twice in the event previously, both times to regular champion Tommy Bowes, who, after blowing the Wembley outing money, had left town in a hurry.

Wilkes was a strong fancy to go one better this year and take the prize and many of his mates had backed him accordingly. He had always been a strong athletic type though one particular incident when he was a schoolboy would have shaken the confidence of most kids.

Alan had won the West Hull School Sports under-15 60-yard dash twice and a hat-trick looked inevitable in his final year at Westbourne Street School. He had hardly broke sweat to win his two Finals and this year most schools neglected to put an entry in as it was thought he was a certainty.

However, lining up for Villa Place School was a newcomer, a skinny kid with the blackest skin any of us had ever seen. His name was Keith and he had arrived in this country from somewhere we had never heard of called British Guyana. Why he was here no-one knew but here he was lining up in lane three of the Final with Alan in lane four.

The starting gun went and Alan got his usual blistering start and was clear at the halfway stage. What happened next went down in history in our small world. Keith came sauntering up to Alan, glanced across and gave him a little smile, then turned on the booster and left him for dead.

The whole place was completely silent for what seemed an eternity. Nobody could believe what they had just witnessed. Alan came back complaining of a 'bad leg' but we all knew we had seen something remarkable. Keith later went on to play professional Rugby League for Hull FC and is still today regarded as one of the fastest wingers ever seen in the sport.

Try-Line Tommy

The rugby league Club has always played a huge part in all aspects of life on Hessle Road and if ever the term Community Club has been earned it's by the Hull FC who play at the famous, and sometimes infamous, Boulevard. Just about everyone is a supporter and the gates for Saturday afternoon matches are huge. At around 2.30pm every other Saturday in winter, every pub and Club on Hessle Road empties as thousands of men head to the ground to watch the Airlie Birds as they are known.

Many of the players are local lads though a small influx of outsiders and foreigners make the team a little more exotic and it's all the better for them. One of the locals who had played for the team a few years earlier had entered the Race and had attracted good support. His name was Tom Parker and was known by one and all as 'Try-line Tommy', for very good reason.

Tom was a big raw-boned second-row forward in his hey-day, without many frills but known in particular for his ferocious tackling and whole-hearted endeavour. He was a big favourite with the supporters though Tom had a bit of a problem that was to hold him back in his career and eventually lead to his downfall – he could hardly see!

Away from the pitch he wore thick black glasses with lenses like bottle-bottoms. Of course he couldn't wear them when playing so he had to do the best he could. He was usually OK when tackling, though there were occasions when he crashed into a poor unsuspecting opposing player who didn't have the ball at the time, but his team mates knew not to pass to him unless it was absolutely necessary as he was more likely to drop the ball than catch it.

The day he earned his unfortunate nickname Hull were playing the powerful Halifax at the Boulevard on a grey, murky day with the ground like a mud bath. It was a third-round cup tie and the visitors had led narrowly for almost all the match and Hull were finding it impossible to break their defence down. That's when Tom Parker became hero and villain in just a very short space of time.

With just a few minutes left and Hull trailing 7-5, they needed something special. Tom, who had worked hard all game without managing anything in particular, crashed into Halifax prop forward Jack Wilkie deep into Hull territory, almost knocking him out and leading him to drop the ball in the process. Even Tom with his terrible eyesight could hardly fail to see the ball at his feet and in one swoop he picked it up and set sail for the opposition try-line.

While never the quickest of players, he was a very determined runner on the few occasions he had the ball in his hands and player after player bounced off him as he crossed the centre circle on the infamous Threepenny Stand side heading for the Halifax line. The visitor's winger came across and looked as though he was about to tackle Tom, who was now in full flow, but discretion got the better part of valour and he chickened out at the last minute.

There was only the full-back to beat now and, as he advanced towards Tom, it looked as though the game was up as he was known as a superb defender. But Tom wasn't to be thwarted and he crashed right through him before diving spectacularly over the line for what would have been the winning score.

Unfortunately it was the wrong line! Tom had dived over the 25-yard line believing it to be the try-line. The whistle blew for full-time, Halifax celebrated, the Hull players were devastated and the crowd went crazy. Poor Tommy, his terrible eyesight had let him down at what should have been the crowning moment of his career. He played on for a couple of seasons but was never the same and it didn't help when the crown chanted 'Try-line Tommy' every time he played.

He still kept himself fit by turning out for one of the local amateur sides but his eyesight was no better though he should have little difficulty following the route of the Race as it was all in a straight line!

A Strong Whiff Of Fish

Another entry with a strong connection to local amateur rugby is George Hartley. George rode up on his bike, as usual with a strong whiff of fish about him, and several people in his near vicinity made their excuses and left quickly when he started talking to them.

George was a simple soul who worked as a fish 'bobber' on the docks. A bobber is someone who unloads the fish from trawlers, usually on a night, and the majority of them have other jobs during the day, often as window cleaners. George doubles-up by working in the fish manure factory, hence his rather unsavoury smell, but he is well liked among the community for the work he does with youngsters at the Fish Trades Boys Club.

George was officially the coach of the under 17's rugby team when I was playing for them, though to be fair he wasn't exactly a top notch coach and like most of his kind would never have heard of a coaching badge, and certainly couldn't have passed one as reading and writing wouldn't have been amongst his strong suits. Most of the lads had experience of playing at school and more or less did as they pleased on the pitch. George's coaching mantra went something like this.

"Now then lads, go out and give 'em some stick."

We lads didn't need much telling. We were a rough and tough bunch playing in a very hard league and liked nothing better than a good thrash around on a Saturday afternoon. George would shout his usual encouragement from the touchline and there was one activity he became well known for.

George would fill his bucket with iced water before a match and, along with the magic sponge, would race onto the field if anyone got injured. The sight of George running towards a player with a bucket of icy water invariably smelling of fish, and the prospect of having a stinking sponge shoved into their face, invariably galvanised any injured player into immediate recovery and it was said that Fish Trades had the hardiest and toughest players in the whole of ruby league.

Ready To Go

The start is now almost upon us and many of the competitors are warming up outside the Club before heading for the starting gate at the St George's Road corner. As this is likely to be the final year of the event, the organisers had no hesitation asking Hessle Road great Johnny Whiteley, captain of the beloved Hull FC and a Great Britain regular, to be the official starter. His duties are to ensure a fair and level start though one or two of those in the line-up are determined to get off to a flyer.

The route is simple – from the Gillette Street and St George's Road junction to Hessle Square and back but along the way passing numerous Hessle Road landmarks. Every road in every town and city in the land would have a few national retailers. The likes of Woolies, Timothy White's chemists, the Co-op and Army And Navy Stores were the bread and butter outlets but also there were little 'one-man' shops everywhere and Hessle Rd was no different in that respect.

One of the first landmarks on the route is the notorious Half Way Hotel, a fishermen's haunt with one of the liveliest, if that's the right word, clientele in the city, including the universally feared Pauline Storr. Whenever trouble raised its ugly head in the pub, as it so often did, it's inevitable that Pauline would be involved and the police almost always have to send for reinforcements to arrest her, though she never goes quietly and generally leaves a few coppers with bloody noses.

Next comes Billy and Dolly Glenton's wet fish shop (better known as Billy Crab-Claw's) and opposite is Mallory's, which constantly stinks of paraffin, then Maltby's pet and garden store, Leo Brown's clog shop and Ernie Parker's 'open all hours' store which sells everything from a bobbin of cotton to the Hull Daily Mail. The Mail is one of the biggest selling regional newspapers in the country and prints at least four editions every day, all of them eagerly anticipated.

The Sport's Mail on Saturday's sells thousands of copies and queues begin forming around Ernie Parker's shop at least half-an-hour before the 6.00pm edition that carries all of the afternoon's racing results plus reviews from the big matches at The Boulevard, Craven Park, Boothferry Park and in the summer the Cricket Circle at Anlaby Road. Mind you, poor Ernie nearly had a riot on his hands one night when the news got out that the Mail had put the price of the sport's edition up from five pence to sixpence.

Billy Crab-Claw's wet fish shop was one of the busiest on the road, despite the fact that hundreds of people were able to obtain their fish for free, or very little. It's wasn't always possible to get things like a bucket of mussels, smoked haddock or a dressed crab from off the dock so Billy's is where most people would go. The little shop was a hive of activity from early morning until tea-time. There were always queues – often a dozen or so crammed into a small space with several waiting outside on the pavement.

There was never any hurry – Dolly would be serving and chatting amiably to the customers while Billy would be ambling in and out of the working area at the back of the shop, in-between nipping out to

281

place a bet or two. Everyone knew each other – or if they didn't when they went in they soon would. We didn't need a newspaper, all we had to do was go to Billy's and learn everything that was going on in the world while waiting for our fish.

It was probably the best place in the whole wide world to start a rumour. One slip of the tongue at Billy Crab-Claws and the whole world would know about it sooner or later – probably sooner. I often heard it told that Hull had signed Billy Boston, Alec Murphy or other notable players while waiting in the queue. Someone once said that he'd actually witnessed Tom Van Vollenhoven signing on the dotted line in Dee Street Club which of course was absolute nonsense but it wasn't long before the whole of Hessle Road had been in Dee Street the night the great South African winger has signed to play at the Boulevard.

Up to Gus Farrow's second-hand emporium then on past the Eureka cinema where the manager 'Eureka Jack' rules with a rod of iron. Jack hates all kids and every Saturday morning matinee where Flash Gordon and Roy Rogers and Trigger are usually the star turns, he deliberately stops the film in the middle while the kids boo and hiss, just for the sheer badness of it.

Wheeler Dealer

Gus Farrow is a wheeler-dealer in the very best tradition. His shop is always filled to the brim with bric-a-brac, old furniture, second-hand sewing machines and other junk that somehow eventually appears in people's houses, mainly thank to Gus's brilliant sales spiel. Gus can sell anything to anyone. If someone walked into the shop asking if he had a cardboard box handy Gus would sell him a suitcase. He deals in everything from dustbins to typewriters, to chickens and even cars. He has a yard in Edinburgh Street where he keeps poultry in a loft and come Christmas the place is a hive of activity as Gus and friends kill and pluck ducks, geese and chickens for the table.

One of my early recollections was of going to Paragon Station goods counter, collecting a couple of boxes of day-old chicks, and carrying them back to Gus's yard on the trolley bus. Gus would pay me half-a-crown for the fare and as a treat and though embarrassing it was just about worth it though carrying boxes of baby chicks, squawking their heads off, on a bus, always attracted plenty of interest.

He and Gerry Malloy go back a very long way, to schooldays in fact. Gerry had helped Gus, who is a daily punter though only in a small way, with the rent when both were starting to make their way in the world and was in partnership with him for many of their money making schemes, some of which came off but others were doomed to failure.

Gerry was a great buyer while Gus was the salesman. Imperial Typewriters had a massive factory on Hedon Road and the pair of them bought the company's rejects for a song, took them back to Hessle Road in Gus's old van, before repairing them and selling them on. Often it was just a case of polishing up a scratch or fixing a loose screw here and there and there were good profits to be made from that little venture.

Another successful opportunity was with 'shop-soiled' sewing machines, also bought as rejects direct from the factory. Sewing machines were an important part of most households and the black, highly-polished Singer machines were excellent sellers which the pair did very well out of. Those machines were a mystery to most fellas but women would make coats, dresses, curtains and many other commodities in order to save money.

One business venture that didn't go according to plan cost Gus and Malloy dearly. Gus had the idea of purchasing baby ducklings and fattening them up for the Christmas table. They would buy the birds in mid-summer and make a killing when they matured at Christmas. Gerry sourced a farm in Lincolnshire that would do business for the right price and the pair set out one mid-June morning to make the journey via the Humber ferry to the farm.

Neither of them had travelled much in the area and rather mistook the distance from New Holland to the farm and back. On arrival Gerry did the buying – for cash of course – and around 500 squawking ducklings were loaded into Gus's battered van for the journey home.

By the time reached the ferry terminal it was early evening and, as luck would have it, the ferry was just sailing out of the terminal which meant a long, hot wait for the next one. The ducklings had been stored in cardboard boxes which by now were beginning to get completely soaked so the intrepid pair decided to open the back door of the van to give them some air.

As Gus opened the door two of the boxes fell onto the floor and burst open, scattering feathers and ducklings all over the ferry terminal and into nearby fields with Gus and Gerry chasing them though without much hope of catching them. In their eagerness to catch the birds they had forgotten to close the back door of the van and by this time ducklings were bursting out of the soaked boxes and making their escape.

What a scene that was. The two budding entrepreneurs chasing hundreds of baby ducklings all over Lincolnshire and by the time the next, and last, ferry of the evening arrived they had rounded up less than a hundred of the birds. With another hundred or so still trapped in their boxes the pair had lost more than half of their stock and limped back to Hessle Road vowing to stay well clear of livestock in the future.

I bought my first car from Gus, a green Ford Popular with a cranked start that needed about half-an-hour's cranking before bursting, if that's the right word, into life. I had passed my driving test after 20 lessons at £1 a time with the Quick Pass School of Motoring in Saville Street. I knew how to drive a car but had absolutely no idea how they worked but that didn't prevent me purchasing the old banger from Gus.

Where he had got it no-one knew and he certainly wasn't telling, probably at a breakers' yard as though it looked quite nice and shiny it was nothing but trouble and, me being a total idiot with any sort of mechanics, rarely helped when things went wrong.

The whole sorry venture into first-time car buying went completely belly-up one day when, as the exhaust pipe came adrift for the umpteenth time, I tied it together with an old rag I found in the shed that unbeknown to me had been used to soak up waste paraffin.

I drove round the block a couple of times congratulating myself on a job worthy of any top mechanic when I smelt burning. Getting out of the vehicle and onto my hands and knees I looked under the car at the errant exhaust pipe only to see flames leaping out of every side. Not surprisingly I quickly left the scene just as the Ford Popular disintegrated in a pall of smoke. Amazingly it didn't blow up – just slowly but surely melted into a mass of twisted metal, watched and cheered on of course by half of Edinburgh Street who had come out to witness the scene.

That was the last car I bought from Gus though it most certainly wasn't the last of my disasters when attempting to fix mechanical problems that were way beyond my level of competence.

Boxing Stable

On the other side of the road is Brighton Street leading to Witty Street where Stan Squires regularly hung out with a few pals. Stan used to rent a large loft above a garage in Madeley Street which housed his stable of professional boxers. Stan had been a very good pro fighter himself and on retiring put together a team of local lads who fought at venues around the country, often at less than a day's notice as they were always fit and ready to do battle.

Amongst those who graced the fight scene in the early years after the war were Jack Carrick, Frankie Jackson, Jos O'Berg, Wilf 'Tiger' Pepper, and numerous others. Bridlington was a well known supplier of fighters thanks to the efforts of Bert Smith, a fighter himself but also a trainer, official and promoter. It was rare for a fight bill in Hull not to feature one of Bert's seaside battlers. Most of these fighters also appeared regularly in the boxing booths when Hull Fair visited every October and there were always long queues to watch these fighting men of the area take on all-comers.

In those days Madeley Street Baths held boxing shows every fortnight and the under-bill was always full of local fighters. The main bout was often an Area Championship which carried a great deal of credibility and would feature boxers from all over Yorkshire, Lincolnshire and the North Midlands. On special occasions the Northern Area title might be up for grabs and fighters from Manchester, Liverpool, Newcastle and other areas would take part, but always on a bill that featured mainly local boxers, many of them trained by Stan Squires above a garage.

Local fish merchant Harry Moody was another 'scrapper' who took on all-comers. Harry was a well known character on the docks who had done well for himself and lived in a large house called 'Ivanhoe' which was right opposite Pickering Park.

One of the best of the locals, and without doubt a future champion, was Wally Mays, an electrician by trade who fought professionally in the early 1950's. Wally was a welterweight and was just beginning to make a real name for himself when he badly injured a forearm in a work-related accident and had to retire.

His final bout with Eddie Phillips at the Embassy Sportsdrome in Birmingham, which he won on points, should have propelled him into a national decider but unfortunately it wasn't to be and Hull-born fighters appear to be cursed when it comes to professional champions despite having numerous ABA title holders.

Madeley Street Baths wasn't the only venue to stage boxing as the early post-war years saw regular fight bills at the White City Stadium on the corner of Calvert Lane and Anlaby Road and also at the Regal Cinema, which once staged a bout featuring the great champion Bruce Woodcock. The promoters at Madeley Street were George Lawson and John Taylor, the latter, a canny Glaswegian who owned the Newington Dance Hall, was also a bookmaker at the dog track.

Jack Wallis once told me a story about John Taylor, which may or not be true (probably not in all honesty) but was typical of a punter-bookie relationship. Wallis said he was going through yet another of his bad spells and asked Taylor to take pity on him and lend him a few quid. He showed the bookie his empty pockets and his threadbare shoes that were flapping in the wind and rain with the soles hanging off.

Taylor, he said, took a wad of notes out of his inside pocket, slowly unbundled them, and handed Wallis the elastic band that held it together, telling him to tie it around his shoe to keep the wet out.

Knockout Smith

Boxing is the one sport which I am loathe to take bets on. I have the greatest admiration for the fighters but quickly realised that they were scrapping for a few quid and it didn't take too much of an inducement for a few of them to 'take a dive' if needs arise.

The majority fought for the sheer love of the sport and to make a few bob to supplement their meagre wages. Middleweight Tommy Mooney was a laundryman by day and a scrapper at night and was thought good enough to join a top London-based 'stable' for a while but the majority fought either in their home town or in places such as Doncaster and Leeds where there were similar promotions.

The main reason I am so reticent to take bets on the fights is that one night, while stood at my pitch at the dogs, I was asked to quote a price about a local scrapper, Tony Smith, failing to last the distance against a journeyman Wakefield fighter called Ernie Jackson.

Smith, a Gypsy who travelled with the fairs but had several connections in East Hull, would have normally looked a good bet to see off Jackson, whose record was nothing to shout home about with many more losses than victories. Indeed I would have expected Smith to knock Jackson out very early in the contest so I was taken aback when several punters came looking for a price for him to be beaten inside the distance.

After taking a few small bets I called time on the wagers reckoning that these punters knew more than I did about the contest and that

Smith, with plenty of pals at the track, had tipped them off that he didn't fancy himself for one reason or another.

Apparently bookmakers all over the north had been inundated with bets on the fight, just about all for Smith to fall early. Just before the fight started the odds had been adjusted to such an extent that Jackson was now a long odds-on favourite to finish his opponent before the final round, which of course meant that Smith was now at very good odds to win the contest.

The bell went for the first round and, after a cagey opening, Smith produced a right hook that would have done Rocky Marciano proud and poor Jackson was carried out of the ring with blood pouring from every orifice.

The crowd, who almost to a man had backed Jackson after being 'given the nod', were booing and screaming foul play but surprisingly Smith, and his corner man, looked rather pleased and so they should have been after availing themselves of the last-minute extended odds available.

So that's the reason I don't get involved with boxing.

The Sawmill

After Manchester Street comes the Liverpool Street tram sheds and Dairycoates Tavern, or Miller's pub as it is better known, on the corner of Hawthorn Avenue, then St Mary's And St Peter's Church and parish hall with the latter having a large crowd watching from the roof.

Just off Hawthorn Avenue is an alleyway known at Patrick's Lane that houses an assortment of buildings, many of the derelict or in need of restoration or better still, demolition. Among them is a sawmill where Ron Jensen makes wooden crates for the fishing industry. Ron is an astute businessman with a good eye for an opportunity and his mill is always very busy. He works almost non-stop in the yard and produces as many crates as his customers require, which is plenty as crates are always being stolen, broken or mislaid.

Ron and his brother Jim are very much in charge as the workforce is made up mainly of youngsters who can't find work anywhere else, not even on the fish dock To be honest it doesn't require an above average IQ to hammer nails into wooden crates and the brothers are the only two in the firm who are capable of using the electric saw. Just about all of the workforce knew they were never going to make it to anything much better but there was one, Gil Murphy, who believed he had a few more brains than he actually had, which is sometimes a dangerous thing.

One day Ron decided he was going to branch out and sell the creosote that he used on the crates to the general public. He asked if any of the lads were interested in taking on the responsibility and Gil, glinting a major opportunity for advancement, volunteered.

Ron set up a separate shed at the bottom of the yard and stored several gallons of creosote for public consumption. A couple of days later a man in overalls cycled up to the yard and spoke to the nearest worker, Jimmy, who was busy sweeping sawdust from the entry.

"Any creosote mate," said the overalls man.

Jimmy, quite surprised at being asked such a profound question, was a little taken aback at first then replied.

"You need to see a guy called Gil at the bottom of the yard, he's in charge of creosote."

The man rested his cycle on a bench and walked down to Gil, who by now was standing proudly in front of the creosote shed, of which he was in sole command.

A small crowd of workers, including Ron, had gathered and were watching and listening as discreetly as possible to Gil's debut as 'Head of creosote'.

"I hear you want some creosote, said Gil, in his most authoritative voice.

"What would you like, brown or black?"

"Er, black please," said overalls man.

"We've only got brown," said Gil.

That was Gil's debut and finale in charge of creosote and he quickly went back to hammering and sweeping like the rest of the workforce.

Along with three of his work colleagues, he is taking part in the great Walk but a regular diet of 'The Bellybuster', an extra large bread cake containing bacon, onions, black pudding, sausage, mushrooms, tomatoes, beans and a dash of tomato ketchup, ensured the quartet would be unlikely winners and all bets are that they won't even finish the course.

Not So Sunny Street

Ron Jensen was also the franchise holder for the dog track and several of the sawmill lads helped out on Thursday and Saturday nights. One of their main duties was working the traps, moving them off the track after the off into the safety of the inside, and also supposedly seeing to security.

One night, an unsavoury character called Isaac Smales, caused havoc in a spectacular way. Smales was a dog owner and gambler who had a bitch called Sunny Street with an equally unappealing trainer called Jim Talbot. The trainer had told Smales that she was a certainty in the third race of the evening and he should put plenty of money on her and when she won he would require a generous back hander, which is generally how things work in dog racing.

Smales told no-one but a few of his pals and waited and watched as the bookies chalked up their prices for the race. The plan was to wait until Sunny Street had drifted in the betting and then to all go down to separate bookies together and pile the money on.

Unfortunately for him, the unscrupulous Talbot also had his henchmen ready to pounce and they got in first, a flood of money causing the bitch to shrink to an unrealistic and virtually unbackable price. Smales was beside himself with fury. By now the dogs had been paraded and were just about to be placed in the traps. Talbot had disappeared back to the kennels and was unreachable so Smales, by now boiling over with rage at having been conned, leapt over the rails onto the track sprinted 100 yards to the traps, grabbed Sunny Street off its handler and jumped back onto the terraces before making off with a yelping greyhound under his arm.

Not surprisingly the stewards warned him off owning greyhounds for ever but Talbot got away scot free as usual and waited for the next mug owner to come along.

Past the sawmill and onto Institute Street then the first and only real obstacle which is the Dairycoates level crossing and footbridge then onto Gypsyville, past the Regis cinema, the Empress Club and Pickering Park before the long haul to Hessle Square via the popular Hessle ex-serviceman's Club.

No time for a breather at the halfway point as it's now be a mad dash home and to the winner a substantial cheque and the kudos of being champion for a year.

Stopped For A 'Jimmy'

As I mentioned earlier, the Rules and Regulations had to be tightened up after instances of scams in earlier races. Before the new Gypsyville Estate was built in the '50s, the area from Pickering Park to Dairycoates was virtually all open fields and allotments. There were major hedgerows on the Askew Avenue side of the road and one year, when the event had only just been reintroduced after a long break, an incident took place that caused the Rulebook to be updated and amended.

That year the field was at least 100 strong though nobody knows exactly how many as there was a much more relaxed feel to the organisation. In fact there was hardly any organisation at all and though there was betting on the outcome it hadn't reached anything like the proportions of later years.

The competitors had each been given a number and were supposed to be members of the Club and their immediate family but one particular member was about to ensure that he would certainly be the winner and collect not just the prize money but also a nice little earner from the bookies.

Les Flanagan, a filleter on the fish dock, was his name and he was about 50 years old, quite fit and though not thought of as one of the favourites he was expected to go quite well for a long way before weakening, as he had done in previous years.

Flanagan had got his usual fast start and had been amongst the front-runners for most of the race but, as expected, he began feeling the pinch just after passing Pickering Park on the home leg. He wasn't far behind the leaders at the time but had mainly managed to conceal himself amongst the throng and never spoke to any of the other competitors.

He stopped abruptly next to a giant tree behind the hedgerow and began fiddling with his shorts in the pretext of going for a 'Jimmy Riddle'. However, hidden behind the tree was his younger brother Ernie, who had the reputation of being a strong sprinter but with little stamina. Les and Ernie had taken the steps of wearing exactly the same tee-shirt and shorts and made every attempt to make themselves indistinguishable.

That was never going to happen as they were not replicas of each other but in their disguises, and in the context of a confused dash for the line, it was highly unlikely that the ruse would be spotted.

Ernie took the numbered vest from Les and immediately began making inroads into the leaders. He cut them down one by one until, with 100 yards to go, there were only two in front of him and they were tiring. With a last-gasp lunge he shot past the pair and breasted the finishing line to snatch the spoils.

In the absolute confusion of that thrilling finish, no-one had noticed the deception and most of the judges and committee men had been having a few free beers in the Club courtesy of the owner.

Ernie Flanagan accepted the not insubstantial winner's cheque and began looking for Alf Morrow, the bookie who he had backed himself (or his brother) with. Unfortunately for him it was Sunday and the bookie, who had watched the race but gone home, wasn't at his pitch that day as there was no racing on Sunday's. He would have to wait until lunchtime tomorrow.

Alf Morrow was at his pitch on Monday lunchtime when someone brought him a copy of the early edition of the Hull Daily Mail. The sports pages were full of Hull City and Hull FC with a few words about Rovers and other minor sports but what stood out were two huge pictures of the start and finish of the St George Club Walking Race.

In the first, the competitors were just setting off and right in the middle of them, wearing number 56, was Les Flanagan, absolutely no question, it was good old Les.

In the second the Mail photographer had done a superb job of capturing an exciting finish and there, passing the winning line in first position, was of course Ernie Flanagan – wearing number 56!

Even Alf, who was blind in one eye, couldn't fail to distinguish the pair and by a sheer coincidence Les Flanagan appeared at the top of the alley in Walcott Street where the bookie had his pitch.

Alf played along with him for a while, taking out of his back pocket the £25 that Flanagan had bet himself (and his brother) to win. Flanagan held out his hand, smiling a contented smile believing he had pulled off an almighty stroke, when the bookie smacked him squarely on the chin with a perfectly executed left jab. He followed up with a right to the solar plexus and Flanagan was screaming and retching on the floor for a good ten minutes.

Meanwhile, Ernie Flanagan, who had been lurking at the top of the alley awaiting his share of the ill-gotten gains, saw what had happened and fled the scene in panic with Alf Morrow chasing but all in vain — after all he was never going to catch the 'winner' of the St George Club Walking Race was he?

The Start

So, Johnny Whiteley is about to get the great St George Club Walking Race on its way and this final year, with such a huge variety of characters taking part, it's more eagerly anticipated than at any time for many years, not least by yours truly who stands to either win or lose a small fortune.

The competitors were a rare sight dressed in an assortment of garbs that made the whole affair look more like a pantomime than a Walking Race. Many of them have been to the local Army and Navy Stores for their rig-outs and brown army surplus tee-shirts, khaki shorts and white sandshoes are the favoured attire.

Some are in suits, others in overalls, and a couple are wearing the clogs that they used for work. Each have a number pinned on to them, either the front or back, and believe me there have been numerous volunteers to help Jo Jones pin hers on her front. Unfortunately for them it was Skipper Unwin who got that particular honour though he decided, just in case any of his family may be watching, to take the back option.

Unfortunately the race didn't get off to the best of starts. The Hawthorne Avenue branch of the Salvation Army band, which gathers at the start every year playing an assortment of favourites, had slowly but surely encroached onto the starting line and there was chaos as the committee men attempted to clear them away. I say an assortment of favourites though in reality the band only had a couple of tunes they knew properly – and one of them was the National Anthem!

The fact is they did have one overriding advantage over other bands from the area – they were free - or at least turned up for just a small donation to bandmaster Walter Wormald, or Wally Worm as everyone knew him. The result was that proceedings were running a little late when Johnny finally fired the starting gun and then all hell broke loose.

Dennis Batte, in his eagerness to get away to a quick start, was pushing and shoving his way past Gil Murphy when the sawmill man threw a right hook that felled him like a sack of coal. In the ensuing melee around a dozen competitors ended up in a giant heap on the floor, one of them Jo Jones, who was roughly manhandled as she attempted to get up.

Skipper Unwin, began fighting with a couple of her supposed helpers and it took several committee men a few minutes to prise them apart amongst accusations of molesting and general foul play.

Gordon 'The Bounder' was oblivious to all of this as he was at the back of the bunch when the original starting shot was fired but with a little persuasion from 'Mrs Bounder' he had worked his way to the front, though swaying somewhat, when the Hull skipper fired the pistol for the second time.

Dennis Batte had made a miraculous recovery from the attack, probably well aware that he had a fortune riding on the result, and was intent on getting a good start again, as was Alan Wilkes, who had sneaked his way into a position where he could get a flyer on the outside. All of their good intentions were prevented once again, however, as 'The Bounder', who had somehow managed to smuggle a silver whisky container into his suit pocket, swerved to such an extent that another melee ensued with several more casualties having to pick themselves off the floor.

Things were now getting desperate. The Sally Army Band was now on its third tune of their less than extensive repertoire and most of the competitors were arguing and jostling among themselves. The watching crowd were booing and jeering and those further up the route were wondering what on earth was going on as the race should have been on its way at least 10 minutes previously.

Thankfully the one man who retained his composure was Johnny Whiteley, who used his exceptional leadership skills to organise everyone into a proper line-up and, when he was satisfied the competitors were ready to go, fired the starting gun for the third time and the St George Club Walking Race was at last on its way.

On Their Way

As usual the early pace-setters went off like bats out of hell but they were of no consequence to the overall result as they would all be done with by halfway, some of them even earlier. One of them, Johnny Bullock, was the perennial early race leader as he had done exactly the same thing for the past eight or nine years.

This was his one moment of glory in an otherwise mundane existence. A road sweeper with the council, he delighted in taking the field along in the early stages, waving to the crowd and blowing kisses to the women along the route but by the time the field had got to Dairycoates and the crowds had thinned out he collapsed in a heap and had yet to finish the race.

The spectacle was certainly a sight for sore eyes as the field sped along the first part of the walk with massive crowds shouting and clapping and the Sally Army band still to be heard in the background, though by now they were back on their opening tune as they had run out of material.

Among the early front-runners were the lads from the sawmill who were hardly taking things seriously, laughing and joking amongst themselves as they went along, much to the annoyance of the serious walkers. Gil Murphy even had a couple of sandwiches in his front pocket, not quite 'Belly Busters' but big enough to cause a bulge that had all the female spectators making rude remarks.

The pace was still far too quick as the field began to approach the level crossing at Dairycoates. The route took them over the iron bridge which had been cleared of normal foot passengers and there was a great deal of pushing, shoving and insults as the walkers jostled for position along the narrow walkway. The sawmill lads were causing havoc with their antics and there were a couple of incidents that could have got out of hand if the stewards hadn't been on the ball but thankfully they were soon to be out of contention as a Mackman's pie shop at the top of Devon Street proved too much of a temptation and they all stopped to refuel.

Meanwhile Gordon 'The Bounder' was already trailing well behind the rest much to the disgust of his wife who could now see the folly of wasting £2 on an entry fee and the same amount in a wager on her feckless husband to win the race.

Gordon was swaying all over the place and by the time the walkers had got to Gypsyville Tavern he took a detour once out of his wife's view. His idea was to join in again when the field came back on the return journey – no-one would mind as he would still be trailing – but like so many of 'The Bounder's' big ideas is ended with him being carried out of the tavern that evening just before midnight, three hours before he was due back on board the trawler that was to take him to the fishing grounds off Bear Island..

Jo Amongst The Leaders

Jimmy Grantham was amongst those tanking along in front and he had a bit of a pedigree in the race having finished in the first half-dozen on a couple of occasions. The serious competitors like Denis, Alan and 'Try-line Tommy' were starting to wonder whether he could keep up this furious pace but the general consensus was that he would tire by halfway.

That wasn't Jimmy's thoughts, however, as he'd been training very hard for the Walk and he felt he could have done better in earlier years with a little more dedication and fitness so he was determined to give it a go this time and had been timing himself on his training walks. He'd also had a nice bet on himself each-way, with me of course, so wasn't about to go down without giving it his best shot.

The next landmark was Pickering Park and the contestants were now in the belief that they were in the countryside as few of them ever ventured this far, apart from the occasional sunny Sunday where families would gather for a game of cricket and a kick-about, and an ice-cream if we were lucky.

By now the race, though still in its relative infancy, was down to around 20 or so serious competitors and surprisingly to most, Jo Jones was amongst them. Jo's walking style wasn't exactly pretty to watch but it was effective and she was quite obviously extremely fit, just as she had told me. Skipper Unwin was unable to last the pace and dropped back quickly just after the park had been reached, no doubt suffering from the previous afternoon's exertions round at Jo's house.

Others amongst those still in the hunt included well known local footballer, Johnny Bidwell, who would have been a clear favourite but for suffering some bad injuries over the past couple of years. He was a very good soccer player at a high level on the amateur scene and for a short spell as a professional but unfortunately spent as much time suspended as on the pitch due to a very short fuse which is probably why he had to endure so many injuries as the opposition just loved to kick the hell out of him at every opportunity.

Bidwell had played for Hull City Boys and represented Yorkshire as a kid and had talent to burn. When he left school he had trials with several top clubs including Sheffield Wednesday and Leeds United but didn't quite make it at that sort of level. However, he was offered terms by Bradford Park Avenue and signed for them for the princely sum of £10.

My dad worked with young Bidwell's father in the railway sheds so we got to follow his career, though unfortunately it turned out to be rather a short one. After he signed on his dad told him he needed to smarten himself up if he wanted to look the part of a professional soccer player so Johnny went to Maurice Lipman's gent's outfitters on Monument Bridge and got himself togged out. He returned with a new blazer and slacks, a shirt and tie and some shoes, all for just over a tenner which Maurice kindly rounded down to the exact amount.

He played a few games for Bradford in the reserves and, with his obvious pace and skill, the manager thought he could do the business in the Third Division North, which is where the team were in the 1950's having been relegated in 1950.

Dad and I went with Johnny for his home debut which was to be against Workington Town, a team not known for their cultured football and always very difficult to beat. Anyway, it took us about three hours to get to Bradford via Pontefract, Knottingley, Selby, York and God knows where else and both dad and I were knackered when we got to the ground. Johnny had then to get ready for his debut in the Football League but he was a naturally fit youth and the long journey never appeared to bother him.

Dad and I stood on the terraces on a cold and miserable afternoon – the wags in the crowd said it was always a cold and miserable afternoon in that area – and waited for Johnny and the team to appear. I can't say I liked the colours – red, amber and black – they looked like a Xmas tree on fire – but we were eagerly awaiting kick-off and the meat pies weren't at all bad.

Bradford kicked off and Johnny was involved quite early without making much of an impression.

"Who's this useless bugger we've signed", was one of the more complimentary shouts from our section of the crowd and neither of us dared mention that we'd come all the way from Hull to see him play. After about half-an-hour the home team's left-half put Johnny through with a cracking ball and he only had the full-back to beat before facing the goalie. Unfortunately for him this full-back was a grizzled old veteran who knew the score and left Johnny writhing on the floor after a viscous tackle.

On came the St John's Ambulance man and along with the club's assistant trainer they helped a badly limping Johnny off the field to the dugout where it looked to us as though they were administering the kiss of life and giving him the last rites. Thankfully Bradford were able to cling on for the next fifteen minutes with ten men and we hoped Johnny would recover in time to come out for the second half.

Johnny came trotting out for the second period and I could see a sort of red mist had descended on him and feared the worst when he confronted the full-back again. Sure enough the next time he got the ball he raced towards his opponent then scooted round him as though he wasn't there, crossing the ball in the process for Park's big brute of a centre forward to head a perfect goal.

The crowd went crazy. "I told you this kid could play" the guy who had originally called him a 'useless bugger' said. I wasn't certain what would happen next as Johnny was acting like a man possessed and the next time he got the ball he again made mincemeat of the veteran full-back. However, just as he was rounding him ready to put in another perfect cross, Workington's centre-half came flying across and kicked Johnny so hard it's a wonder he didn't end up in the stands.

Johnny had had enough by this time and promptly stuck the nut on the centre-half, then planted a left hook firmly on the jaw of the full-back. Even this incompetent referee knew he had no option but to send Johnny off. With ten men for the rest of the match Bradford were unable to cling to their lead and eventually lost 3-1.

Johnny was suspended for three matches and fined two week's wages which meant he was well and truly out of pocket, even with his signing on fee included. We waited at the gates for him, but he had gone to the post-match reception with the rest of the team and the visitors where they tucked in to boiled ham sandwiches provided by the chairman, a local butcher.

Johnny came out and we started looking for a bus stop to take us back into the station but we then had a stroke of good fortune. The chairman was also on his way out with the manager and he asked if we wanted a lift, which of course was gratefully accepted. The manager never spoke, obviously miffed with Johnny for getting sent off, but Johnny asked the chairman if there was any chance of being reimbursed with his travelling expenses.

I thought the chairman, who was driving a huge shiny black Humber motor car, was about to have a fit so hard was he coughing and spluttering. He never replied and when he dropped us and the manager off at the station the manager went berserk.

"Never, ever ask the chairman a question like that again, he screamed.

"I deal with all money matters and you're just an employee here, remember that.

"Who do you think you are, Tom Finney?"

It was a long journey home. Johnny was quite badly hurt with a huge bruise and gash on his leg but no-one had mentioned treatment – he was expected to take care of stuff like that himself.

He played a few more games in the reserves then went back in the first team when a couple cried off for the trip to Barrow, which they again lost. And that was more or less it as what with the travelling, injuries, fines and poor pay he felt he would be better off getting a proper job and never played in the Football League again.

He ended up playing as a part-time pro, earning a few quid on the side and working as an insurance salesman though almost every season he played he spent more time either on the treatment table or watching from the touchline while suspended. Anyway, there he was in about sixth place and still going strongly – a definite contender in what was becoming an intriguing battle.

Took A Gamble

Past the popular Empress Club now towards the Maritime Museum with its huge whale skeleton and then along Hessle High Road with the orphans' home coming into view and mainly clear countryside with just a few houses and a couple of shops between the walkers and Hessle. No crowds along the route and it was mainly deathly silent with just the heavy breathing and occasional coughing and spluttering of the walkers to fill the air.

As Hessle Ex-Serviceman's Club and the halfway point approached, Jimmy Bullock was still in the lead followed by Alan Wilkes, Denis Batte, 'Try-line' Tommy, Rodney O'Dowd and regular walker Jack Turner, who had done well enough in previous races to believe he was in with a chance, Johnny Bidwell and, most surprisingly Jo Jones, who was in about seventh or eighth place. 'Slaughterman Sam's' cousin Jake had long since departed and those who had backed him had known their fate before the field had gone much further than Dairycoates as he had dropped a long way off the pace and was obviously struggling.

Charlie Dudgeon had also gone having exited just before the halfway point, just in time to catch the next bus back.

At this stage of proceedings, I certainly wouldn't have been too happy, though I wasn't to know it at the time as I was enjoying a pint in the Club. Four of those in the leading position, Dennis, Alan, Johnny and Tommy, had been very well supported and Jimmy

312

Bullock had also received plenty of attention in the betting though he was still a winner in my book, albeit a small one.

Denis was by far the worst loser but both Alan and Tommy took out plenty of win money and those who believe bookies never lose would have been amazed just how unbalanced my betting book was. For once in my life I had taken a gamble on an event and had decided that an outsider would win this year with dire consequences for my finances if proved wrong.

The halfway point came and went and the walkers began the long march for home. The dozen or so leaders were passing the stragglers along Hessle High Road and by the time Pickering Park came into view the field was strung out like washing.

Jimmy Bullock was now beginning to show the first signs of weariness and Denis Batte felt it was time to exert some pressure. He went past him just before Gypsyville Tavern approached, giving a cheeky grin as he did so, and quickly established a lead of about twenty yards. He was being cheered on by several supporters and followers who had all backed him to win after he'd told them he was all but home and hosed and the others may as well not bother.

Meanwhile Alan Wilkes had covered Denis' move and went in hot pursuit followed by Try-line Tommy and Sam Cassidy with Jo Jones and Johnny Bidwell just behind and the weakening Jimmy Bullock now looking a spent force.

The race was now approaching its most crucial point and as the field approached the level crossing at Dairycoates and came into full view of those who were on the roof of the parish hall, a cheer went up which turned into something of a crescendo as the walkers crossed the footbridge and onto the finishing straight.

Dennis was now in full flight and was beginning to count his winnings already though the punishment he had taken at the start of the race was beginning to tell and he was in severe pain. Alan now sensed his chance and went after him but Try-line Tommy had no more to give and dropped tamely away. Rodney O'Dowd and Johnny Bidwell were also done with but amazingly Jo Jones had moved into third place with just a few hundreds yards to cover.

The Finish

By now I confess to being in a terrible sweat as I was facing a massive payout if either Batte or Wilkes won the race. My only hope was that Jo Jones could somehow find the energy to get past the pair in front though at this stage my thoughts were that all was lost.

Batte was holding on for grim life as he heard Wilkes coming up behind and now, with just 100 yards left and the crowd screaming encouragement, he made one last lung-busting thrust as he saw pound notes fluttering before his eyes. Not only was he to receive a big winner's cheque but he hated me with venom as he had lost many a week's wages at the dog track and I would have to dig deep and provide him with a huge payout, the biggest in a lifetime of gambling, all he had to do was hold on for the last few yards.

Wilkes was trying for dear life to catch up but he was making inroads too slowly and time was running out. Meanwhile Jo Jones was slowly catching him and it now looked a race for second spot as Batte looked a certain winner. That scenario would be no good to me as Jo had backed herself each-way and I had laid off with Malloy but to win only.

With a final lung-bursting effort, Batte crossed the tape about eight yards clear with Wilkes and Jo Jones battling it out for a place. The stewards at the finish put the tape back across the line just as the pair approached and they crossed the line virtually together.

Unfortunately for poor Wilkes, Jo had a big advantage, or two rather big advantages, and it was her heaving bosom that touched the tape first.

She had finished second – the first woman ever to take part in the great event and she had defied all predictions and prejudices to finish runner-up with a very nice prize and an each-way bet to boot. Wilkes was an exhausted third, Cassidy fourth, Try-line Tommy stayed on again into fifth, and Turner came through late to finish a very creditable sixth.

The crowd were screaming, most in admiration for a truly brilliant effort from Jo, but also for all those who had taken part in what had been a memorable race. But suddenly everything changed and mayhem was on the agenda.

Few people had noticed that I had slipped out of the Club just as the walkers were reaching the finishing straight. Realising a huge payout was pending I had begun planning a possible escape route long before the end of the race. Situated 100 yards from the finish was Doug Joplin, a Club committee member and a steward for the day.

Most people had plenty of time for 'good old Doug', a fitter on the railway and of excellent character. He liked a bet, as many working men did in those days, but he also had a secret that was about to come home to roost.

Doug liked more than just a small bet; in fact he was a compulsive gambler, especially at the dog track, and was in hock to yours truly for a lot of money, almost two months wages. There was no possible way he could pay that amount back – or was there?

I realised Joplin was a much respected steward and had hatched a plan even before the race had begun. I explained to him that it might be worth his while to position himself not far from the finish and though Joplin didn't understand why he was happy to oblige if it meant relieving a little of his debt.

Before Batte had even crossed the finish line I was whispering into Joplin's ear. I said to the horrified steward: "You'll have to disqualify him, he was running the last few yards."

"How the hell can I do that, said the railwayman.

"It's too bloody late, he's already finished."

I then persuaded Joplin that if he went to the Chairman right now and told him that Batte had been running and that he, Joplin, couldn't keep up with him, the Chairman would have to initiate an enquiry and the result could be invalidated.

Joplin was about to protest the futility of such a deed but I casually mentioned that if he didn't comply then the IOU's I was coincidentally carrying in my pocket would be shown to everyone, including his wife and family, and that his reputation would be ruined.

If he agreed to the plan and Batte was thrown out then all debts would be wiped out.

Joplin had approximately 30 seconds to decide which way to jump – and thankfully he jumped my way.

Setting off like a scalded cat and blowing the whistle that all stewards had been allocated, he passed the cheering throng and found Chairman Walker.

"What the hell are you blowing that whistle for? said the Chairman.

"The race is finished."

"Batte broke into a run just to keep ahead, said Joplin, and I must say very convincingly.

"He was going so quick I couldn't catch him and my whistle seized up.

"He was definitely running and has to be thrown out."

Persuading The Stewards

By now the crowd were realising something wasn't right and began circling the committee members who had gathered in a bunch to see what was going on. The Sally Army band's rendition of God Save The Queen was halted abruptly in the second verse as the bandsmen and women were straining to find out the cause of the commotion that was now ensuing.

Denis Batte, who a few minutes earlier had been whooping and hollering like a the winner he believed himself to be, was now a deathly white having suddenly realised his world could just about to be crumbling.

And me? I was busying ingratiating myself with Committee members, suggesting of course that Joplin was a man of such exceptional character that if he said someone was running then that was surely the case.

I also had the foresight to take the Chairman aside just before the melee enveloped him and offered to sponsor the Club's next major concert night, an offer that of course 'Wasn't subject to Batte being disqualified' though thankfully for me, Walker quickly got the message.

The Committee had just two options.

1: To enforce the letter of the law that stated a steward had to blow his whistle immediately when suspecting someone of breaking the Rules.

319

2: To accept that Batte had indeed broken into a trot to keep ahead in the final stages and that Joplin had no hope of catching up with him.

After a short deliberation, very short as the crowd were by now baying for blood, Chairman Walker announced that option two had been taken and that Batte had been disqualified and Jo Jones was the winner of the St George Club Walking Race.

To say pandemonium broke out would be greatly understating things. Batte went crazy, physically attacking Walker and any other Committee member who got in his way. His many supporters were also screaming abuse at the Chairman but Joplin, with a little help from you-know-who, had managed to slip away unnoticed, like myself and Jo, the day's big winner.

I was of course absolutely delighted to be paying out. Only Jo had backed herself to win while the each-way money amounted to very little. But easily the most satisfying aspect was that I had £1010 to come from Malloy. I had made a killing – the best result I'd had in all the years I had been making a book on the race, or anything else for that matter.

Malloy was not best pleased. There he was, the owner of the Club from where the race took place, being well and truly turned over. He realised of course that my intervention had been fraudulent but couldn't do a thing about it. Joplin certainly wasn't talking having got himself out of big trouble.

Although I was the only one to back Jo to win and he had taken plenty of money on losers, it was still a terrible race financially and he decided to give up being a bookie and concentrate on his other business interests.

Batte, instead of being well in front with the winner's cheque and his successful bet, had done his dough big-time and it took him a very long time to get over the incident. However, he was still issuing challenges and was last seen attempting to swim across the River Humber for a bet – in a Batman suit!

Alan Wilkes won just a few quid but had to endure much taunting from his friends about being beaten in a photo-finish by a 'mere woman'.

Try-line Tommy bought some new glasses.

As for me, the result turned out much better than I could possibly have envisaged – well certainly for myself and Jo. I had taken a real shine to Jo by now, and it most certainly wasn't just the money talking.

She had quickly ditched Skipper Unwin, whose luck had taken a turn for the worse after he ran his ship aground and was now out of work. His floosy of a wife had also done a runner so he was back living with his mother in Devon Street.

I did feel sorry for her husband Ronnie but he very quickly bounced back and the last I heard he was shacked up with one of the McKeown sisters – let's hope he doesn't fall out with her father!

With my winnings I bought some premises in Withernsea where I opened a betting shop and lived in the flat above. It was a nice, spacious flat, just big enough for the three of us; myself, Jo and little Andrea.

The business was a bit quiet in the winter but Jo helped out in the Spread Eagle and during the summer it was booming and I was able to welcome many of my old friends and punters from Hessle Road, still taking their annual holidays in caravans parks around the town.

Life is full of surprises – sometimes shocks – and I'd had plenty of them but there was an unforeseen surprise for me the very first day I opened the shop. Just before racing was due to start who should walk through the door but my old nemesis Baz Shorthouse.

'Oh no, I thought, here we go again'.

"Now then 'ow are yer?" Shorthouse said with a somewhat more jovial touch than I expected.

"Haven't seen you for ages."

The last bit was no real surprise as the previous time I had seen Shorthouse he was in a heap on the floor of a drainage ditch, where I had deposited him a few moments earlier.

"Not so bad thanks Baz, I said.

"Ow's yerself?"

He then proceeded to tell me that he'd got a job with Holderness County Council working on the roads and had been given a council house for himself, his wife and two little daughters. I didn't even know he'd got married but here he was showing me pictures of his family, a very smart looking wife and two gorgeous little girls.

He was obviously besotted with them and had turned his life around completely. His job started early in the morning and he was finished just after lunch and was a regular visitor in the shop though by no means a big punter. After a couple of weeks I asked him if he fancied helping me out by chalking the board on busy days and he readily agreed.

There was I, doing something that would have been unthinkable a few years earlier, employing a once mortal enemy but Baz had got over his early demons thanks to his wife and was now a greatly reformed character. He even asked me to be Godfather to the latest offspring and I was proud to accept.

I spent a very long time searching for my sister Kathleen, who had more or less disappeared from the face of the earth after the revelation about her parentage a few years earlier. Although unsuccessful so far I believe she is still in France, close to the border with Spain and living amongst a community of artists.

I am convinced I'll find her one day and she can be reunited with her family. She may officially be my cousin not my sister but nothing has changed as far as I'm concerned and I'll keep searching.

The real hero of this story though is of course Gordon 'The Bounder' Bailey. He's still spending 20 days trawling for fish in the most inhospitable of environments – still having three days at home to get plastered, have a bet and see his ever growing offspring – and his wife still believes he's her hero.

I have bought a modern caravan on Highfield in Withernsea which I intend to rent out and every year 'Mrs Bounder' and her ever-growing brood, plus Gordon whenever he's available, will have a rent-free fortnight courtesy of yours truly.

I don't even mind when he backs a winner or two in the betting shop, or when he shouts the immortal words: "Come on you bounder."

THE END

4013339R00180

Printed in Great Britain
by Amazon.co.uk, Ltd.,
Marston Gate.